THE MANDOLIN LUNCH

Date: 2/15/22

FIC VAUN
Vaun, Missouri,
The mandolin lunch /

What Reviewers Say
About Missouri Vaun's Work

The Sea Within

"This is an amazing book. *The Sea Within* by Missouri Vaun is an exciting dystopian adventure and romance that will have you reading on the edge of your seat."—*Rainbow Reflections*

Chasing Sunset

"A road trip romance with good characters that had some nice chemistry."—Kat Adams, Bookseller (QBD Books, Australia)

"*Chasing Sunset* is a fun and enjoyable ride off into the sunset. Colorful characters, laughs and a sweet romance blend together to make a tasty read."—*Aspen Tree Book Reviews*

"This is a lovely summer romance. It has all the elements that you want in this type of novel: beautiful characters, great chemistry, lovely settings, and best of all, a nostalgic road trip across the country."—*Rainbow Reflections*

"I really liked this one! I found both Finn and Iris to be well fleshed out characters. Both women are trying to figure out their next steps, and that makes them both insecure about where their relationship is going. They have some major communication issues, but I found that, too, realistic. This was a low key read but very enjoyable. Recommended!" —Rebekah Miller, Librarian (University of Pittsburgh)

"The love story was tender and emotional and the sex was steamy and told so much about how intense their relationship was. I really enjoyed this story. Missouri Vaun has become one of my favourite authors and I'm never disappointed."—*Kitty Kat's Book Review Blog*

Spencer's Cove

"Just when I thought I knew where this story was going and who everyone was, Missouri Vaun took me on a ride that totally exceeded my expectations. …It was a magical tale and I absolutely adored it. Highly recommended."—*Kitty Kat's Book Reviews*

"The book is great fun. The chemistry between Abby and Foster is practically tangible. …Anyone who has seen and enjoyed the series *Charmed*, is going to be completely charmed by this rollicking romance."—*reviewer@large*

"Missouri Vaun has this way of taking me into the world she has created and does not let me out until I've finished the book." —*Les Rêveur*

"I was 100% all in after the first couple of pages and I wanted to call in sick, so I could stay home from work to immerse myself in this story. I've always enjoyed Missouri Vaun's books and I'm impressed with how she moves between genres with such ease. As paranormal stories go, this one left me thinking, 'Hmm, I wish I was part of that world,' and I've never read a book featuring vampires or weres that left me with that feeling. To sum it up, witches rock and Vaun made me a believer."—*Lesbian Review*

Take My Hand

"The chemistry between River and Clay is off the charts and their sex scenes were just plain hot!"—*Les Rêveur*

"The small town charms of *Take My Hand* evoke the heady perfume of pine needles and undergrowth, birdsong, and summer cocktails with friends."—*Omnivore Bibliosaur*

Love at Cooper's Creek

"Blown away…how have I not read a book by Missouri Vaun before. What a beautiful love story which, honestly, I wasn't ready to finish. Kate and Shaw's chemistry was instantaneous and as the reader I could feel it radiating off the page."—*Les Rêveur*

"*Love at Cooper's Creek* is a gentle, warm hug of a book."—*Lesbian Review*

"As always another well written book from Missouri Vaun— sweet romance with very little angst, well developed and likeable lead characters and a little family drama to spice things up." —Melina Bickard, Librarian, Waterloo Library (UK)

Crossing the Wide Forever

"*Crossing the Wide Forever* is a near-heroic love story set in an epic time, told with almost lyrical prose. Words on the page will carry the reader, along with the main characters, back into history and into adventure. It's a tale that's easy to read, with enchanting main characters, despicable villains, and supportive friendships, producing a fascinating account of passion and adventure."—*Lambda Literary Review*

Birthright

"The author develops a world that has a medieval feeling, complete with monasteries and vassal farmers, while also being a place and time where a lesbian relationship is just as legitimate and open as a heterosexual one. This kept pleasantly surprising me throughout my reading of the book. The adventure part of the story was fun, including traveling across kingdoms, on "wind-ships" across deserts, and plenty of sword fighting. …This book is worth reading for its fantasy world alone. In our world, where those in the LGBTQ communities still often face derision, prejudice, and danger for living

and loving openly, being immersed in a world where the Queen can openly love another woman is a refreshing break from reality."
—Amanda Chapman, Librarian, Davisville Free Library (RI)

"*Birthright* by Missouri Vaun is one of the smoothest reads I've had my hands on in a long time."—*Lesbian Review*

The Time Before Now

"[*The Time Before Now*] is just so good. Vaun's character work in this novel is flawless. She told a compelling story about a person so real you could just about reach out and touch her."—*Lesbian Review*

The Ground Beneath

"One of my favourite things about Missouri Vaun's writing is her ability to write the attraction between two women. Somehow she manages to get that twinkle in the stomach just right and she makes me feel as if I am falling in love with my wife all over again."
—*Lesbian Review*

All Things Rise

"The futuristic world that author Missouri Vaun has brought to life is as interesting as it is plausible. The sci-fi aspect, though, is not hard-core which makes for easy reading and understanding of the technology prevalent in the cloud cities. ...[T]he focus was really on the dynamics of the characters especially Cole, Ava and Audrey—whether they were interacting on the ground or above the clouds. From the first page to the last, the writing was just perfect."—*AoBibliosphere*

"This is a lovely little Sci-Fi romance, well worth a read for anyone looking for something different. I will be keeping an eye out for future works by Missouri Vaun."—*Lesbian Review*

"Simply put, this book is easy to love. Everything about it makes for a wonderful read and re-read. I was able to go on a journey with these characters, an emotional, internal journey where I was able to take a look at the fact that while society and technology can change vastly until almost nothing remains the same, there are some fundamentals that never change, like hope, the raw emotion of human nature, and the far reaching search for the person who is able to soothe the fire in our souls with the love in theirs."
—*Roses and Whimsy*

Writing as Paige Braddock

Jane's World and the Case of the Mail Order Bride

"This is such a quirky, sweet novel with a cast of memorable characters. It has laugh out loud moments and will leave you feeling charmed."—*Lesbian Review*

Visit us at www.boldstrokesbooks.com

By the Author

All Things Rise

The Time Before Now

The Ground Beneath

Whiskey Sunrise

Valley of Fire

Death by Cocktail Straw

One More Reason to Leave Orlando

Smothered and Covered

Privacy Glass

Birthright

Crossing the Wide Forever

Love at Cooper's Creek

Take My Hand

Proxima Five

Spencer's Cove

Chasing Sunset

The Sea Within

Writing as Paige Braddock:

Jane's World: The Case of the Mail Order Bride

THE MANDOLIN LUNCH

by

Missouri Vaun

2021

THE MANDOLIN LUNCH

ISBN 13: 978-1-63555-566-0

This Trade Paperback Original Is Published By
Bold Strokes Books, Inc.
P.O. Box 249
Valley Falls, NY 12185

First Edition: January 2021

CREDITS
EDITOR: CINDY CRESAP
PRODUCTION DESIGN: SUSAN RAMUNDO
COVER DESIGN BY TAMMY SEIDICK

Acknowledgments

A few things happened to jump-start this story. Evelyn and I visited a small, charming town called Dillsboro, North Carolina, and I thought to myself, this would be a great setting for a romance novel. I made notes and took pictures, embellished a bit, and kept the location in a drawer for a couple of years until the actual story presented itself. That part happened one night over dinner with our friends Renee and Karen. We were each retelling "how we met" stories. Theirs involved a mandolin repair at a music shop and an accidental lunch (I'm taking some narrative license here), but the end result was an encounter that I started calling "The Mandolin Lunch." So, special thanks to Renee and Karen for allowing me to use this as the title for the book. And, Renee, I really appreciate all your input about music, performing, and the mandolin. Renee is part of a Bay Area band called Blame Sally. Do yourself a favor and look them up.

I would also like to add a special thank you to Jenny Harmon. Her years as a teacher made her a huge asset in the crafting of this story.

As always, gratitude to the Bold Strokes dream team: Rad, Sandy, Cindy, Ruth, and Carsen. You guys are the best. And to my beta readers, Vanessa, Alena, Rachel, and Karen. And to my wife, Evelyn, whose love inspired me to write romance in the first place.

My intention was to write a sweet, hopeful story for a time when we need one most. To my readers, I hope you enjoy it.

Dedication

To Renee and Karen

CHAPTER ONE

Garet Allen stood in the middle of the upstairs bedroom with the empty duffel bag drooping from a strap across her shoulder. Welcome to the beginning of another end. She and Jillian were over, finished, done. All that remained was the last scene and then—exit, stage right. Garet exhaled, a long slow breath.

The antique oak dresser squeaked in complaint as Garet tugged the drawer free. A picture frame on top of the dresser wobbled and loudly plunked facedown. Balancing the drawer on her hip with one arm, she righted the small frame. It was a photo of Jillian and her at a black-tie fundraiser for the Human Rights Campaign right after they'd first started dating. She shifted the drawer, holding it in front of her as she studied the photograph. Jillian had insisted on buying her the suit. Jillian was wearing a sleek black dress, and her slender, pale arm was draped through Garet's casually as they'd posed for the photo. From the outside, they probably looked like a perfect match.

The truth was never that simple.

Relationships were nothing but layered complications beneath a veneer of attraction. Maybe that was the problem. Garet got so distracted by the attraction part that she failed to notice all the ways *a relationship would never work* in the long-term. Half the time she wondered if it really *was* all her fault. If relationships failed because she aspired to be the person she thought her partner wanted her to be, rather than the person she really was. Usually, she was unable to maintain the I'm-a-grownup facade for more than a couple of months. That's when problems started to show up. Luckily, Garet had a system, more accurately, an exit strategy for when the problems began to reach a critical level, as they inevitably did.

Garet's basic strategy, for her own sanity, was to keep the level of commitment limited to one drawer. Regardless of how in the beginning she thought every relationship would last forever. What did forever look like anyway? Anything more than one drawer of clothing stored at your girlfriend's place and you were bound to lose something valuable, including your autonomy.

Everything Garet needed to pack was in one dresser drawer, except for the suit that mocked her from the open closet door. She should never have allowed Jillian to buy it. She'd looked like a Jane Bond imposter the entire evening.

Garet had given Jillian the wrong impression right from the start. Garet had let Jillian think her wardrobe, and her life, needed improvement. Both probably did, but any improvement was bound to be short-lived because the truth was Garet liked herself the way she was.

Just after college, Garet had fallen head over heels for a therapist, Kelly. People might say falling for a therapist was her first mistake, but she was certain her larger mistake was filling up an entire dresser with clothing at Kelly's apartment. She was too young to know that was three drawers too many. She'd lost several of her favorite T-shirts in the breakup. Because inevitably when you've got several drawers full of stuff at someone's house, something is bound to be in the hamper waiting to be washed when you hurriedly pack to leave.

It's hard to move freely when you're traveling with too many things.

It was also impossible for Garet to ever win an argument with Kelly. Therapists were always taking every situation apart to examine the inner workings, or Garet's inner workings. Either way, Garet had gotten in over her head, with the drawers of stuff to prove it.

That breakup with Kelly taught Garet some hard lessons.

That epic breakup was the genesis of the one-drawer rule. Sorting out her inner workings still hadn't happened, not by Garet or any of the well-intentioned exes who'd come after Kelly. In Garet's opinion, if you took something apart—separated it into too many smaller pieces—they never fit back together again. Better not to put things under a microscope, especially messy things like needs and feelings. Besides, Garet didn't really want to change.

With a sweeping motion, Garet upended the drawer into the duffel bag on the floor at her feet.

"Go ahead, leave." That sounded like a dare. Jillian, her ex-girlfriend as of five minutes ago, stood in the bedroom doorway with her hands on her hips.

Wasn't that exactly what she was in the process of doing—leaving?

"You're so immature."

"Sticks and stones, Jillian, sticks and stones." Garet wasn't going to get pulled into another argument she would inevitably lose. This six-month relationship had lasted four months longer than it should have. She chided herself for not packing up her single drawer sooner.

She glanced up at Jillian's reflection in the mirror over the dresser. Jillian's pencil skirt and dark, fitted blazer hugged her subtle curves. She'd obviously come straight from the law office. Whereas Garet was in her usual *I'm an artist and I work from home* attire. Her faded, ripped jeans were only one rung above flannel lounge pants. Her short hair was askew, falling into her eyes, and she'd only just noticed a coffee stain on her gray T-shirt. She and Jillian were a case study in opposites and why, even if opposites initially attract, they inevitably repel each other like inverted magnets.

"I should have known you'd never really commit to this relationship. Just like everything else in your life. You're afraid of anything that gets too serious. Afraid to actually need someone or, heaven forbid, for them to need you." Jillian didn't even raise her voice. She was in lawyer mode—calm, tactical, and self-righteous.

Garet wondered if it was tiresome for Jillian to always be right.

"That's not entirely true." Garet zipped the duffel with one swift swipe.

"Which part?"

"I do take things seriously." She stood and faced Jillian with the bag in her hand. "Look, I'm doing you a favor. Be honest, you're not even that upset about this. And now you can go find someone who's a better fit for you. Someone who makes six figures and drives a BMW. That's who you really want and you and I both know it." That sounded a little callous, but it was also true.

"So, I should thank you?"

"Well, only if you really want to." She didn't mean to sound like a jerk, but she feared she was treading very close to jerk territory. They'd been arguing a lot and she just wasn't in the mood to argue any more. It was all such a waste of mental energy.

Jillian deserved a serious girlfriend, a girlfriend who'd lie in bed on Sunday and read the *New York Times* with her. A girlfriend who liked her coffee in a French press. Jillian deserved a serious, adult girlfriend—a grown-up—and that was not Garet. She knew it and she was sure Jillian knew it too. This whole breakup scene was simply a formality for something that should have happened weeks ago.

Garet paused to give the moment some air, to give Jillian a chance to get any remaining grievances off her chest. When Jillian said nothing, Garet slipped past her and trotted down the stairs. At this point Garet wasn't even angry, she just wanted to be somewhere quiet, alone with her thoughts.

"You should do something with your life. You know that, right?" Jillian remained on the top step and didn't follow. "You should create *real* art instead of wasting your talent drawing cartoons."

"They're not cartoons, they're children's literature!" Garet slammed the door, blocking out any response from Jillian.

Six months together and Jillian still hadn't taken time to figure out the difference between cartoons and the storybooks Garet created. Who was it that didn't take things seriously? Jillian said she cared, but she continually minimized Garet's work as juvenile. In truth, the books she created *were* for kids, but she hoped they were anything but insubstantial. She was actually striving for something magical, something meaningful, something to inspire kids to feel empowered and dream big.

She tossed the faded canvas duffel bag onto the passenger seat and climbed into her vintage Volvo station wagon. The boxy 1980 wagon was a hand-me-down ride from her grandmother, proof that she was suffering for her art. In fact, suffering to the point of being unable to afford a modern automobile, let alone a BMW.

Garet gave the car a moment to warm up and then eased away from the curb. She didn't need to make a fast getaway. It wasn't as if she was running away. Although, the odometer, which currently read two hundred eighty-seven thousand miles, might tell a different story.

Afternoon traffic on the connector was thick. Garet merged, but given the advanced age of her car, she didn't angle for the fast lane. She hugged the shoulder as she followed the throng of taillights toward downtown Atlanta.

CHAPTER TWO

Tess Hill stood for a moment, taking in the last warmth of summer. The grass around the turn of the century, two-story, wood-framed house was thick, lush, and green. A hint of smoke was in the air, tinted with the scent of an outdoor barbeque. One of her neighbors was grilling something savory. She loved this neighborhood. Here, she felt sheltered and cared for. It was a good habit she figured, to take moments every now and then to acknowledge all the ways in which you were blessed. A place to call home was one of them.

Tess bent down as she returned to one of her weekly chores—laundry. She shook the damp fabric as she pulled it from the basket. She stretched to her full five foot six inches and folded the edge of the sheet over the clothesline. She'd left the dangling corner in the laundry basket to keep it off the ground, but that didn't stop a ladybug from lightly traveling up from the lush grass. The bug's bright red wings were a tiny pop of color against the white cotton cloth. She clipped the sagging side of the flat sheet with a clothes pin and then swept her fingers across the fabric to smooth it into the warm breeze. The small red-winged passenger took flight as the sheet fluffed and billowed.

Lady bugs were good luck, right?

The thought of it made her smile.

She loved the smell of clean, line-dried bed linens. To Tess, almost nothing smelled more like summer. It was mid-September and the warm days would soon transition to autumn, so she wanted to take advantage of line drying the laundry as often as possible until the weather changed. Not to mention the added bonus of lowering her electric bill.

The pillowcases filled the last two spaces on the clothesline strung between crosspieces, mounted on sturdy four-by-four posts along the side of the house. Getting her brother Nathan to install the clothesline after they moved in had been the answer to one of her little hopes. Tess measured them out in small batches, little hopes and wishes. She paced herself, not expecting for so much as to be disappointed. Actually, she was rarely disappointed, one of the byproducts of keeping expectations low. Even still, it wasn't as if she wasn't optimistic. She practiced optimism daily, making a conscious effort to love the life her choices had made. It wasn't that she regretted how her life had been changed by that one night so long ago. Every time she thought back, she knew, even if she could go back in time she would still make the same decisions.

She'd gone to the lake with friends. It had been the last week before she was supposed to start grad school. Everyone was coupling up, and she was smitten with this French exchange student who'd joined the party late. She was usually attracted to women, but for some reason the young Frenchman caught her eye. He was more androgynous than masculine, and she was curious, in a *why not* sort of way. She'd only ever been with one guy, briefly, in high school. Those liaisons had been mostly awkward teen exploration. Wasn't college all about trying new things? Maybe she'd had too much white wine. Or maybe it was his azure blue eyes. Francois was sensitive, attentive, and sexy. She'd had fun and enjoyed his attentions, but Tess wasn't about to switch teams for good. They'd had one night, that night by the lake, and then he'd flown back to his home country. She'd had no plans or expectations to see him again. She literally didn't even get his last name. It took another three weeks for Tess to realize she was pregnant.

For the briefest moment Tess considered alternatives. None felt right. She couldn't explain it, and if she'd tried no one would have believed her, but before the baby was born, she could hear the infant's voice sometimes in her head. Somehow, she knew that having the baby was something she needed to do, *had* to do. Luckily, Tess's mom and dad got on board with the idea of being grandparents. Her parents lovingly supported her through the pregnancy, and she ended up getting a teaching job back home after the baby was born. A girl. She'd named her June.

Grad school had morphed into one year following undergrad to get a teaching certificate, but she had no regrets. It was strange how everything just seemed to work out, as if fate had planned things out this way all along. Everything just fell into place. Tess was a single mom at twenty-three, and that was okay.

Over the past six years, she'd crafted a full life, on an inadequate income. This feat required constant ingenuity. Her teaching salary paid just enough, if she budgeted carefully and worked at the music store during the summer. She even took weekend shifts sometimes during the school year. And then there was also the occasional performance at the local café, but that was really just for fun and tips.

Tess picked up the empty laundry basket and turned toward the house, but then it struck her that the yard was very quiet. Maybe too quiet. She shielded her eyes from the sun with her hand and searched in the darker, shady areas at the edge of the lawn for her daughter. She dropped the basket on the front steps and rounded the corner of the house in search of June.

June sat cross-legged on a beach towel, facing her neighbor's dog, Richard. A tea set was unevenly balanced on the towel between them. Richard had a red scarf around his neck, no doubt a wardrobe embellishment deemed necessary by June for a formal afternoon tea.

Tess was fond of her neighbors Betty and Ray. They'd been retired for several years, and when their daughter accepted a new job that required lots of travel, they'd dutifully agreed to take care of her dog, Richard. Betty and Ray were cat people, and Richard seemed to good-naturedly tolerate their indifference to his canine habits. Richard was equal parts wire-haired terrier and mystery mutt, medium sized, and adorably fluffy in all the right places. He had a black nose and shining dark orbs for eyes peeking out from beneath bushy eyebrows.

June badly wanted a dog of her own, but thankfully had agreed to settle for playdates with Richard for now. Motherhood, a full-time teaching job, and a part-time job was almost more than she could handle. Throw in afterschool activities and there was no way she could add pet care to the mix. These were the moments when she wished she weren't alone. If she had a partner, June could have a dog. What else was June missing out on simply because Tess couldn't do everything alone? It wasn't only June's needs, what about hers?

Sometimes the loneliness was so real that it occupied space in the house. But that was mostly late at night when she couldn't sleep, or when she longed to be held, or…

She let the thoughts trail off. Tess tried dating when June was younger and it was too complicated. She either didn't want to share June with someone else, or didn't trust them to have any parental-type role in June's life. She'd felt guilty that she was putting her needs above her child's needs every time she went out with anyone. In the end, it just wasn't worth it. They had a good thing going. They were happy.

Tess stood at the corner of the house watching June, who was lost in her own world.

"Sweetie, I'm not sure Richard should eat cookies." Tess had gotten close enough to see that June was feeding him.

"Mom, they're not cookies, they're animal crackers." June, all of six years old, was sometimes too clever for her own good.

"Whether they are cookies or crackers is not the issue. They're shaped like animals, not *for* animals."

Richard gently accepted another cookie from June's tiny palm.

"I'm serious, June Bug. You'll make him sick."

"But he likes them." June whined a little.

"I'm sure he does." Tess retrieved her basket. "Sometimes we like things that aren't good for us." She waited until she saw June close the box of animal crackers before she headed up the steps and into the house.

It was getting late. She had just enough time to change clothes and drop June off at her mother's place before heading into work. She usually went into the music store in the afternoon to give Mark, the owner, a break. She'd give lessons, or work alongside him assisting customers. For some reason, this past summer, everyone wanted guitar lessons. The mandolin was her preferred string instrument, but she was quite capable of conducting guitar lessons for beginners.

School had started already so she'd dropped back to only helping Mark on Saturdays. Sunday was her day with June.

"Please take Richard home. I have to go to work in a few minutes." She talked through the open bedroom window as she buttoned a fresh blouse. "Come on now, don't dawdle."

Tess glanced in the mirror over the bathroom sink. She ran damp fingers through her hair and tucked a few unruly strands behind her ears and then applied just a little eyeliner.

"June! Did you hear me say, no dawdling!" She watched at the window until June actually got up and led Richard by the collar back to his own house.

She returned to the mirror to add lipstick.

Dawdle? Since when did she say dawdle? She was beginning to sound like her mother.

CHAPTER THREE

The Peach Café wasn't that busy for a Saturday. Maybe the first wave of the breakfast rush had passed. Several years ago, the Peach, as the locals referred to it, had been purchased and turned into a franchise. Now they were in multiple locations, but none had the shabby chic charm of the original. Seating was limited in the cozy café located in a small storefront near Candler Park, a quaint in-town Atlanta neighborhood. The Peach served breakfast all day. Garet loved breakfast, any time of day.

On weekends, half the fun was grabbing a coffee from the *Help yourself* table out front and then loitering on the sidewalk with your friends, while you waited for a table to open up. Back in the day, she'd be feeling sleep-deprived and on occasion, hung over and not quite ready for eggs, in any form, until late morning. But that was a long time ago. Garet was two years past thirty and too mature for all the late-night shenanigans, right?

Garet scanned the brightly colored interior for her best friend, Lane. There was no sign of her, so Garet grabbed an open table and ordered a coffee. Lane was dependably five to seven minutes late for everything. Garet was doctoring her coffee with cream and raw brown sugar when the bell over the door chimed. She glanced up as Lane ambled toward the table.

Lane Westridge looked like a woman in need of a few more hours of sleep. Her T-shirt had that rumpled, slept-in look, and her jeans were faded with smudges of oil stains across the thighs. Lane owned Westridge Motors, a woman-friendly garage located in an old brick front industrial building along Dekalb Avenue. The shop was literally a five-minute drive from the restaurant, but Lane didn't really look as if she'd come from work. It wasn't as if she had to work anyway. Thanks to her family's money, work for Lane was more of a hobby. She took off her sunglasses, squinted at the waitress, and ordered a coffee. She slouched in the seat across from Garet.

People sometimes assumed Lane and Garet were related. They probably did have enough similarities to pass for cousins. They had a similar lanky build and a shared affection for classic Levi's and plaid shirts. Most people weren't observant enough to notice that Lane's eyes were brown and Garet's were blue. Garet's brown hair was also a few shades darker. But they were both almost five ten, and slender, with similar mannerisms. They'd roomed together in college so they'd definitely rubbed off on each other. Garet figured that was why people mistook them for family. They *were* family, just not the DNA variety.

"I think I figured out why you love this place so much." Lane brushed a clump of hair away from her forehead.

"You mean besides breakfast all day?" Garet sipped her coffee loudly. It was hot and she didn't want to burn her tongue.

"Yeah, besides that."

"Because I love the biscuits?"

"The biscuits are amazing, but no. Because it looks like someone decorated it using every color from a giant box of crayons." The waitress returned with Lane's coffee and she glanced up. "Thank you."

"I'll give ya'll a minute to look at the menu." The waitress returned to the counter to pick up food for another table.

"I do like lots of color." Garet responded to Lane's original comment. Even the Fiestaware dishes were every shade of the rainbow.

"Well, the walls in here are bright enough to wake the dead. Or the extremely hung over." Lane surveyed the room as she sipped her black coffee.

"You have the look of someone who might fall into the latter category."

"Long night." Lane gave the waitress her full attention.

"Ya'll ready to order?" Her pen hovered over a small wire-bound note pad. The edges of it were darkened from use and coffee spills.

Neither of them needed to check the menu. They ate at the Peach often enough to know what they wanted. The Piedmont omelet with creamy grits for Lane and the turkey pot roast with eggs for Garet.

"Are you all packed?" asked Lane.

"Yeah, the car is loaded. I was gonna leave after breakfast." She searched in her jeans pocket for the keys to her apartment and handed them to Lane.

"You're really saving my ass, you know."

"Yeah, yeah, not like it's the first time." Garet smiled. She gratefully accepted a warmup for her coffee from the waitress.

Lane and her girlfriend had broken up just a few days earlier and Lane had agreed to move out but hadn't found a place. Sleeping on the living room couch in the apartment you shared with your ex was no way to survive a breakup.

"When do you start the teaching gig?"

"Monday." Garet rested her elbows at the edge of the table. "I figure I'll have the weekend to get settled and then be ready to start on Monday. You staying at my apartment while I'm away saves me all kinds of headaches. Maybe, just this once, you're saving *my* ass."

The waitress showed up with their order. Garet leaned back to make room for a heaping plate of food.

"Let's just call it mutual ass saving and be thankful it worked out." Lane gave Garet a sincere look with her fork midair. "So, you and Jillian?"

"Over. Beyond over."

"Good." Lane forked a huge bite of the omelet. "She wasn't right for you."

"Says the dating expert."

"Hey, I'm an expert on what doesn't work."

"That you are."

They both laughed.

Deep down, Garet wondered if the laughter was born of some sadness that neither of them wanted to face. It was true that they both loved their freedom and Lane and Garet had helped each other through numerous dating disasters. But they were both just beyond thirty. Shouldn't they be figuring out how to avoid some of the romantic drama they seemed to continually stumble into?

Maybe the best course of action for Garet would be to remain single. Then she could focus on her work, drama free, without feeling guilty for ignoring her girlfriend with all the late nights she spent drawing.

"Are you sure about this teaching thing?" Lane looked serious. "You know there are children involved, right?"

"Hey, I have nothing against kids. I write and draw stories for children, remember?"

"Yeah, but I always just assumed those stories were sourced from your own personal immaturity, not based on any insights gained from hanging out with *actual* children."

"Ha ha, very funny." Garet shook her head. "You know I've been doing some substitute teaching for extra money. This assignment will just be a bit longer."

"Listen, if it's simply a money thing, you know I could float you a loan, I really don't mind—"

"No, thanks. I've got this."

Lane could easily loan Garet cash without hardship. But Garet made a rule early in their friendship to never take advantage of Lane's generosity in that way. She'd seen the way people sometimes used Lane for her charitable nature, or tried to, even though Lane refused to see it. Money could ruin a friendship and Garet had every intention of protecting theirs. Besides, Garet liked to make her own way, even if it was in a lower tax bracket than Lane's.

"Okay, okay, I know how you feel about borrowing money." Lane put her hands up in surrender. "Just know that I'm always here for you if you need me."

"Thanks." It was nice to know that Lane really meant it.

"So, back to this teaching adventure of yours. Three months is a lot of quality time with kids. That's all I'm sayin'." Lane sipped her coffee. "I mean, I don't personally know any children, but I've heard stories."

"It's gonna be a piece of cake."

"Said no teacher, ever."

Garet laughed, as if in the face of looming danger, and then got this weird little twist in the pit of her stomach. She hoped like hell she knew what she was getting into.

"You'll drive up and hang out with me sometime, right? It's a cute little touristy place. There's even a microbrewery in the old train depot."

"Yeah, yeah. I'll rescue you from boredom. At least once or twice. You know, if things don't get too busy here."

Garet knew what "busy" was code for.

"Who is she?"

Lane smiled broadly, a twinkle in her eyes, and waved the waitress over for a coffee refill.

❖

"Can we please get in the car?" Tess did her best to gather June and her backpack and hustle them toward the door.

For a six-year-old, June had mastered the art of general *foot dragging* when there was something she didn't want to do. Tess knew that June loved spending time with her grandmother, so that wasn't anything she usually tried to avoid. Probably she just hadn't been ready to relinquish her afternoon tea with Richard. A very long three minutes later, Tess backed her Subaru SUV out of the driveway and turned in the direction of her mother's house. With any luck, she could still make it to the music store almost on time.

"Maybe you and Gran can make some cookies today." Tess glanced up at the rearview mirror. In the back seat, June shrugged and looked out the window. She was definitely in some sort of funk. Possibly having to cut her play time with Richard short had put her in a bad mood.

They were quiet for a few minutes. The blinker sounded particularly loud in the silent interior of the car.

"What are you thinking about, June Bug?"

"I was thinking about owls." June rubbed her eyes.

Maybe she needed a nap.

"Owls are very interesting."

"Yeah." June yawned.

"You know, owls are nocturnal."

"Yes, Mom…I know owls are *not* turtles."

Tess laughed, which made June look in her direction for the first time.

"What's so funny?" June frowned.

"Nothing, sweetheart."

A few minutes later, she turned into the driveway of her parents' single level, brick house. It was a ranch style, three-bedroom place with a nice-sized yard that featured a few older hardwoods. Her mother had grown up in Shadetree and wanted to move the family back there. Tess's father had taken a job in Shadetree when she was a teen, so she'd sort of grown up in this house. Theirs had been a tight family unit. She and her brother were only a little more than two years apart and had been very close. Actually, they were still close, but life and adulthood sometimes kept them apart. Her brother traveled for work. He and his wife lived in the Atlanta suburbs, closer to the airport.

It was an odd experience to return to your childhood home as a grown-up. She saw everything now through adult eyes. Rooms that had seemed so big, choices her parents made that seemed odd—she now realized some of those choices had been sacrifices made for the sake of family. Her mother had worked outside the home before they moved back to Shadetree. Her father made a modest income working as the county fire chief. Her dad was quite popular in that role; she always joked with him that he was the unofficial mayor of Shadetree. It was amazing now to think that her folks had been able to own a home *and* help with her college expenses.

Everyone always said that things were different back then, that the middle class had actually been able to afford to own a home and a car and even take vacations. Tess knew she was lucky to be able to live in her aunt's house for almost next to nothing. She paid a below average rental fee to her aunt, who now lived in a condo down in Florida. Mostly, her "fee" for living there was keeping the place up.

Although, without her dad around, she wasn't quite as handy with repairs.

Tess missed her father. He was the sort of guy who never met a problem he couldn't solve. He could basically fix anything, mechanical or otherwise. She frequently missed being able to go to him when she needed to talk something through. He passed away suddenly from a heart attack only two years earlier.

Tess parked behind her mother's car. June sprang from the back seat, suddenly finding a spurt of energy that had been missing during their drive over. June only made it a few feet before realizing not only had she forgotten to close the car door, but she'd also left her bright pink backpack on the back seat. It was packed with coloring books, crayons, and her current favorite storybook. An afternoon without coloring books would be a terrible thing to endure. Tess had no doubt that her mother would be asked to read *Marty Moose's Big Day Out* at least twice before the day was over.

June bounded through the door and Tess followed.

"Don't run in the house!" But it was too late. June dropped her backpack in the living room and bolted out the screen door at the back of the house. The wood-framed door banged loudly.

Tess stood and watched for a moment. Her mother was in the garden. June ran to her, chatting excitedly about something that Tess was unable to hear from the house. She waved to her mother from the doorway.

"I'll be back by six."

"Will you stay for dinner?" Her mother stopped what she was doing and straightened, leaning against the long handle of the rake.

"Sure. Do you need me to pick up anything at the store?"

"No, I have everything."

"Okay, Mom. See you later." Tess paused and waited for June to look her way, but she was already digging into the dirt. "Good-bye, June Bug."

She knew she was lucky in so many ways. One of them was having her mother's help with June. That was huge and she tried her best not to take it for granted.

CHAPTER FOUR

Garet steered her faded blue Volvo onto Front Street. She slowed to a crawl and craned her neck to take in the architectural details of the vintage train depot turned microbrewery as she passed. She made a mental note to come back and sketch the historic structure. She was always scouting locations that she could use in her books. She had sketchbooks full of reference drawings for buildings, settings, and characters.

There was no way to deny that Shadetree, Georgia, was charming and quaint. Front Street ran east to west, parallel to the long-dormant railway, along the bank of the Tuskahee River. The old path of the railway had been turned into a bike path and walking trail. The south side of Front Street was the river and on the north side a thriving village peppered with all manner of shops housed in turn of the century Victorians interspersed with a few touristy gift shops and a tea house. Shadetree was small but busy, and the autumn tourist season was probably just beginning to ramp up.

The settlement had been officially named in 1883, for the grouping of willow trees that shadily lined the river's edge. The town didn't really come into its own until 1889 when the new railroad first began to bring tourists to the area. Just before the turn of the century, Shadetree was the largest non-county seat northeast of Atlanta. It was easy to see the allure for visitors, with its cool summers and beautiful mountain scenery.

Garet wondered why she hadn't escaped the heated asphalt of Hotlanta sooner for a weekend in Shadetree. It was romantically picturesque, a perfect getaway.

A pickup truck passed with a Confederate flag sticker on the back window, and she was reminded of why she hadn't visited sooner. Oh yeah, because despite how cute and quaint this town was, its fringes might be populated with rednecks who in all likelihood loathed gays, liberals, and kale.

Good thing she wasn't planning to stay for very long. This was a place where it might be hard for her to blend in. Not that she was particularly sophisticated or anything. She could definitely do a great imitation of a redneck in her beat-up University of Georgia ballcap and faded Levi's on weekends, but she had a hard time keeping quiet about social politics. And inevitably, that could get her into trouble. She wasn't sure why she'd agreed to accept a temporary teaching position at a small public school in the foothills of the Blue Ridge Mountains.

Due to the remoteness of the area, the county was required to keep the school open, otherwise kids would have to be bussed at least forty-five minutes away across the ring of mountains that surrounded the valley of unincorporated Tanner County. There were only about one hundred kids, kindergarten through twelfth grade. She wasn't sure if the smallness of the number made her more or less nervous.

Garet would be teaching art. One of the things she'd realized as a result of her occasional, scratch that—rare—substitute teaching posts was that art *theory* and art *practice* were two very different things. She was a working illustrator; she did art for a living. Reason would seem to support the notion that she knew what she was talking about, but there were rules about teaching the basics she'd need to follow before she embellished with her own, personal *real world* experiences. Might as well allow the kids to remain idealistic about the world of art for as long as possible.

She'd started filling in as a teacher for selfish reasons. It was true that Garet wrote and illustrated books for children, but she didn't actually have kids and she didn't really hang out with kids. At some point she decided a little market research would benefit her work. Substitute teaching allowed her to get paid for essentially doing research. And the kids got to learn from a professional artist. She figured it was a win-win.

In order to be certified, she had to go through some training, but that wasn't too bad. With a few extra classes and a four-year degree, she was able to substitute teach anywhere in Georgia. In her limited experience in the classroom it didn't seem that the educational training was nearly as important as the ability to wrangle a roomful of children. Garet knew she still had a lot to learn in that department. Kids tended not to respect Garet as a figure of authority. She was fairly certain that was equally her fault because she didn't really care for authority herself and took every opportunity to avoid it in her own life. It was only natural that students picked up on that when she was in the classroom. They could probably sense her disdain for authority. At any rate, this particular trait was something that made her popular with pupils, but not so much with the other teachers.

Since this was a longer post than just for a day or two, she'd have to be a little more buttoned up when it came to discipline. It was one thing to let the kids have their fun if you were only going to be with them for a day, but this was at least a three-month assignment.

Garet was at the far end of town now. She slowed so that she could more easily read the numbers on each mailbox. She was looking for—there it was. The name *H. Green* was hand painted on a mailbox at the end of a white picket fence. Garet turned into the driveway and parked near a neat row of groomed boxwoods. The house was tidy and well-kept. Its architecture looked to be from the early 1930s, but the paint looked new. She'd always been partial to light blue houses with white trim and she wasn't even sure why.

After knocking lightly on the front door, she rotated to survey the yard. A wooden chair swing hung under a large tree in the center of the front lawn. The slats were gray from sun and weather. A couple of faded cushions adorned the seat back. The swing looked well loved. Movement caught her eye farther up in the sprawling oak, a flash of color. A blue jay rested for an instant and then took flight.

"Hello. You must be Garet." A cheerful woman probably in her early forties, who was well-dressed for a Saturday, held the door open and motioned her inside. She wore a floral silk blouse and capris slacks. Sensible, low-heeled pumps rounded out the ensemble. She looked as if she were about to attend a country club garden party. "I'm Hildy Green. We spoke last week."

"Yes. Thank you for renting the unit to me over the phone." She followed Hildy into the cool interior. A ceiling fan created a welcomed breeze.

"Well, the school had already checked your credentials. You know, the principal, Henry Carlisle, is a deacon in my church. If he thinks you're okay, then that's good enough for me."

A town this small would be hard to live in. Garet was suddenly appreciating the anonymity of living in a large city. Atlanta could at times feel like it was small too, but not this small.

Hildy was in the kitchen, searching through a drawer.

"There it is." She smiled and held up a key. "Would you like to see the cottage?"

"Yes, thank you. I was hoping to move in tonight and have the rest of the weekend to get settled before school on Monday. If that's all right with you."

"Of course. It's just this way." Hildy led Garet through the kitchen and out the back door. "It's a granny unit and mine now lives in a condo in Destin, Florida, so I figured I might as well rent it out. You're my first tenant."

She smiled at Garet over her shoulder as if she'd just revealed some top-secret information. Hildy's entire demeanor sparkled with playfulness, despite her professional looking attire.

The backyard cottage was painted to match the house. It had a little covered front stoop adorned with potted plants. Hildy ushered them inside.

"Like I said over the phone, it's furnished and it has a wall unit for air conditioning. Although, you won't need it in another week or so at night. It'll start cooling off soon. The same unit gives heat too, when you need it." Hildy glanced around the space and then handed Garet the key.

The kitchen was visible from the living room. Basically, the cottage was one big room, with the sitting area on one side and a kitchenette on the other, divided by a counter and stools for seating. A bedroom and bathroom were off the living room. It was small but this was all Garet needed. This was a short-term thing. The main room had good light from a large bay window. Yes, this was going to work well. She could do the teaching job during the day and the rest of the time she'd work on the pages of artwork for the book. Three months without distraction was just what she needed to finish. The whole setup was sort of genius on her part. She mentally patted herself on the back.

Normally she'd have to take additional freelance art and design jobs to pay her bills until the second half of the advance money for a book came through. Freelance work was a terrible distraction and it sapped her energy for drawing. This teaching job was going to give her several weeks of steady pay without all the headaches of dealing with clients and chasing payment. For an instant, Garet wondered whether kids would be easier than clients. She hoped so. They had to be, right?

"Well, what do you think?"

Garet had been off on a side trip inside her head and had sort of forgotten that Hildy was still there.

"This seems great. I have cash for the first month's rent in my car." She motioned over her shoulder with her thumb. "Should I get it now?"

"That would be perfect, thank you." Hildy smiled.

Hildy had a very simple one-page rental agreement that basically covered the monthly fee and due dates. After Garet gave Hildy the first month's rent, Hildy even helped her carry in a few boxes. Garet hadn't packed too much, just enough to get by. Luckily, the cottage was furnished, so within an hour she'd unloaded and almost unpacked. Her drawing equipment wasn't set up, but she decided to take a stroll around town and set up her work space later. She wanted to get more of a feel for the place, and the best way to do that was on foot.

Garet locked the door, sauntered down the driveway, and made a left on Front Street.

CHAPTER FIVE

After dropping June off with her mom, Tess stopped into the Cookie Company for a latte before heading down the street to the music shop. She'd run out of time so she'd skipped lunch. The vegan backpacker cookie she inhaled as she walked, plus the latte chaser, would have to cover her until dinner.

Tess arrived for her afternoon shift, and the store was buzzing. Mark's Guitar Shop on Front Street also specialized in dulcimers, mandolins, and banjos. While he did have a decent selection of guitars, bluegrass was his first love, dulcimers were the instruments he preferred. Mark was known for crafting his own series of instruments that were sort of a cross between a banjo and an Appalachian dulcimer. They were made to be played upright like a banjo, but having the dulcimer construction made them especially suited to play bluegrass and Celtic music. Mark was also one of the members of the group she played with every third Sunday. They'd been playing together since high school.

Tess loved to play bluegrass. She'd grown up listening to it at her grandparents' place. Bluegrass was always on the radio in the kitchen while her grandmother was baking. The tune of "Foggy Mountain Breakdown" conjured the scent of baked apple pies. Music, memories, and food—all of it would come rushing back in an instant. The ability of music to alter place and time and mood always inspired her. The transformative power of music was something she tried to share every day in class with her students.

Tess immediately got to work when she arrived, walking up to a customer waiting near the dulcimer display.

"Can I help you with something?" Tess stowed her purse behind the counter and spoke to the customer with short dark hair who was eyeing the instruments hanging along the wall. At first glance, from behind, Tess had assumed the person was a guy. Now that Tess was facing her it was obvious this person was a woman. Androgynous, yes, but definitely a woman.

"I've never played a dulcimer, but they look really interesting."

The woman facing her was wearing a vintage Star Wars T-shirt featuring a nearly completely faded image of an X-wing fighter. Tess knew this because her brother had been a Star Wars fanboy when they were kids. Over the T-shirt the woman wore a lightweight unzipped gray hoodie. Her jeans were faded, and her Converse sneakers had seen some serious mileage. Her dark hair was short and stylishly tousled. Her blue eyes sparkled with curiosity and were at the moment laser focused on Tess. The attention made Tess wish she'd done something with her hair or possibly worn a different shirt. After a moment, she looked away, focusing on the instruments rather than the adorable woman with the ice blue eyes.

"I haven't seen you in the store before. Are you a musician?" Tess didn't usually ask personal questions, but something about this woman's innocent and open demeanor gave her the impression she could.

"I'm new in town, just rented a place today." She held out her hand to Tess. "I'm Garet."

Garet was tall and leanly fit but didn't strike her as someone particularly into athletics. Garet had more of a bookish air. She was fashionably nerdy. The only thing missing was horn-rimmed glasses. Garet had the look of someone who would make a great friend, or possibly even something more. Tess tried not to stare, tried not to notice the smoothness of Garet's neck or her slender fingers resting on the glass case. There were black smudges on the fingers of Garet's right hand that conjured questions, but she set them aside. She was at work and Garet was a customer. Even still, there was no harm in being cordial to someone who'd just moved to Tess's little corner of the world.

"I'm Tess." She accepted Garet's hand. Warmth seeped up her arm from their clasped fingers. "So, you're interested in a dulcimer?"

"I don't know much about them, but I was drawn to all the different shapes. And the wood is beautiful." Garet seemed suddenly self-conscious. She sunk her hands into her pockets and took a step away from the glass-topped counter that separated them.

"Well, each one is different. The voice and personality vary from instrument to instrument." Tess reached for one of the four-stringed dulcimers and handed it to Garet. "This one has more of a banjo twang." She waited a few minutes while Garet lightly strummed, then reached for another instrument for her to try. "This one has a more rounded, mellow sound."

"You're right, they each sound so different." Garet placed the second instrument on top of the glass case alongside the first one. She rubbed the dark walnut face of the dulcimer with her fingertips.

Garet was probably in her late twenties, maybe early thirties, and definitely had more of an urban look. Tess wondered if she played music regularly. Sometimes customers volunteered personal information while shopping. Something about music and sampling the instruments inspired people to share. Tess liked the way music opened people up.

"This one is the lightest and easiest to learn." Tess held a small dulcimer and deftly played a simple tune as she talked. "It has three strings all tuned to the same note, high and low. It has seven diatonic frets, which means you get an instrument that literally has no wrong notes."

"Says the woman who just played...was that a Beatles song?"

"Good ear." Tess handed the instrument to Garet for her to try. "It has the tone of a mandolin, which makes it my personal favorite."

Garet really had no interest in learning to play a dulcimer. She'd strolled by the music shop only to have boredom and curiosity lure her in. And now that she was talking to Tess she had the urge to try every instrument in the store. Especially if Tess sampled a tune on each one. The expression on Tess's face changed when she played. As if for an instant she was somewhere else, maybe on a different plane, or in some ethereal parallel universe. It was magical to watch and inspired Garet to linger.

Tess had layered, strawberry blond hair that she wore in a loose, three-strand braid that began low, below her collar and then extended just past her shoulder. The relaxed, open texture of the braid allowed a few shorter strands to curve, framing Tess's face in such a way as to perfectly accentuate her cheek bones. Though her delicate facial features would have looked at home in an eighteenth-century oil painting, her casual emerald blouse, skinny jeans, and slight build set her apart from the scruffy, mostly older, shoppers that populated the rustic music store. Her curve-hugging dark jeans were tucked into tall boots. Not the sort of boots someone would wear hiking. These were black leather boots with low heels that came almost to her knees. If she was wearing any makeup she did it so naturally that it was barely noticeable except for a little eyeliner accentuating her brown eyes. Tess was empirically, undeniably, distractingly pretty.

"Oh yes, I think this one is my favorite too." Garet strummed and smiled. She was stalling, enjoying Tess's attention. If she hadn't known it previously, she was now certain that she had no talent for music whatsoever.

Wait, what was she doing? She'd been single for less than twenty-four hours and she was already crushed out and flirting with the first beautiful woman she'd met in Shadetree. Get serious.

"We have songbooks that use a numbering system that makes it very easy to learn."

"Oh, so even someone as clueless as me can manage to learn to play?"

"Well, I haven't known you long enough to describe you as clueless. But yes, this simple instrument gives even novices an entry point."

Tess smiled and the temperature inside Garet's hoodie spiked upward.

Garet wanted to keep Tess engaged as long as possible. When Tess talked about the instruments her entire face lit up like sunlight on a shimmering lake. Her eyes sparkled and her obvious love of music was infectious.

Garet tried to think of something clever to say but was feeling conversationally inept. There was an awkward moment or two of silence between them. The corner of Tess's mouth quirked up in a half smile. A hum of random strains of music and voices filled the space as people chatted and sampled instruments. Was it suddenly louder than it had been a few minutes ago? Unsure of how else to break the silence between them, Garet picked up the dulcimer and strummed.

"I think you'd be very happy with that one." Tess made lingering eye contact.

Garet wasn't actually planning to purchase anything, and when another salesperson showed up with a vibe of closing the deal, she figured she'd lingered too long.

"That's a good choice." The man nodded his approval. "I can ring this up." He spoke to Tess. "Charlotte just dropped in to see you." He motioned toward the front of the shop with a tip of his head.

"Garet, it was nice to meet you."

Don't leave yet. Once again, Garet wanted to impress Tess with a clever turn of phrase, a response, anything, but once again, she just stood there, staring.

"This is Mark. He's the shop owner. He can answer any additional questions you might have. Oh, and welcome to Shadetree." Tess smiled as she slipped from behind the counter.

And just like that, she was gone. It was almost as if the light in the room left with her when she departed.

Mark waited patiently while Garet pretended to consider the instrument. Mark was probably close to her age, early thirties, tall and slim, with a thin beard. Both his beard and his short, shaggy hair were light brown. He owned the scruffy musician look.

"Would you like a case for that one?" Mark pressed her to make a decision or move along.

"I think I'll look around a bit more." She set the dulcimer on the glass surface. "Thank you." Garet ambled around the store, glancing every so often over her shoulder in Tess's direction. But she couldn't figure out a way to linger without coming off as a stalker, a very *not* musically inclined stalker.

CHAPTER SIX

Tess wouldn't have minded a few more minutes with Garet. She'd literally only discovered her name and nothing else. It was rare that someone—anyone—moved to Shadetree, let alone someone who caught her attention so immediately. But that was how things went, right? Timing was everything, or mostly everything. Garet had an adorably approachable air about her and she even smelled good. Tess had noticed when she stepped past Garet that she smelled deliciously inviting—vanilla with a hint of sandalwood. But Charlotte was waiting, so Tess didn't linger even if her curiosity inspired her to do so.

She met Charlotte near the front of the store and hugged her warmly.

"Hey, I'm sorry to bother you at work." Charlotte rubbed her hands on her belly. "Ow."

"Is the baby kicking?" Tess placed one hand over Charlotte's.

"Like a future soccer player."

"I can't believe you won't be at school Monday. Things will be so weird without you there." Tess was trying to mentally prepare to function without Charlotte for the next three months, but it was hard to imagine.

Charlotte was not only Tess's coworker, she was also one of her closest friends. The teacher's lounge and their shared classroom would feel very empty without Charlotte's sweet, calming presence. The children loved Charlotte. The timing of the pregnancy had been a bit of a surprise, but Tess knew Charlotte had wanted to have a baby for a while. Tess worried that Tim, Charlotte's boyfriend, might not be as ready. At any rate, maternity leave was inevitable at some point and Tess was excited for Charlotte.

"Text me if you need anything, or just need to vent about work." Charlotte shifted her weight from one foot to the other.

"I'll try not to bother you with school drama while you're out."

"Do you know who's covering my classes?"

"Someone from Atlanta. I hope I like her." Shadetree's school was small, and the student body so sparse, that art and music shared a classroom. It would be stressful to share the space with a stranger while Charlotte was out, but she'd try to be positive for Charlotte's sake.

"I think Tim is nervous." Charlotte bit her lower lip.

He should be, thought Tess. Having a baby was a big, life-altering, event. She knew that from personal experience. Charlotte was the adult in that relationship and Tim's world was about to be turned upside down. He needed to grow up, for Charlotte's sake, and the baby's.

"Being nervous is completely normal." Tess hugged Charlotte again. She wanted to soothe Charlotte's worries, even though she shared them. "Listen, call me if you guys need anything. No matter what time of day…well, I mean if it's during school I might not be able to leave, but any time, really. I mean it."

"I should probably let you get back to work. When I saw your car I just wanted to stop in and say hi and wish you luck next week."

"I'm sure it'll be okay, but definitely not the same without you." Tess glanced over her shoulder. Mark was outnumbered by customers.

The realization that Garet was no longer in the shop was a disappointment. She must have slipped out while Tess was focused on Charlotte. It was just as well. Between school and being a single parent, Tess really had no free time to date anyway. Funny, her thoughts had jumped from *nice to meet you* to a date. A mental leap like that hadn't happened in a long time.

❖

"Hi, Mom, it's just me," Tess called out as she opened the door. It took a moment to dislodge the key from the vintage lock. The doors and hardware were original to the house.

Her mother had only recently started locking the front door. A year or so after losing her father, her mother had begun to feel nervous alone in the house. Tess could relate. There were times when she was really glad that June was with her. Even though June was only six, she was a large presence in the house. June took up space and made Tess feel less alone. Sometimes, after June was in bed and the house grew quiet and dark, Tess lounged on the couch and tried to imagine having a partner. What would it be like to have someone to come home to at the end of the day, to share life's joys and struggles? It was hard to picture a stranger integrating into their little family unit, but sometimes, every now and then, Tess longed for someone to lean on. Not that she was particularly needy. But it would just be nice to have someone to share her life, someone who would hold her late at night and tell her everything would be okay.

She'd have those lonely moments and then they would quickly pass the second she tried to imagine anyone with any sort of parental role in June's life. June was a precious thing and the thought of trusting anyone with her child shut down any notions of dating. She'd tried a few times when June was a toddler and it just hadn't worked. Plus, there weren't many people interested in an instant family.

"We're in the kitchen." Her mother's voice was followed by the sound of dishware clinking.

Tess dropped her shoulder bag off in the living room and walked toward the noise. June was perched on her knees on a stool, her elbows rested on the countertop.

"June, please sit on the stool before you fall."

June huffed but did as she was told. She was wearing bright red rubber boots with shorts and a T-shirt. From the condition of her shorts, Tess assumed June had been helping her grandmother in the garden most of the afternoon. Mud and grass stains were evident.

"Are you hungry, sweetheart? I made dinner." Her mother swiveled and set a casserole dish on a wooden trivet near the stove.

Her gray hair fluffed around her face as she turned. She was wearing a lightweight blue work shirt, with the sleeves rolled up to her elbows. The knees of her khaki slacks were scuffed with dirt and grass stains to match June's shorts.

"I'm starved." The cookie and latte had evaporated long ago. She kissed her mother's cheek and then snagged a carrot stick from a nearby dish. "Thank you for making dinner."

"June, would you set the table please?" Her mother motioned with a nod of her head toward the silverware drawer.

"Sure." June hopped down.

"What do we say?" Tess prompted her.

"Yes, ma'am." June was barely tall enough to peer inside the drawer as she fished out forks and then got cloth napkins from the next drawer down.

"Did you make iced tea or should I just get water for all of us?" Tess pulled three glasses from the cabinet.

"I didn't make tea. I'm trying to cut down on my caffeine so I sleep better." Her mother served generous helpings of the casserole onto plates and carried each one to the table.

"Water is good for me too." Tess was sure she didn't drink enough to offset all the coffee she consumed. There was free coffee in the teacher's lounge so she was pretty sure she overindulged. Maybe she should cut back. She'd been staying up too late and her brain just wouldn't shut down at night.

The three of them settled around the table and they let June say grace.

"God is good, God is great. God, thank you for our daily bread. Amen." June rushed through the brief prayer.

"Is that the way the prayer goes?" Tess arched an eyebrow.

"That's my version." June shrugged and spooned food into her mouth.

"How was the store today? Busy?" Her mother offered her a plate with dinner rolls.

"It was steady. Pretty normal for a Saturday." Her mother's chicken casserole was one of Tess's favorites. It was like chicken and dressing all in one entree. She frequently made it herself. There was nothing handier than a one-dish meal. Especially one that could easily be reheated for leftovers. "What did you two get into today?"

"Weeds." June scrunched her nose.

"June Bug helped me with some weeding." Her mother smiled at June. "I'm not sure June enjoys gardening as much as I do, but she was very helpful."

"She may have inherited my non-green thumb." Tess was terrible at gardening.

She literally couldn't even seem to keep a house plant alive for more than two weeks, whereas her mother could probably get butter lettuce to grow in the desert. It was a talent that Tess didn't share. But Tess could practically play any musical instrument someone handed her, whereas her mother had no ear for music at all. Maybe the gardening gene and the music gene were mutually exclusive.

"Have you seen Charlotte?" her mother asked.

"I saw her today. She stopped by the shop for a minute."

"How is she? Is next week her first week of maternity leave?"

"Yes, it is. She's doing good. She said Tim is nervous."

Her mother huffed. "That boy...I'm concerned about that entire situation."

"I know what you mean." Tess worried that having a baby would end the relationship. Especially if Charlotte was ready for a family and Tim wasn't. It wasn't that Tim was a bad guy. He was just, well, immature. Tess didn't want to say more in front of June. Six-year-olds had no filter, and she was afraid June might blurt something out in front of Charlotte.

"What's wrong with Tim?" June asked.

"Nothing. He's about to become a father." Tess focused on June. "And remember what we said about talking with food in our mouth?"

"Yes, ma'am," June answered before swallowing.

Chapter Seven

Garet yawned and stretched. It was Sunday morning. What did people do here on Sunday morning? Probably attend church. Driving into town, she'd noticed far too many churches for such a small town. There'd been the Living Waters Fellowship, Victory Baptist Church, New Life Missionary Church, and about six others. There were so many churches here it almost made Garet nervous. If someone needed to find religion, this was the place to do it. Religion wasn't really Garet's thing, not since elementary school. To be exact, not since second grade, which was the last time her mother managed to get her into a dress for Easter.

These days, the only morning ritual she practiced religiously was the acquisition of good coffee. There'd been a couple of coffee options when she'd done her walking tour of Shadetree. Surely one of those spots also served Sunday brunch. If she got dressed and left now she'd beat the church crowd. That was assuming the local pastors were long-winded and wouldn't release congregations until twelve thirty.

She rubbed her eyes and checked the time on her phone. It was nine thirty. There was also a text from Lane. It was highly unusual to hear from Lane so early on a Sunday.

Lane's text read, *Want to do brunch?*

Was Lane driving out to see her already? Garet's mood brightened.

Just got up. What time and where? Garet propped up against her pillow and waited for a response.

I'm already driving. One hour. Your place. Text me the address.

Lane obviously needed to get out of town. Something must have gone sideways with the new girl. That hadn't taken very long—not good.

Garet got out of bed and sent Lane the address for the cottage as she headed for the shower.

Forty minutes later, Garet stepped outside to check the temperature. It was a sunny autumn day, probably in the sixties. Not a cloud in the sky. Nice.

"Well, hello there, neighbor." Hildy waved from the back door.

Garet wasn't used to having someone close enough to notice or care about her comings and goings. This would take a little getting used to.

"Good morning." Southern manners demanded a cordial response. Even if Garet wasn't really in the mood for small talk.

"Come have a coffee with me." Hildy waved her over.

"I was just about to go for a walk." *And get coffee elsewhere.* But Garet didn't say that last part out loud.

"Oh good. I'm glad I caught you then." Hildy's hospitality was clearly going to be hard to avoid, or refuse. "You can have a cup of hot coffee before you go for a walk."

Garet turned toward the back of the house where Hildy stood holding the door open for her just when Lane showed up. The driveway was nice and wide. At some point, the cottage had probably been a two-car garage. Lane pulled her V8 Mustang into the space behind Garet's aging Volvo. She wasn't sure what modifications Lane had done to make the Ford sound like there was a jet engine under the hood, but her arrival always got attention. It seemed even Hildy wasn't immune to the butch charm of a muscle car.

Lane unfolded her long legs from the driver's seat and Garet was fairly certain Hildy swooned just a little. Was her landlord a lesbian? Lane swept off her aviator sunglasses and smiled, first at Garet and then at Hildy.

"Oh, I'm sorry. I hope I didn't disturb your quiet Sunday morning." Lane took a few steps in Garet's direction, but she was talking to Hildy.

"Oh, not at all. I was just about to share a cup of coffee with Garet. I mean, not share…she would have her own cup and I would have mine."

Oh, good Lord, Hildy *was* swooning. Lane loved to flirt. And Hildy Green, despite signs of maturity, at least superficially, was clearly not immune to Lane's skillful charms. Great, her first morning in Shadetree was starting off with a bang.

"Mrs. Green, this is a friend of mine from Atlanta, Lane Westridge." Hildy stepped down from the back stoop as Lane and Garet approached. They crossed the grassy patch of backyard that separated the main house from the cottage.

"It's a pleasure to meet you, Mrs. Green." Lane held on to Hildy's hand for longer than necessary, and for a minute, Garet thought she might kiss it.

"That's *Miss* Green. But, please, call me Hildy."

"We should probably get going." Garet tried to hasten their departure. "I'll take a rain check on the coffee if you don't mind. Lane and I were planning to get brunch downtown."

"Of course, another time." Hildy hugged herself. "You should try the Riverside Café. It's next to the old train depot. They do a great brunch."

"Thank you, we'll do that." Garet put her hand on Lane's shoulder in an effort to usher her in the direction of Front Street.

"Very nice to meet you, Hildy." Lane walked backward for a few paces, smiling at Hildy. After several steps, she put her sunglasses back on and fell in beside Garet.

"Dude, you failed to mention that your landlord is a hotty." Lane playfully punched Garet's shoulder.

"I had no idea she was a lesbian until *you* arrived." Garet scowled. Lane was like some sort of lesbian litmus test.

"You're welcome." Lane grinned. "And by the way, your gaydar sucks."

They strolled along the sidewalk, in and out of shady spaces. Most of the quaint shops along Front Street, including Mark's Guitar Shop, were closed on Sunday. The parking spaces around the old train depot were mostly all occupied though, signaling that indeed the Riverside Café was the place to be for brunch. There were a few people seated on the deck overlooking the river drinking coffee, but it seemed that if you wanted real food and table service you had to sit inside.

There were four people in front of them. Garet surveyed the bustling room as they waited. The crowd was pretty much what she'd expected. Old guys in trucker hats, couples with children. Only a few people close to her age. It seemed the population of Shadetree was mostly retired folks and families. What had she expected? A rural gay getaway in the mountains?

"Party of two?" A matronly woman sized them up as she shuffled menus.

"Yes, ma'am." Garet nodded.

She and Lane followed the woman over to a two-top near the windows overlooking the river. Lucky seating. Garet took the chair that faced the windows, which meant she didn't have to look in the direction of the busy restaurant. Too much activity before coffee visually stressed her out. She preferred the view of the slow-moving, swirling water.

"Hey, it looks like there's going to be a band playing." Lane sounded happy about the discovery. "Someone is over there setting up speakers."

"Hmm, cool." Garet didn't turn around. She was singularly focused on the menu at the moment. Atlanta had a great live music scene, so a band playing during brunch sort of seemed normal.

"Hello, darlin', can I get two coffees here?" A woman with a serious southern drawl stood at the side of their table. Her nametag read Candi and she was wearing a snug, curve hugging T-shirt with the caption *Disastrously Pretty* in loopy letters. She had long, wavy blond hair loosely pulled up at the back.

"Yes, two coffees would be great." Lane propped her sunglasses on top of her head for a better view of Candi.

Candi was swallowed up by the crowded café. She returned swiftly holding two mugs with one hand and a coffee pot with the other. She plunked the white diner style mugs on the table and filled each to the brim. Then she propped her hand on one hip and looked them over.

"Are ya'll from out of town?"

"Yes—No." Lane and Garet answered in unison.

"Well, which is it? Yes or no?"

Candi was definitely flirting with Lane. Or maybe she was flirting with both of them, or possibly just *really* friendly. Sometimes with southern women it was hard to discern the difference, and Garet wasn't caffeinated enough to know for sure which it was.

"I just moved here," Garet offered. "She's visiting from Atlanta." Garet motioned in Lane's direction.

"Well, welcome to Shadetree." Candi pulled a small notebook from the tiny apron tied around her waist. She settled the coffee pot on the table so that she could write on the pad. "Do ya'll know what you want?"

"Hey, is there music today?" Lane was distracted.

Garet wanted to get food ordered before the place got any busier.

"Yes, didn't you see the sign in the window?" Candi pointed with her neon pink ballpoint pen. "Every third Sunday we host a Bluegrass Brunch."

"Excellent." Lane grinned and returned her attention to the menu. "I'll have a waffle and two eggs over easy."

"And for you, sweetie?" Candi looked at Garet.

"Um, two scrambled eggs and bacon…oh, and a biscuit. Thanks." She handed the folded menu to Candi.

She and Lane were quiet for a couple of minutes while they each doctored their coffees to taste. Garet sipped cautiously, but there'd been no need to worry. The coffee was quite good. Her mood instantly brightened and she regretted not adding a short stack of buttermilk pancakes to her order. Why was she so hungry?

Oh yeah, Jillian wasn't here. She and Jillian had broken up. She was happy. Happiness always improved her appetite.

"So, I didn't expect to see you so soon." Garet sipped the coffee. "I mean, not that I'm not happy you're here." It was always easier to navigate a new place with a wingman.

"Yeah, I needed to get out of town for a few hours and clear my head. Driving always clears my head." Lane slouched in her chair.

"What happened that required therapeutic driving?"

"Remember that girl I told you about over breakfast?"

"Yeah, as in, yesterday?" So much had happened, this weekend felt four days long. "Umm, Andi, Alicia, Anna—"

"Alice."

"Right, Alice." It was hard to keep track. At least she'd remembered that her name started with an "A."

"Well, Alice was not technically single."

"What does that mean?"

"It means that in her mind, she'd broken up with her girlfriend." Lane touched her temple with her finger. "But she hadn't remembered to actually inform the girlfriend."

"Oh, dang."

"Yeah…we were in the middle of a big make out session on the sofa last night when the girlfriend showed up. Needless to say, *girlfriend* was *not* happy." Lane took a swig of her coffee. "And neither was I."

Lane liked to play the field, but she wasn't a home wrecker. She'd dated a lot of women, some in rapid succession, but she was honest with all of them and she didn't mess around with women who were already involved with someone else. But not everyone had such clear boundaries.

"I'm sorry." The dating scene in Atlanta could get complicated, and messy. She was glad to be out of it for a while. She'd voluntarily put herself in rural, lesbian exile. Behind her, the random sounds of stringed instruments being tuned merged with the loud murmur of voices in the café, but Garet was enjoying her window seat overlooking the water and didn't turn around.

"Okay, ladies. Here ya go. Let me know if you need anything else." Candi delivered two plates of food.

"Can I get a refill?" Garet held up her mug.

"Sure thing, sugah, just give me a sec."

CHAPTER EIGHT

The music started and the volume of voices in the room sank beneath it. Garet wasn't a huge fan of bluegrass, but this wasn't what she'd call true bluegrass. This sounded like something one of her favorite folk trios might play. Actually, this tune sounded like a cover from one of Hem's songs. Threads of "Half Acre" swirled around her as she watched the river slowly churn past.

Curiosity got the better of her and Garet rotated in her chair to get a look at the band. On the far end of the quartet, she recognized a familiar face.

"Uh…" She blinked and set her coffee cup down almost missing the edge of the table.

"Hey, careful there." Candi righted her cup and then filled it.

Garet leaned past Candi to get another view of Tess, who smiled when they made eye contact. Lane angled out on the other side and then Candi rotated, following her gaze.

"The band is really good, huh? They're all local musicians." Candi left a ticket for the meal on the table. "Ya'll just wave if you need anything else. No rush."

To say Garet was surprised to see Tess wasn't quite accurate. Under normal circumstances a random retail encounter wouldn't have stayed with her, but Garet hadn't quite been able to get Tess out of her head. It wasn't as if they'd even really talked about anything in particular at the music store, but Tess had real presence. Garet had been drawn to her in a way that fell beyond simply a physical attraction. She'd been puzzling over the chance meeting since yesterday. In the dance of desire, sometimes it was what you didn't say that mattered. From her perspective, during that ten-minute encounter in Mark's Music Shop, Tess had *not* said many things and Garet had gotten the message loud and clear.

"Hey, Garet, do you know the woman playing the mandolin? Dude, she's super cute." Lane was starstruck. "You've been holding out on me."

"I was gonna mention it." But Garet wasn't so sure she would have. "I only just met her yesterday."

"She looks like that really pretty actress. You know, the one with the British accent and elegant cheek bones."

"I know the one."

"You always watch her movies like a hundred times."

"We all have our weaknesses." Garet sipped the coffee loudly, her eyes glued to the stage. Was it just wishful thinking or was Tess playing this song especially for her?

"Man, she can't take her eyes off you." Lane voiced Garet's unspoken thought.

Garet and Lane lingered through a third cup of coffee, as the bluegrass ensemble played at least five or six more songs. Garet sort of lost track, seeing as how her attention was completely focused on Tess. She didn't have the right vocabulary to describe Tess's performance, her music. Tess's instrumental phrasing was so sensitive to the shifts of harmony that she won Garet over to bluegrass fandom. The mandolin glowed with soft-spoken brilliance. Bluegrass was suddenly and unexpectedly the most beautiful thing Garet had ever heard, her new favorite genre. When the music stopped, Garet felt the absence of it like an emptiness in her chest. She looked away from the stage for fear she'd give something away, and instead, focused intently on her coffee.

"Don't look now, but *dream girl* is walking this way."

"What?" She looked up just in time to see Tess winding her way through the tables in her direction. Tess was wearing a modern, stylish version of a prairie dress, the skirt of which teasingly swayed as she walked. Garet lurched to her feet. She fumbled her mug, dribbling dark spots down the front of her shirt. She wiped at the spill and then glanced up to greet Tess.

Garet was taller than Tess remembered, a few inches taller than she was, probably close to five feet ten inches. Garet seemed adorably nervous for some reason. She was wearing a denim jacket over a white T-shirt with khaki trousers and the same well-traveled Converse sneakers as before.

"Hi." She gave a little wave.

"Hi." Garet wiped at the front of her T-shirt with her napkin.

"Did your beverage get away from you?" There were light brown splotches at the hem of Garet's otherwise perfectly stark white T-shirt.

"Uh, yeah, I guess I'm not really awake yet." Garet made an excuse.

"Hi, I'm Tess." She pivoted and introduced herself to Garet's striking tablemate.

"Nice to meet you. I'm Lane." Lane stood and offered her hand to Tess.

Lane was good-looking, but definitely gave off a player vibe. Tess returned her attention to Garet.

"Sorry, I should have introduced you. Lane, this is Tess…Tess, this is my friend Lane." Garet blushed.

"I think we just took care of that ourselves, chief." Lane patted Garet on the shoulder. "Tess, would you like to join us? I'm sure I can find an extra chair."

"Oh…yeah, would you like to join us?" Garet repeated the invitation as if she was the first one to think of it. "You play really well, by the way. I mean, not by the way as in…what I meant to say was, you're an amazing musician."

Tess found Garet's nervous floundering endearing, cute even. She hadn't gotten this sort of reaction from someone in a while and she'd forgotten how that made her feel—young, desirable, pretty.

"Thanks for the invitation, but I've got to get back. We're playing one more set." She motioned with her thumb over her shoulder. "I just wanted to say hello. It's nice to see you again, Garet."

"Um, it's really nice to see you too." Garet stood with her hands shoved in her trouser pockets. Lane had taken her seat with an amused expression.

"Okay, then." She started to turn but hesitated. "Nice to meet you, Lane. Enjoy your coffee." She made a point of making eye contact with Garet when she said that last part before walking toward the makeshift stage.

Tess looked back once. Garet was still standing, making no attempt to hide the fact that she was staring. The honesty of Garet's attentive gaze warmed her skin. Her fellow musicians were tuning their instruments. She picked up the mandolin to do the same.

Tess focused on Mark, to her right as he counted off. She joined after the first refrain, trying her best to focus on the music and not on Garet. A rush of nerves shot through her when she'd spotted Garet seated near the windows. At first, Garet faced the river, outside the windows, rather than the stage. She tried not to take it personally. Maybe Garet had other things on her mind. But then Garet had turned, they'd locked gazes, and Tess had to redirect her focus so as not to lose the thread of the song they were right in the middle of.

The coolest thing about performing was that an energy occurred between the players on the stage and the audience. There was a flow of energy that traveled constantly, going back and forth. It was a unique feeling. In this instance, the energy rebounding from Garet pulsed around her; she felt it in her chest. She was certain that if she hadn't been holding the instrument so tightly for each chord progression that her fingers would have been shaking.

There was a normal rush from performing live, but this was different. She stopped playing for a moment, pretending that she needed to wait for the refrain. She turned her focus to Mark to get her head back into the right space. Mark was a rock on stage; he never got flustered.

Tess faced away from the crowded café to retune between songs and regroup.

When she turned back after a few moments, Garet and her friend Lane were gone.

❖

Garet exited the café and took a few deep breaths to settle. Her insides churned as if a hundred butterflies had taken up residence in her stomach.

"Are you sure you want to leave?"

"I didn't want to camp out in there. Did you see how many people were waiting for a table?" Garet couldn't help the empathetic streak, and maybe that wasn't the only reason to leave. She blinked and swallowed.

"Hey, man, are you okay?" Lane's hand was on her shoulder.

"Yeah, I'm fine."

"You don't seem fine." Lane gave Garet a friendly one-armed hug as they walked down the paved path along the river. "You seem completely rattled by Tess."

"Maybe."

"I mean, I don't blame you. She's...wow...Tess has a great ass, the sort of ass that fills out a form-fitted dress in all the right ways, and small firm breasts, breasts that would fit perfectly in your cupped palm—"

"You're not going to ask her out, are you?" For some reason, Lane's glowing review inspired a surge of jealousy and protectiveness.

"So, you do like her." Lane grinned. "I would never ask her out given how smitten you clearly are by her."

"I'm sorry." She genuinely was. "I don't even know Tess, but... she makes me feel...rattled."

"That's a good thing, my friend." Lane smiled.

"It is?"

"I haven't seen you rattled, in a good way, since college." Lane slid her sunglasses off the top of her head and put them on. "You're way overdue."

They walked in silence for a few minutes. The wind stirred the branches of a willow tree overhead creating shifting shadowed patterns on the sidewalk.

"Too bad you didn't get her phone number." There was humor in Lane's statement.

Garet came to an abrupt stop. *Damn.* She didn't have Tess's number. She glanced at Lane.

"Don't look so forlorn, buddy." Lane patted her back. "It's a small town, I'm sure you'll see her again."

In this instance, rural geography wasn't the least bit comforting.

"What am I doing?" Garet started to walk briskly and talk with her hands. Lane hustled to catch up. "Jillian and I only just broke up the day before yesterday. I've got no business getting anyone's number. I came up here to finish my book. I need to stay focused on my work."

"That's a great pep talk, but I'd like to point out that I never saw you look at Jillian the way you just looked at *Mandolin Girl.*" Lane sidestepped beside Garet and pointed back toward the café.

"Really?" Garet stopped and faced Lane.

"Yes, really." Lane was serious. "Maybe you can focus on work *and* have a date with a nice girl at the same time."

"Maybe." But she wasn't at all sure that was possible. Tess, so pretty and sweet, was the poster girl for beautiful distraction. And distraction was the absolute last thing she needed.

CHAPTER NINE

While June retrieved her stuffed narwhal, Chester, from the living room, Tess took a moment to notice the long shadows from the bedroom window. Moonlight filtered between the branches of the old growth poplar at the back of the house, casting jagged crisscrossed shadows on the hardwood floor. A minute later, June bounded into the room and onto the bed.

The long day was coming to a close for Tess. Playing with the band was energizing and exhausting at the same time. She pulled the covers up to June's shoulders as June snuggled in. Sometimes bedtime was easy and sometimes not. It often depended on how much sugar June consumed late in the day and whether or not she'd settle down and agree to get ready for bed. Tonight, things had gone pretty smoothly, which was great, since tomorrow was Monday. It was never good to start a week of school feeling sleep deprived.

"Are you and Chester all cozy now?" Tess was sitting on the edge of the bed.

"Yes." June drowsily yawned.

Tess fussed with the quilt, tucking it around June.

"Mama, why do some kids have two parents and I only have one?"

Tess was taken aback. That was a big question and not easily answered.

"That's just how things work out sometimes." She stroked June's forehead. "Why do you ask? Did someone at school say something?"

June shook her head. But Tess could tell there was another question coming.

"If I had two parents could I have a dog?"

This was kid logic at its best. She'd told June repeatedly that as a single parent she couldn't take on the additional responsibility of raising a puppy. June just couldn't let it go.

"We'll talk about getting a dog when you're older, okay?"

June seemed to accept that response for now.

"Did you and Grandma have fun today?"

June nodded and yawned again.

"Sweet dreams." She kissed June's forehead.

"Night, Mama." June rolled onto her side and draped her arm over the well-loved plush toy.

Tess turned off the bedside lamp and left the door ajar. She stood for a moment to make sure June was settled and then went to the kitchen to make a cup of herbal tea.

She studied the darkness outside the kitchen window absently as she lifted the tea bag from the cup and dropped it into the sink. Somehow, she'd managed to bump into Garet two days in a row. That seemed like an odd coincidence. What did that mean? Tess was definitely intrigued by Garet. Maybe she should have asked Garet to meet for a coffee or something.

She shook her head. Coffee would probably only start something that had nowhere to go. She'd tried dating on rare occasions and it hadn't gone so well. It was very tricky to date as a single mom. Not only was she very selective about who she spent time with, but she was even more discerning about who she allowed to spend time around June. Was she too protective? Maybe.

Was Garet someone who even liked kids?

If Garet knew Tess had a child, would she run in the opposite direction?

She'd probably never find out and that was just as well.

Sometimes a very specific sort of loneliness settled in her chest. Tess wasn't really alone, because she had June. But this was the sort of loneliness and longing that only a lover could fill. In quiet moments, late at night, it was hard to find much comfort in singleness. It was less complicated to be single, but sometimes not very satisfying.

June was singularly precious to her.

June came first, everything else came second. Any other way and she was awash with guilt. She set aside her desire to have it all—a happy, well-adjusted child and a fulfilling love life.

Tess sipped the soothing tea as she padded barefoot up the stairs and along the cool hardwood floor toward her bedroom. The house was quiet and dark, except for the ambient light seeping into the hallway from her bedroom. She set her tea on the nightstand and lingered in the open window before closing it. There was a slight chill in the air and the scent of wood smoke from someone's chimney. Autumn was only days away. The poplars and oaks around the house already had hints of amber and red. A few more chilly days and they would blaze the hillsides with color. She slid the old wooden window frame down and sank under her comforter to finish the last of her chamomile tea.

CHAPTER TEN

Monday morning arrived too quickly, and too early. Garet stood at the small window over the kitchen sink and stirred cream into her coffee. She hadn't slept particularly well. Some really great ideas had popped into her head at two in the morning. Sometimes it was hard to differentiate a dream from an inspired idea. On occasion they ended up being the same thing. All the lights in her head would flip to the *on* switch—thoughts swirled, dendrites flared, and synapses fired in an electrical storm inside her head right about the time she should be slipping into REM sleep.

Sometimes Garet gave in to it. Life was short and sometimes days seemed even shorter. She hated to give in to sleep if she was feeling particularly inspired. Last night had been one of those nights. Maybe it was sleeping in a strange place. The hum of city sounds were missing. The quiet was almost unnerving. She'd stepped outside after midnight just to get a sense of where she was. With fewer electric lights, the sky was too big. It made her feel unsettled, small, insignificant, and alone.

Unable to get back to sleep, Garet decided to stay up and do some drawings. She'd brought a portable slant board with her and set it up on the counter between the kitchen and the main living space. Once she lost herself in drawing, in the little world she'd created, she began to settle. The infinite darkness above that was too large became less unnerving when she focused on the small world she was creating on paper.

But now, sipping coffee, she was wishing, uncharacteristically, that she'd gotten a few more hours of sleep before the first day at a new job.

Sunday, after Lane's departure, had been spent settling into her unfamiliar, temporary quarters. She'd made a run to the local market to stock the refrigerator and had taken another stroll around town in the hopes that she might bump into Tess. Most shops were closed by Sunday afternoon, except for the microbrewery which was open for dinner. There weren't very many people out and about. The sidewalks probably rolled up in town by eight most nights. At least that was the impression she got. She basically made the whole circuit through town within a half hour and was back at the rental unit without even breaking a sweat.

Garet finished the last of her peanut butter toast. The breakfast of champions. And slipped her sketchbook into her messenger bag. She had a few choice pencils, a brush marker, and her cell phone. This was like any first day at something new. She didn't really know what to expect so she tried to pack light but at the same time be prepared for anything.

The Tanner County School building was on the opposite side of town from her place. Garet probably could have walked the distance in twenty minutes but decided to drive in case she needed to make a quick getaway for some reason. That thought made her laugh. There was nothing quick about her hand-me-down Volvo. This car did zero to sixty in about seven minutes. Maybe she should get a bicycle while she was in Shadetree. Lane had more than one. Surely, she could spare a loaner. Actually, the Volvo had been acting twitchy lately. Having backup transportation was probably a good idea anyway. She made a mental note to text Lane about it later.

Garet parked in a spot marked for teachers out in front of the school and watched the parade of kids entering the building. One kid, or even two, wasn't that intimidating. But a herd of kids was a little unnerving. She'd be outnumbered all day. Lane's words of doubt echoed inside her head.

After a minute, she got out of the car, shouldered her bag, and tried to act as if she knew what she was doing, which she didn't.

She wondered if children could sense fear the way dogs could. That thought made her smile. At least she had the advantage of age and experience over most of the kids she saw filing into the building. A young woman and a little boy approached the door at the same moment. Garet smiled and held the door for them. Before she could step through herself, a gaggle of children rushed by in the still open doorway. The woman she'd originally held the door for was swallowed up by the stream of students.

"You're welcome," she said to no one and quickly stepped inside before she ended up as doorman for the entire student body.

The principal's office was just past the main entrance. Garet made that her first stop since she had no idea where her classroom was. After brief introductions around the office, the principal, Henry Carlisle, offered to walk Garet down to her classroom. Henry was what she pictured when she imagined a stereotypical small town principal. He had a receding hairline and an advancing waistline. His shirt, pants, and shoes were various shades of tan and brown. His plaid tie was a couple decades too wide and wasn't quite long enough to span the entire bulge of his stomach. He seemed like the sort of guy who'd stopped updating his wardrobe sometime in the early eighties. Garet wondered absently what Henry had done for work before he was a principal. Toll booth attendant? Mall cop? It was hard to guess.

Schools were such strange places. She looked side-to-side, taking in details as she walked with Henry down the long corridor lined with lockers. The smell was hard to describe, but every school had it. The scent was some combination of paper, crayons, and sweaty gym shoes. And even though she was supposed to be a teacher in this scenario, she couldn't ignore that familiar *new kid* nervousness in her gut.

"Here we are." Henry stopped and motioned toward a half-open door. "As I said, the art classes alternate with the music classes and share this room. Ms. Hill is the music teacher and I'm sure she can answer any questions we haven't covered about the schedule."

"Thank you, I'm sure I'll be fine."

"The first hour is free to prep for both art and music, so you'll at least have a little time to get acclimated and talk with Ms. Hill." He pushed the door open. "I'll introduce you."

Garet came to a full stop, her eyes widened.

In the center of the room, adjusting chairs, was Tess.

"Tess Hill, I'd like to introduce you to Garet Allen." Henry grandly swept his arm out in Garet's direction.

"Hi." Garet considered offering her hand, just for the chance to hold Tess's for a moment. Tess seemed as surprised as she was that they'd bumped into each other, again. What was the saying? The third time was the charm?

Should she act as if they hadn't already met?

Tess suddenly had the watchful look of someone who didn't trust easily, and who probably kept a cushion of protected personal space around her at all times. This was a different woman than the one she'd bumped into at the café, friendly, open, and casually conjuring bluegrass tunes with her fellow band mates.

Once again, Garet had the thought that Tess was distractingly pretty, and now that they were in a professional setting, aloof. It was easy to imagine lots of students having crushes on her. Yes, Tess Hill was most definitely crush material.

"It's nice to see you again." Tess dipped her head in greeting.

Tess regarded her with a look that Garet couldn't quite decipher, but it didn't strike her as approval. Garet shifted uncomfortably under Tess's appraisal. She adjusted the strap of her bag across her chest in an effort to seem unaffected by Tess's lingering gaze.

"Oh, you've met already. Excellent. Well, I'll leave you two to get settled." He didn't seem curious about how or where they'd met. He turned back just before he left the room. "And don't hesitate to find me, Ms. Allen, if you need any assistance."

CHAPTER ELEVEN

Tess was trying to recover from the shock of Garet showing up in her classroom. She hadn't thought for a second that Garet might be Charlotte's substitute. Nothing about Garet signaled that she was a teacher. First off, she dressed more like a student than any sort of authority figure. Today she'd raised the bar a little from T-shirts and sneakers. Garet was wearing a white oxford shirt, French tucked to expose a wide belt, navy trousers, and scuffed espresso colored leather, cap toe shoes. Garet was definitely cute, but now she knew why Garet had moved to Shadetree. For a temporary job. Everything about Garet was transitory, and short-term was not a place Tess wanted to invest time in. At least now part of the mystery surrounding Ms. New-In-Town had been resolved.

Garet removed the messenger bag and dropped it into a nearby chair. Her movements were slow and deliberate but vibrated with energy. Garet looked at her with a smile that was easily distracting, and after a few seconds, Tess averted her eyes. She cleared her throat and returned to her task of moving chairs into neat rows while Garet looked on.

Normally, she arrived early to set the classroom up and have a moment to gather her thoughts before the students arrived, but June had been slow to eat breakfast and get dressed, so they'd arrived later than usual. It worked in her favor that the first hour was free for prep. Being a single parent meant sometimes complications hindered her prompt arrival.

"Can I help set up the room?" Garet stepped back as Tess adjusted the placement of the chairs near where she was standing.

"I'm almost finished." Tess was trying to focus on her routine and *not* on Garet.

"Oh." Garet shifted, as if she were unsure of where to stand. "Um, your band sounded really good yesterday."

"Thank you." Tess stopped and faced Garet. "I suppose I should have asked why you'd moved to Shadetree. To be honest, and don't take this the wrong way, but you just didn't strike me as a teacher."

"It's not my usual profession."

Now Tess was a little worried. What exactly did she mean by that?

"How much teaching experience do you have?" Tess was afraid she already knew the answer.

"I've been a substitute teacher a few times."

"Define few."

"Three."

She couldn't help but stare at Garet. *Three?*

"As in, three years?" Tess tried to be hopeful.

"Three days. Not all at the same school." Garet cleared her throat. "I um, I've only just started this substitute teaching thing."

Tess took a deep breath. She might as well just cover Charlotte's classes herself for all the help Garet was going to be. Garet would probably end up being little more than a glorified babysitter.

"At least tell me you know something about art." It wasn't really a question and she didn't mean for the statement to sound as sternly disapproving as it probably did to Garet.

"Oh, yeah, of course…I mean, that's why they hired me…I think."

Garet seemed completely unconcerned about her lack of experience in the classroom. It was going to be equal parts painful and entertaining to watch the kids walk all over her. Well, if the school administration thought an inexperienced teacher could handle the classes, then it wasn't her problem to solve. However, it did annoy her that the students might somehow suffer due to Garet's lack of training. Public schools struggled enough without throwing an inexperienced instructor into the mix. Whatever attraction or curiosity she'd had for Garet had been quickly replaced by apprehension.

"So, Henry, I mean, Mr. Carlisle." Garet was holding a sheet of paper she'd pulled from her bag. "Are first names okay?" She looked up at Tess.

Garet had a practiced innocence about her, but Tess wasn't falling for it. The last thing Tess needed was one more child to manage.

"First names are acceptable, but not in front of the students. They should be taught to respect adults." This was like classroom etiquette for beginners. Tess shook her head.

"Is something wrong?" Garet was watching her.

"No, nothing is wrong." Yes, something was wrong, but if Garet didn't already know what it was, then it wasn't worth explaining. "Did you have a question about Henry?"

"Well, I was just going to say he seems pretty mellow for a principal."

"That's because he has good teachers at this school and they do all the real work."

"Oh, sorry." Garet shifted her weight. "I didn't mean to hit a nerve."

"You didn't." But maybe she had. The question was, which nerve? All Tess could think about was how this was gearing up to be the longest three months of her life. She was going to have to carry most of the load while Charlotte was out. Garet obviously wasn't prepared. And in addition to everything else was the nagging annoyance that despite Garet's inexperience and general cluelessness, Tess found her distractingly attractive.

This was a disaster. What could Henry possibly have been thinking when he hired Garet? Whatever his thought process, Garet would be faced with the reality of her situation soon enough. It wasn't Tess's job to spell it out for her. Tess checked the wall clock. In fact, the first class would start in fifteen minutes. Music was first, so Garet had about forty-five minutes of blissful ignorance before mayhem ensued.

CHAPTER TWELVE

Garet sat in a chair along the back wall during the first music class, which was chorus. There was an upright piano near the front of the room. Tess had arranged the chairs in a semicircle. She played and simultaneously directed the class. Every so often she stopped and focused on getting a particular kid on key. She'd strike a note on the piano and ask the student to match the tone. The kids weren't really singing a song as much as practicing scales. At least that's what it sounded like to Garet. She realized she didn't know that much about the mechanics of music. She enjoyed it, without really understanding how it worked, or being musically inclined herself.

At least once, Tess stopped and helped a student who seemed to be struggling to read the music. Once the students actually began to sing a song, there were reminders from Tess about measures and time signatures. She'd clap her hands to illustrate the note durations of quarter notes and half notes in four-four time.

Garet tried to busy herself with drawings in her sketchbook but found Tess a little too distracting. The best she could manage was to pretend she was doodling so that Tess would hopefully not notice she was watching. What were the odds that the two of them would end up sharing a classroom? She still couldn't quite believe it and she hadn't had a chance to text Lane and share the shocking news.

The period lasted for forty-five minutes and then the bell sounded. It was Garet's turn to command the shared space. She wasn't sure what to expect, but she knew the room arrangement had to shift. Tess was kind enough to assist in arranging the chairs around two rectangular tables. There were art supplies stored in plastic bins along the wall. Garet took pencils and sheets of white paper and placed them at even intervals around the tables.

Students began to file in. She knew from the roster that this class would be fourth graders, all together, twelve students. That was a manageable group. Henry Carlisle had explained to her that students could opt for either music or art, sometimes both. But in order to accommodate everyone who requested those classes, students alternated. Fourth through sixth grades on Mondays. First through third grades had music and art on Tuesdays, and so on and so on. Garet didn't have the entire schedule clear in her head, but she did understand that she wouldn't see the same students every day. At some point during the week she'd have every grade between first and twelfth. The thought of facing a room full of teenagers was pretty dang intimidating.

Garet took a deep breath and tried to channel her inner grown-up. The important thing was to project confidence. At least, that's what she told herself as the last kid took his seat and Tess chose a chair at the back of the class. Tess sat stiffly with her arms folded, as if evaluating Garet's every move. Garet sighed and tried to ignore her, an almost impossible task.

❖

Tess adjusted for a more comfortable position to enjoy the show. Not that she was wishing for Garet to fail or anything, she just couldn't quite figure out how this was going to go down. Things were already off to a rocky start. Garet waited too long to get the students to be quiet. They fidgeted and grabbed for paper and pencils while Garet made an attempt to get their attention.

After a few painful moments, she decided to come to Garet's rescue. After all, she'd been a new teacher once and she still remembered what that felt like.

"Quiet now!" Tess clapped her hands. "Eyes forward."

The chatter died down immediately and Garet regarded her with an expression of gratitude.

"Class, this is Ms. Allen. She will be teaching art classes until Ms. Hastings returns."

"Are you a boy or a girl?" A boy blurted the question.

"Anthony!" Tess tersely called him by name.

"It's okay." Garet stepped forward. "I'm a girl. My mother's maiden name was Garet so that's what she named me. I know it's a bit unusual for a girl's name, but I kinda like it."

The children giggled and Anthony grinned. Garet didn't seem embarrassed at all by his query. No doubt she'd heard the question before.

"Thank you for the introduction, Ms. Hill." Garet nodded at her and smiled.

This was her signal to sit down. She'd done her part to help out. Now Garet was on her own.

"Are there any other questions before we begin?"

Tess wanted to warn Garet that opening up the floor to general questions was a bad idea, but it was too late.

"How much money does a teacher make?" Lucinda asked the question with a raised hand.

"Um, I think it varies depending on experience." Garet started to turn toward the blackboard, but Jeffry shouted out the next question.

"Can you really see Russia from Alaska?" he blurted.

"No, that's an urban myth." Garet paused. "Any other questions?"

Three more hands shot up.

"What is reincarnation?" Raymond adjusted the oversized dark framed glasses that were always slipping down his nose.

"Well, it's…" Garet quirked an eyebrow and crossed her arms. "Maybe that's a question for you to ask your parents."

Yes, redirect, thought Tess.

Best not to discuss religious beliefs if possible to avoid them.

"Okay, my turn." Garet reached for a piece of chalk. "How many of you like to draw?"

Garet had pivoted smoothly. Nicely done. A few raised hands shot up. Others were more measured, only half-heartedly raising their hands.

"I like to draw too." Garet smiled and seemed to relax.

That first question was followed by other questions about form, perspective, and composition. Mostly, the students had approximate answers, but it was obvious they were a bit fuzzy on some of the fundamentals of art. Garet seemed to be genuinely interested in getting a handle on what the level of skill was for this group. She might not be an experienced teacher, but Garet did seem to have an easy rapport with kids.

Tess found herself rather captivated as she watched Garet draw shapes on the chalkboard.

"Does anyone know what perspective means?"

No one raised a hand.

"Okay, who'd like to help me with a demonstration?" Garet turned toward the class.

Anthony raised his hand and Garet motioned him forward.

"Draw a simple cube, a box." Garet handed him the chalk.

He hesitated for a moment as if visualizing the shape in his head, then drew the outline of a square. It looked more like a Cubist version of a square shape, than an actual box.

"Okay, good try." Garet took a step back. "Does this look like a box to you?"

"Sort of." Anthony scrunched his nose.

"Perspective means that as things move away from the viewer they seem to get smaller. It's an optical illusion of sorts." Garet drew a straight line across the box and then drew a dot off to one side. "Every object has a horizon line." She set the chalk point on the dot. "This is the vanishing point." She started drawing lines from each corner of the front plane of the box to the vanishing point. And then constructed the sides and top, based on those guiding lines.

"It looks like a real box now." Anthony sounded impressed.

"Here, now you try it. And everyone else…try this on the paper in front of you." They moved to the clean side of the board and she stood aside as Anthony mimicked what she'd just showed the class.

It was amazing. In a matter of minutes, Anthony had learned to draw a box in proper perspective.

"This is boring." One of the other boys in the class sat back in his chair with his arms crossed.

"This might seem boring, but if you master the simple fundamentals of art you can literally draw anything. Even much more complex objects." Garet didn't seem at all fazed by his grumbling. "Watch this." She erased the box and started to draw again. This time, a long, circular tube. "What is this?"

"A sausage!"

"A pipe."

Kids called out various guesses.

"Nope." Garet added a few more details. "It's a submarine."

The children were attentive now.

"See, I started with a simple shape, drew in the proper perspective, and from that I was able to draw a more complex object. Every complex shape can be broken up into smaller, simple shapes. Combining the components of those simpler shapes helps us draw." She was quiet for a minute or so, allowing what she'd said to sink in. "Okay, now. Let's see you draw some boxes."

CHAPTER THIRTEEN

The morning passed quickly, and before Garet knew it, the bell for lunch rang. It was only midday and she was exhausted. Would she be this tired every day or was it simply because there was so much *newness* to contend with? Garet was a creature of habit. She liked her routine and that routine normally included coffee around ten o'clock, which hadn't happened, and lots of breaks. She was caffeine deficient and she needed a snack.

"I'm going to the teacher's lounge to get my lunch." Tess was halfway to the door.

Was that an invitation?

"Can I walk with you?" Garet started following her without waiting for confirmation. "It'd be nice to know where the lounge is."

Tess nodded and waited for Garet to catch up.

"Have you been teaching here long?" Garet grimaced internally at her lame small talk attempt.

"Almost six years." They'd walked the length of the hallway. Tess stopped at the door marked *Teacher's Lounge* and motioned for Garet to enter.

Hmm, with that sort of labeling it wouldn't have been that hard to find.

"Please, you first." Garet reached around Tess and placed her palm on the frosted glass to prop the door open. Based on her expression it was clearly going to take more than chivalry to win Tess over.

Garet was starving, but all she'd thought to pack was a granola bar. With any luck there'd be a food or drink machine in the lounge so that she could supplement her meager meal. Tomorrow she'd get her act together and pack an actual sandwich.

She was eager for lunch, but the introvert side of her wasn't looking forward to the forced chitchat of the staff room. She took a deep breath and followed Tess, allowing the door to softly close behind her.

Garet was immediately reminded of study hall and the dry smell of chalk. There was a well-built athletic looking woman near the coffee pot, wearing fancy sweatpants and a polo shirt with sleeves that hugged her muscled biceps. The woman looked like a professional tennis player or something. She smiled broadly at Tess and offered to pour a cup of coffee for her. Her teeth were super white against her suntanned skin and her short blond hair was almost white on top, probably from lots of hours outside.

Yeah, Sporty Spice definitely had a thing for Tess. Actually, the entire small gathering seemed to brighten the minute Tess walked into the room. Tess was definitely well liked by her colleagues. Hell, she liked Tess too, but she wasn't so sure the feeling was mutual. It was weird. Garet could have sworn they'd had some little connection at the café the previous day. But it was possible that the tingly nervous stomach was all on her side of the equation.

"Hello." The woman holding the coffee pot greeted Tess and then gave Garet a sideways glance.

"This is Garet Allen." Tess held a cup out for coffee. "She's covering for Charlotte."

"Hi." Garet smiled and tried not to feel as if she were the new kid and this was her first day at school, although, both things were true.

"Garet, this is Riley Caldwell. She teaches phys ed."

That seemed obvious.

Riley was a walking reminder of how unathletic Garet was. And Riley was definitely crushed out on Tess. She didn't even need eyes to see that. Garet wondered if Tess knew and chose to ignore it, because while she was polite to Riley, Tess certainly wasn't flirtatious. Not even in a friendly sort of way.

"Coffee?" Riley motioned with the pot in her direction.

Was it possible that Riley actually just flexed her bicep to show off?

"Sure, thanks." Garet refused to be intimidated by the butch display. She chose a mug from the open cabinet near the sink and held it as Riley poured. She seemed to like her role as lounge ambassador.

"This is Mary Thomas, Anna Larkin, and Rupert Brooks." Tess introduced the three other people in the room.

Mary was probably in her sixties. She had the look of a stern librarian as she riffled in her lunch bag while standing in the open door of the refrigerator. Anna Larkin was closer to Tess's age, which Garet guessed to be late twenties or early thirties. Anna had brown skin and black curls that framed her pretty, oval face. She seemed like the friendliest of the three. She smiled and nodded to Garet as she added sugar to hot tea. Rupert looked like her kind of guy— nerdy, introverted, bad at sports. She could tell he was tall even though he was seated, and rail thin. He wore a garish purple tie and black thick rimmed glasses.

Garet wasn't sure if she should sit or stand. Should she go back to the classroom and take a look at the art supplies while she munched on the granola bar? Indecision rooted her in place.

"Take your time, Ms. Allen. I'm going back to the room. I'd planned to eat at my desk and work on the music for the fall festival production." Tess retrieved a container from the communal fridge and started for the door.

Ms. Allen? What was that about? Garet had assumed they were on a first-name basis in front of fellow teachers.

"I'll walk with you." Riley followed on Tess's heels like a puppy dog.

She considered going with them but didn't want to seem needy.

Garet turned and faced the others for a moment, sipped her coffee, and then smiled.

Awkward.

So much for scuttling back to the class to eat her meager snack. She might as well stay and make nice. The granola bar wrapper sounded unusually loud as she did her best to open it while everyone stared.

Just focus on the wrapper, not them.

The door opening diverted everyone's attention. A woman approached the group, carrying what looked like a frosted Bundt cake. She leaned past Garet to bestow the delicious looking cake in the center of the table.

"Carol, this is Garet. She's covering for Charlotte." Anna wasted no time. She fetched several small plates from the cupboard and returned to cut the first piece.

"Nice to meet you, Garet." Carol rested her hands on her hips. She had the look of someone who'd just delivered treasure to pirates. "Don't think ill of us, but if we'd brought this cake in earlier, when Riley was here, she'd practically eat the entire thing by herself."

"There's always some shared food in here—doughnuts, cookies, and cakes. Or leftover Halloween candy, or produce from someone's garden—something is always out on the tables." Mary explained. "But Riley is known to brag that she never has to bring her own lunch because she can always find something up for grabs in the staff room."

"So, if anyone has something super good to share and wants to make sure that we all get a chance to try it, they hide it in my office next door. I'm the school secretary." Carol sighed. "She never catches on, bless her heart."

Garet felt pleased that she was getting let in on this little secret. She probably didn't pose much of a long-term threat to free snacks since she was only on staff for a short period of time. Anna offered her a piece of cake and she gladly set the granola bar aside, the fruity nut bar being soundly upstaged by frosted lemon Bundt cake.

"And I know what you're thinking." Carol pursed her lips and nodded at Garet.

"Uh…" Garet didn't even know what she was thinking, so how could Carol know?

"You're thinking where does Riley put it all, right?" Carol shook her head. "The world just isn't fair. She eats everything in sight and still looks that good."

"She probably runs a lot, or something." Riley did look way too fit. That just wasn't normal in Garet's opinion. Her idea of exercise was walking from the couch to the refrigerator and back.

No one responded to her remark about exercise. Everyone was focused for the moment on enjoying the cake.

"So, what do you teach?" Garet looked at Anna first, since she seemed to be the friendliest.

"I teach first grade." Anna motioned to her right. "And I've gotta run." She finished the last bite of her cake as she moved toward the door. "Good luck with the rest of your day."

Somehow, the way she said *good luck* sounded ominous.

"I teach fifth grade." Rupert's voice was barely audible. He cleared his throat. "I teach fifth grade." The second time with more volume.

"Eighth grade." Mary made a slight wave with her hand holding a celery stick.

Celery as a snack was just plain wrong. No one ate celery willingly or with any real joy. Celery was like chewing wet air with texture and was just about as satisfying.

"I teach art. But I guess you knew that already since I'm filling in for Charlotte." Garet nodded as if to confirm her own statement. "So, you guys usually eat lunch in the lounge?"

"There isn't really enough time to leave." Mary finished a small container of yogurt before sampling the cake.

"The lunch room is chaos. I only go there when I'm required to chaperone." Rupert stared off into space as he forked a rather large bite of cake and then methodically chewed.

"Will you take a piece of cake to Tess?" Mary looked at Garet as she sliced a generous portion onto a small plate. "Just make sure Riley isn't there when you deliver it."

"You're here just in time to start working with the art students on backdrops." Rupert finished the last bite. Was he talking to her?

"Sorry, what? Did you mention backdrops?" she asked.

"The music and art classes always work together to put on the play for the fall festival." Mary answered her question instead of Rupert.

"We have to put on a play?" The cake became a gooey lump as she tried to swallow. She didn't know anything about stage backdrops. She'd never hung out with the drama nerds in high school or college.

"Next month, for the fall festival." Rupert rinsed his plate in the sink. "I should get going." His bedside manner was less than zero. She couldn't tell if he was giving her a hard time, or seriously trying to psych her out, or just bored. His tone and mood were impossible to read.

"I should get back too." Mary covered what was left of the cake. "Nice to meet you, Garet."

It seemed as if lunch breaks were short if they happened at all and everyone had prep work to do in their respective classrooms. Garet should probably be prepping too, although, she didn't quite know what to expect next. She figured today would be mostly spent winging it. So far, that plan had worked. Except now she had some stage production to worry about. Surely, they didn't expect a substitute teacher to deal with that.

CHAPTER FOURTEEN

Riley lingered and Tess really wanted her to leave. She didn't want to eat with an audience or feel pressure to chat between bites. Riley wasn't taking any subtle hints so Tess would have to be more direct.

"I'd love to chat, Riley, but I have some work to take care of."

"Oh, yeah, sure." She started to leave but then hesitated. "Hey, would you like—"

Tess's phone buzzed and she glanced at the name on the screen.

"I really should get this." Charlotte's call had saved Tess from another awkward invitation to drink or dine out. She liked Riley well enough, but she was definitely not interested in dating her. Even more so because they worked together.

She nodded and waved as the phone buzzed again.

"Hello, Charlotte?"

"Hi, Tess, this is Tim. I'm calling from Charlotte's phone." He sounded as if he'd just run sprints.

"Tim, is everything okay?" The fact that he was calling from Charlotte's cell and sounded so winded made her worry.

"No, no, everything is fine...I mean, everything is mostly fine." He took a breath. "I just wanted to let you know, we're at the hospital. Charlotte is having contractions."

"Do you need me?" Tess mentally calculated leaving work early. Could she even make that happen? Could Garet manage to cover things the rest of the day? *Unknown.* Regardless, Garet might have to jump into the deep end without Tess to play lifeguard.

"I—" His voice broke. Was he crying?

"I'm on my way."

"Thank you." Tim's relief was evident. "Thank you, Tess."

Her hands were shaking when she clicked off. Why was she so nervous? She wasn't the one having a baby. She stood quickly causing the chair to tip over. It banged loudly on the tile floor. The noise made her jump. Garet had just entered the room holding a slice of cake. Garet strode toward her and reached for the toppled furniture.

Garet hadn't touched Tess, but when Garet reached past her shoulder for the fallen chair she disturbed the air. And Tess registered the disturbance immediately. There was an uneasy twinge, a tightening deep inside, a pulse of desire she hadn't felt in a long time. She brushed the sensation aside as some involuntary response. A symptom of too many nights alone, a superficial attraction to Garet, and nervousness for Charlotte.

"Hey, is everything all right?" Garet had righted the chair and lightly rested her fingers on the back of it. "Oh, and this is for you." She held out the cake as if it were a peace offering.

"I'm fine." Shaking her head, she waved the cake away and took a step back from Garet. "Charlotte, the woman you're subbing for, has gone into labor."

"Oh…so, there's like, a medical emergency?" Garet held the dessert in both hands. She seemed unsure what to do with it.

"Well, yes, you could call it that." Tess couldn't help noticing how cluelessly cute Garet was. "That was Charlotte's boyfriend on the phone. He sounded overwhelmed and upset. I think I need to be there." She began to shuffle papers on her desk and stow them in her shoulder bag. "Can you cover things for the rest of the day? I'll let the office know I'm leaving."

"You mean, teach your music classes?" Garet's voice went up a notch.

"No, you can just have them read or something." Tess shouldered her large leather satchel. "Tell them to treat the hour like study hall, just for today."

"Okay, yeah…sure." Except that Garet sounded anything but sure.

"You'll be fine. I'll stop by Mary's class on the way out and ask her to check in on you."

"Maybe I should have your cell number, you know, in case there's an emergency…I mean, a non-medical emergency."

"Right, that's probably not a bad idea."

They traded phones so they could share contact info.

"Thanks again for covering my classes. Mary will be great backup."

Garet stood like a cake-wielding statue in the center of the room as she pulled the door closed. The bell rang and students flooded the hallway. She dodged and angled toward Mary's class first. Five minutes later, she was outside and rummaging for her phone to pull up her mother's number. If she was at the hospital for more than a couple of hours, which was highly likely, then her mother would need to pick up June from school. The distance to her mother's house was probably walkable, but she'd feel better if June had a ride.

She transferred the call to the car's Bluetooth as she backed out of the parking space.

"Hi, Tess dear." Her mother sounded chipper, although a bit out of breath. Maybe she was in the garden again. "How is it that I rated a call in the middle of the day?"

"Hi, Mom, I have a favor to ask."

❖

Tess parked in the visitor's lot and hurried toward the main entrance of the Tanner County Regional Hospital forty-five minutes from Shadetree. Anything that couldn't be handled by the local volunteer rescue squad got transported to the Regional Hospital. Maternity was on the second floor. The woman at the front desk directed Tess toward the elevators. She spotted Tim first. He was in the waiting area with his face in his hands.

"I can't go back in there." He looked very sleep deprived and the baby hadn't even arrived. "She hates me."

"Women say crazy things during labor. Don't take it to heart." Tess patted his hunched shoulder.

Tess hardly remembered the pain of childbirth now. It was as if her brain had glazed over all of it. Since she'd had no partner at the time, her mother had stayed in the room with her the entire time. She'd been so relieved to have her there.

"Where is Charlotte?"

With a shaky finger, he pointed down the hallway.

"Room 315."

This could have been a scene from some romantic comedy where the husband was completely frazzled and had been thrown out by his screaming wife. Only, there was no hair and makeup on the set—this was the real thing. Tess hurried down the corridor. Charlotte looked up when she peeked around the partially open door. Before Tess could say anything, Charlotte grimaced and moaned, clutching her stomach.

"Oh my God…Tess, it hurts."

"I know." She set her bag on the nearest chair and reached for Charlotte's hand.

"Tim is no good in here. He almost passed out and hardly anything has even happened yet." Charlotte winced.

Tess suspected it was something more than the anticipated goriness of childbirth that unsettled him. Tim was probably terrified of fatherhood itself—parenthood he might not be prepared to shoulder.

"How are you holding up?" She offered Charlotte some water.

Every woman's labor was unique. No one knew what to expect until it happened.

"Okay. Mostly…I felt mild contractions last night. We didn't actually get here to the hospital until this morning." Charlotte gripped Tess's hand, her face contorted with pain.

It was all coming back to Tess. Active labor was where all the fun stopped. The contractions were stronger, your legs cramped, and you felt nauseous. You began to have second thoughts about *everything*.

"My lower back is killing me."

"Roll onto your side. I'll rub your back." She knew from experience, that for a first-time mother this could take hours.

She'd been lucky. She'd returned home for June's birth, and her mother had been a rock through the entire pregnancy. Even her father had finally gotten on board. Initially, he'd wanted to track down June's father, more accurately—the sperm donor—and lay some heavy-handed paternal guilt on him. But having June was ultimately Tess's decision and she made that decision knowing she'd be doing it as a single parent. She had no regrets and she couldn't imagine her life now without June.

Charlotte moaned, calling her attention back to the moment at hand.

"Breathe through it. Just breathe, Charlotte."

Charlotte nodded silently as she inhaled and then exhaled, until the contraction eased.

"Thank you for coming." Charlotte sank into the pillow.

"I'll stay as long as you want. Okay?" She let her palm rest on Charlotte's damp forehead.

CHAPTER FIFTEEN

It was about five minutes past three. Garet only had to hang on for another few minutes and then the *longest day ever* would be over. Mary had stopped by to check on her once an hour or so after Tess's abrupt departure. The kids had immediately quieted down when Mary stepped into the room. Of course, mere seconds after Mary left, mayhem resumed.

Didn't first graders ever run out of energy? Shouldn't they be tired by now?

"Hey, quiet down." Garet tried to regain control. "And you, striped shirt, stop running. Everyone in your seats." But no one was listening.

Garet sank to a chair, folded her arms on the table, and rested her forehead on her arm. She released a long, slow breath and tried to channel some distant sense of calm. She only had to manage to keep everyone from jettisoning into orbit for another ten minutes. Not much could go wrong in ten minutes, right?

She felt someone tap on her arm and turned her head to see who'd touched her. She opened one eye to see a cute kid with short blond hair and huge brown eyes. Her button nose had a smattering of freckles. Her faded pink T-shirt bore the stains of juice, probably grape, and the legs of her jeans were tucked into red rubber rain boots.

"You're not very good at this." The little girl's statement sounded more like a wise observation than a criticism.

"Thank you for noticing." Garet sat up in her chair and sighed. "Tell me your name again?"

"June."

"So, June, what's going on right there?" Garet touched her own front tooth indicating the space where June had none. A dull roar of excited voices vibrated all around them like a high-pitched gathering storm.

"I've lost three teeth." June filled the empty space with her tongue for emphasis.

"Three, huh?"

"And this one is loose, see?" June wiggled another tooth with her fingertip.

"What did you get from the tooth fairy for the others?" Garet was genuinely curious.

"A dollar."

"A dollar for each one or all three?"

"A dollar for each one."

"Wow. I guess that's inflation. I'm pretty sure I only got fifty cents when I was a kid."

"You can't buy very much with fifty cents."

"You're right about that." Garet reached for a box of crayons just as they were about to careen to the floor.

"You'll get better at this teacher stuff. You just need practice." June sounded so certain.

Before Garet could respond, the last bell of the day rang. Relief cascaded through her system like floodwaters down a staircase.

Students grabbed backpacks and scurried toward the door. June hadn't moved.

"Aren't you...I mean, don't you need to catch a bus or something?" Garet moved chairs so that they were more orderly around the tables.

"I'm supposed to wait here for my mom."

"Oh, really? Who's your mom?"

"Tess Hill. She teaches in this class too."

Garet stopped and gave June her full attention. Of course, the resemblance was so obvious now.

"Um, your mom had to leave early. Are you sure—"

"Hi, June Bug. Are you ready to go?" An older woman breezed into the classroom. June trotted toward her and then fell into a hug. The woman looked up and smiled at Garet while still holding June. "You must be covering for Charlotte."

"She's not very good at it," June volunteered.

"June!" The woman frowned and shook her head. "That isn't a very nice thing to say."

"It's okay." Garet sighed and crossed her arms. "June and I were just discussing how I might need some practice. I'm Garet Allen, by the way."

"I'm June's grandmother, Adelle. And I think June owes you an apology."

June scrunched her nose and cocked her head.

"We're waiting." Adelle's hand was on her hip. Meeting June and now Adelle was like getting a glimpse of three stages of Tess—young, adult, and older. Tess had a strong resemblance to her mother. Adelle was fit for her age, with shortish gray hair and eyes that sparkled with friendliness.

"I'm sorry?"

"An apology is not a question." Adelle coached June. She was kind, but firm.

"I'm sorry." This time June shifted her weight from foot to foot and bit her lower lip.

"Apology accepted." Garet extended her hand. "Friends?"

A huge grin exposed the open space between June's teeth as she placed her tiny hand in Garet's.

"All right then, your mother had something to do so you and I are having dinner. Gather your things." Adelle waited while June retrieved her backpack and pencil case. "It was nice to meet you, Ms. Allen."

"Please, call me Garet."

She smiled at Garet as she held June's hand and was tugged through the doorway.

Garet dropped to the nearest seat and slouched, stretching her legs out in front of her. She could have sworn that at least twelve hours had passed since Tess left for the hospital. In reality it had been only a little more than three hours. Three hours of managing kids had been like a grueling marathon. At least that's what she suspected the exhaustion of a marathon might feel like. She'd never actually been much of a runner. So much for her genius plan that she'd teach, get out around three, and then go home and work on her picture book project. She was completely depleted. There probably wasn't enough coffee in the world to jump-start her system. She wasn't just tired, she was mentally fatigued and physically spent. For a minute, she considered crawling under the table and going to sleep.

How did teachers do this every day?

Garet suddenly had a renewed appreciation for every teacher she'd ever had, even the ones whose classes she didn't enjoy.

CHAPTER SIXTEEN

Garet trudged into the house, let her shoulder bag slide off her arm onto the floor, and walked through the tiny kitchen to the bedroom where she flopped like a felled tree face-first onto the bed. She was exhausted, beyond exhausted—wiped out, empty, depleted, and defeated. Teaching was much harder than she'd thought it would be. She rotated her face on the soft fabric of the bedspread so that she could breathe. She blew out a breath.

How was she ever going to last for three months when she'd barely survived the first eight hours on the job? She was screwed.

She sighed and tried to relax the tense muscles in her back. Maybe she just needed a little power nap to recharge. Yeah, that was it.

A brief rest with her eyes closed would leave her refreshed and ready to work.

Events of the day circled in her head. Then, certain visuals came forward and maintained her focus. Tess had a starring role in every one of those replayed scenes.

The way Tess tilted her head when she smiled, an alluring combination of shyness and flirtation. Garet imagined herself responding.

Garet brought Tess a slice of cake from the teacher's lounge. Tess set the dessert offering aside and stepped into Garet's personal space. Tess brushed hair off her forehead with a tender gesture. They were close now. Tess's lips mere inches from hers, parted in invitation. Garet drew her close. The press of Tess's body against hers was painfully delicious. An ache deep inside began to rise up.

Garet placed one hand on Tess's hip, the other at the base of her neck, and closed the space between them. The kiss was deliciously slow, an exploration, a connection unspoken yet deep.

The room shifted and they were lying down. Garet shifted her thigh between Tess's and trailed her palm down the outside curve of Tess's breast and across her ribs. The never-ending kiss began to deepen, her tongue teased Tess's with need and desperation.

A low repetitive banging sound invaded the room.

What was *that* noise?

Garet jolted awake. There was a loud knock at the door. She'd been dreaming. She must have dozed off for real. Her neck was stiff from the angle of her head on the mattress. And she was so turned on. Another rap on the door.

Who would be knocking?

She didn't even know anyone here. Getting off the bed was a struggle, but finally she made it to a standing position. Garet squinted at the shape of someone standing in the doorway, backlit. In her extreme mental fatigue had she forgotten to close the door? As she drew nearer she realized Hildy Green was at the door holding a cardboard to-go container of something.

"I hope I'm not interrupting?"

Interrupting? Yes, the best dream ever. Garet checked to make sure there was no residue of afternoon nap drool on her shirt.

"No, I was just…hanging out." Admitting she'd been asleep at four in the afternoon on a weekday was far too lame.

"I thought you'd be adjusting to your first day in class and that you might not have stocked the kitchen yet." Hildy offered up the cardboard container. "The tea house does breakfast and lunch until three thirty. I brought you a chicken sandwich and iced tea."

"Hildy, you might have just saved my life." Garet gratefully accepted the boxed meal. She shook her head in a failed attempt to dislodge the memory of Tess from her dream.

"Takeout to the rescue." Hildy smiled and followed her to the kitchen still holding the iced tea. "You just sit down, I'll get a plate for you. You're not vegetarian, are you? I suppose I should have asked. That's a chicken salad sandwich." She swiveled from the cabinet with a plate and handed it to Garet.

Hildy obviously knew her way around this kitchen, technically, it was *her* kitchen.

"So, you're teaching art, then you must be sharing the class with Tess Hill. Isn't she adorable?" Hildy sat opposite her, with elbows on the counter and her chin in her hand.

Garet had just taken a big bite from the sandwich and almost swallowed it whole. Adorable? Yes, absolutely. But the description sounded strange coming from her landlord. Although, adorable was the sort of word older southern women used for a variety of things— babies, puppies, and apparently, small town music teachers. Despite seeming more uptight in the classroom than she'd been at the café the previous day, Tess was undeniably adorable.

Tess, unfortunately, was also most definitely Garet's type. Unfortunate because now Tess wasn't just some cute woman she'd met at the music store, and again at the café, Tess was a coworker. Despite Tess's physical charms, which Garet took a moment to mentally catalog. She shook her head again. She was beginning to act like Lane, who was much more of a player than she was. Sure, Garet had her one-drawer rule, but that was more about keeping things clean, more about boundaries than it was about jumping from one woman rapidly to the next. No, Garet did *not* have the emotional fortitude to be a player in the true sense of the word; she was much too sensitive.

Garet slowly chewed, realizing Hildy had been silently watching as she ran through mental gymnastics regarding Tess.

"You know Tess?" She took a sip of tea from the glass Hildy placed in front of her. She must have seemed as if she needed a drink. The thick sourdough bread was sort of stuck in her throat, or was that knot her feelings of regret about Tess because she was never going to be able to act on them?

"Why yes, it's a small town you know." Hildy smiled.

It seemed Hildy was planning to stay while Garet ate. She'd plunked herself down on a stool with no sign of leaving.

"What does her husband do?" She might as well find out what she could if Hildy was in the mood to share.

"She's not married."

"Oh." Garet took another bite.

"I don't even think she's had a girlfriend in several years." Hildy angled her head as if she were trying to look for answers on the ceiling. "No, not since June was much younger. I'm sure it's not easy to date when you're a single mom."

So, Tess was a lesbian. Garet had gotten a slight flirtatious vibe when they'd first met at the music store. And Lane had insisted that Tess was focused on her while the bluegrass band played at the cafe, but that certainly wasn't conclusive. This was a welcomed bit of confirmation. Wait, what did it matter if Tess was a lesbian or not? It would be very messy to date a coworker, very messy indeed. Hang on, rewind, how did Hildy even know that Tess was a lesbian? Was Hildy a lesbian too? She'd wondered after Lane's visit. She was about to ask more questions when Hildy spoke.

"It's not like Shadetree is a hotbed for lesbian dating options." Hildy rolled her eyes. "I mean, you've only just arrived, but you'll see what I mean."

Garet coughed and took a sip of tea. All she could do was nod.

It seemed obvious that either Hildy had assumed Garet was gay too or at the very least that she was okay with gayness in general. Was this Hildy's way of letting Garet know that she was also a lesbian?

So far, this conversation had given Garet a lot to process.

Her thoughts returned to Tess. Garet wondered if it was a problem for a teacher in Shadetree to be openly gay. She knew it wasn't an issue in Metro Atlanta, but she hadn't really taken time to consider that it might be more of an issue in a small town like this. Although, she wasn't getting that impression from Hildy. There didn't seem to be any hint of judgment, simply good-natured gossip about a person Hildy clearly liked.

Thinking about small towns conjured memories of high school and her mother finding out she was a lesbian. It wasn't as if her mother and father had disowned her, but they weren't ecstatic either.

Even though there was no such thing as a Presbyterian convent, Garet knew her mother still held hope to this day that she'd take a vow of celibacy rather than committing to a relationship with a woman. So far, Garet's one-drawer rule had worked in her mother's favor.

Garet finished off the sandwich and thanked Hildy. She had a ton of questions, things she'd love to know about Tess. Hildy gave the impression that she'd be happy to share more, but Garet wanted to hear details from Tess or not at all.

Garet used the excuse of work she needed to return to in order to encourage Hildy to leave. She closed the door and leaned against it as she surveyed the tiny cottage. Could she even get her head in the right space to work?

She had to.

That's why she'd taken this teaching gig in the first place.

Within a half hour, the slant board was set up and she was staring at a blank sheet of Bristol board. Thoughts of Tess swirled inside her head. This entire situation with Tess was going to end up being a painful combination of attraction and restraint.

Garet chewed her lower lip.

Just focus on the work.

She coached herself in hopes that she might actually listen. Garet unzipped the pen case and put an array of pencils and a few pens on the countertop next to the slant board. She'd already figured out the trim size for the book and had lined off a few pages to get her started. There was nothing worse than "getting in the zone" creatively, on a roll, only to have to stop what you were sketching to do something mechanical like line off a page.

Actually, the technical aspects of penciling a book were Garet's least favorite part of the process. She tried to do all that stuff up front, saving the good stuff—the drawing and painting—for last. There were thumbnail sketches that broke the story up into the right plot points and the proper page count. Garet flipped through it and settled on a page in the middle to begin with. Part of her methodology was to start in the middle, work to the end, then go back to the beginning. That way, you were completely warmed up and on model at the very beginning of the book and you hid any rookie mistakes in the middle.

Character sketches were taped to the top few inches of the slant board. Views of the bear from the front, side, and back. The same for the kitten.

Kittens were so hard to draw. A caricature of a bear was easy. He was all hulking fur with a square snout and big teeth. In contrast, the kitten had been designed for maximum cuteness—big head, large eyes, and tiny little kitten feet.

Garet roughed in the larger shapes on the Bristol board, then set about adding details lightly in pencil. She'd watercolor everything and then go back in with ink for the final pass. But first things first, penciling the entire book and getting sign off from her editor in New York.

As she worked, the day slipped away. The distraction of Tess, her insecurities teaching, even her fatigue, slowly evaporated with the Zen-like soft scratching of the pencil against the paper. Garet was lost now, in a magical world of her own making.

CHAPTER SEVENTEEN

The alarm rudely ejected Garet from sleep. She'd stayed up too late working on drawings. Once she'd gotten into the rhythm of it she hadn't been able to bring herself to stop. It was probably close to three before she crawled into bed, and now she was feeling it.

Garet covered another yawn with her hand, then sipped coffee from the oversized yeti mug she'd discovered in a cabinet in the cottage. She needed as much caffeine as was humanly possible to consume before the bell rang for classes to start.

Tess was writing notes on the chalkboard when she stepped into the classroom. Despite her efforts to not care, her heart rate spiked briefly at the sight of Tess. The sensation reminded her of one time when she was a kid and accidentally touched an electrical fence. Luckily, it had been a low wattage fence, but the tingly buzz was similar.

"Hi." Garet stowed her messenger bag behind the large desk they shared.

"Good morning." Tess looked as if she needed a bit more sleep also.

"How is your friend? How is Charlotte?"

"She gave birth to a healthy baby boy." Tess smiled at Garet, causing her heart to do that little staccato jolt again. "His name is Tucker and he weighed eight pounds."

"Tucker is a nice name."

"It was a long night." Tess set the chalk aside and dusted her fingers together.

"Hey, you know, if you need to take off early and rest…well, I can handle things."

"That's nice of you to offer." The bell rang and the first group of students for the day began to file in. "I'll be okay."

She'd proposed covering the classes to be nice, to be a team player, but was extremely relieved that Tess declined. Tess was back and she wouldn't have to handle all the kids on her own. Relief settled her system a bit.

Garet moved to one of the chairs along the back wall with her giant to-go cup of coffee. She wasn't sure if there were rules about bringing beverages to class, but what were they going to do, fire her? She didn't even really work there. This was a temporary gig. Surely breaking a few rules was allowed if you were only substituting for the *real* teacher.

Garet did her best to be helpful, and if not helpful, at least less annoying than some clueless novice, which she was now pretty sure she was. Whatever arrogant bravado she'd had going into the first day of class had been completely crushed by reality.

The last bell rang, and noisy kids jammed the hallway.

Garet began straightening the chairs for the next day's class. She wanted to ask Tess to have dinner, or something, as an apology of sorts, but then chided herself. Dinner was a bad idea. Dinner would just lead to complications. She was completely inside her own head as she slid the last chair into place. So much so that she almost bumped into Tess when she spun around.

"Oh, sorry." She was surprised by Tess's proximity.

"Listen, remember our conversation earlier about the production for the fall festival?"

Garet nodded.

She'd asked Tess about it after hearing other teachers in the lounge mention it. She'd been extremely relieved when Tess said she didn't need Garet's help. Not that she didn't want to be helpful, but she did have the graphic novel to finish, and she was on a deadline. That was supposed to be her afternoon job, not a kid's production.

"I've been reflecting on it all day and...well, I don't think I can manage it by myself." Tess folded her arms. It seemed she needed assistance but wasn't happy about asking for it. "If you could work with the art classes on the backdrops that would be really helpful."

"Sure." Garet had no idea how to create backdrops, but she definitely wasn't going to reveal that to Tess. And the fact that Tess needed something from Garet was an opportunity not to be missed, in her opinion. This was a chance to redeem herself a bit in Tess's eyes.

"Great." Tess crossed the room to retrieve her shoulder bag.

"Just out of curiosity, has the play been selected already?" Garet wanted to know what she was getting into. She hoped it wasn't Shakespeare. That would not be her favorite.

"We're doing *The Wizard of Oz*. Charlotte and I let the kids vote before she left on maternity leave."

"Good...The Emerald City and the yellow brick road and stuff." She could already picture key visuals in her head.

Tess studied Garet. The students took the entire endeavor very seriously and she worried that Garet's recap of the story was a bit too loose.

"Don't forget the poppy fields. The one where they fall asleep." Tess arched an eyebrow, curious to find out how well Garet knew the storyline.

"Yeah...poppies, right before the flying monkeys." Garet grinned.

Tess almost laughed but fought the urge. She was trying hard not to fall for Garet's easy charm. Besides, Garet struck her as the sort of woman who preferred to keep her distance. The sort of emotional anarchy that Tess could never quite manage. Women like Garet gently mocked the trappings of commitment, in both work and relationships. It was obvious. Tess was probably too much like Dorothy Gale in search of the Emerald City and a way home. Tess had a tendency to trust people too easily. She was co-teaching and producing a play with someone who was only in this for a short-term gain. She needed to remember that, regardless of how distractingly cute Garet was. She shook her head.

"Did I say something wrong?" Garet seemed genuinely concerned.

"No, I was just thinking it might be wise if you familiarized yourself with the material before we involve the kids in constructing props and backdrops."

"Oh, yeah, sure, that's a good idea." Garet nodded, and then turned back to Tess. "Um, how should I do that?"

"Maybe you should rent the movie."

"I don't have a TV."

"Or, you know, stream it on your laptop."

"Yeah, I suppose that would work—"

"Or you could come over and watch it at our house. I think we have it on DVD. It's one of June's favorites." She blinked rapidly. Her mouth had gotten way ahead of her brain and she'd just invited Garet to her home without really meaning to. "You probably don't—"

"That'd be great." Garet's eyes lit up at the invitation.

Now Tess felt guilty about rescinding the invite. What was the best way to gracefully backtrack? Tess tried to quickly flip through options in her head.

"Hi, Mama!"

Too late. Before she could think of anything, June bounced into the room and wrapped her arms around Tess's waist.

"Hi, June." Garet gave a little wave with one hand as she braced her other hand on the back of a nearby chair.

"Hi, Garet."

"That's Ms. Allen, June," Tess corrected her.

"But she doesn't look like a *Miss* to me." June rotated to face Garet, with her back against Tess. She rested her hands affectionately on June's tiny shoulders.

"She can call me Garet. I don't mind."

"How did you two even meet?" Tess wasn't crazy about the idea of June striking up a friendship with the object of her distraction.

"Yesterday, when you were gone." June tilted her head to look up at Tess. "She's not a very good teacher. Maybe you could give her some lessons."

Garet laughed.

"I'm so sorry." Tess apologized for June's rudeness.

"No, don't worry. She told me the same thing yesterday." Garet looked down at June and grinned. "June and I have a very honest friendship, don't we?"

June nodded emphatically.

"Are we watching a movie tonight?" June sounded hopeful. "I heard you say we might watch a movie."

June was at the age where it was almost impossible to sneak anything past her. At six years old, she was practically all ears. June retained everything and seemed to have a gift for repeating things she'd overheard, but didn't completely comprehend, at the absolute worst moments.

"I invited Garet over to watch *The Wizard of Oz*…sometime."

"Tonight! Tonight! Tonight!" June did little jumps up and down. "Let's watch it tonight. And get pizza!" She turned to Garet. "Do you like pizza?"

"I…" Garet let her response trail off as she made eye contact with Tess.

It was so hard to say no when June was so excited about it. And they did need to watch it so that she and Garet could make plans for the production. She felt a bit outnumbered, but in a good way.

"Okay, June Bug." Tess smiled. "Movie and pizza night, it is."

CHAPTER EIGHTEEN

Garet volunteered to pick up the pizza and drive it over. That would give Tess an hour or so to help June with any homework before she arrived. She ended up waiting at the café for the pizza, rather than calling it in. She figured she could get some sketching done while she waited. She carried a sketchbook with her everywhere to utilize any free time to think and make story notes and work out problem scenes or character designs.

"Are you an artist?" Candi, the waitress from Sunday brunch, angled her head for a better look.

"Yes, most of the time." Garet glanced up to see Candi holding a pizza box.

"You're really good." Candi sounded impressed.

"Thanks. These are just rough drawings…nothing finished." Garet closed the sketchbook and slid it into her messenger bag.

"Do you need utensils or anything with this?" Candi offered her the slender box.

"No, I'm good." Warmth radiated through the cardboard.

"Party for one, huh?" Candi braced her hands on her hips. "There's nights when I can eat a whole pizza myself too. Now don't go hatin' yourself in the morning for it. We all deserve to indulge every now and then." Candi playfully touched her arm. "Besides, you could stand to gain a few pizza pounds."

"Ha ha." Garet laughed nervously.

This was a lot more nosiness and advice than she'd expected. It was a good reminder that news in this small town probably traveled lightning fast. She was really thankful she hadn't mentioned that she was taking the pizza over to Tess's place.

Candi was in the middle of totaling up the order when the phone near the register rang.

"Riverside Café, this is Candi, how can I help you?" She cradled the cordless phone against her shoulder as she rang up the ticket. "Yes, she is." She glanced up at Garet and a huge smile spread across her face. "Sure thing, sweetie." She hung the phone up. "Tess wants you to bring a lemonade for June Bug." She winked at Garet. "I'll just add that to the tab."

"Okay." Garet stood like a statue holding the pizza in both hands. She wasn't sure what else to say.

Maybe Tess didn't care if anyone knew she was going over to her house for dinner. Maybe Tess invited all the new substitute teachers over for dinner and Garet was the only one wishfully reading into things. She signed the screen and waited for Candi to return with the to-go cup of lemonade.

"You and Tess have a nice evening now." Candi's slow drawl sounded very suggestive.

Did Candi know something Garet didn't?

"For sure. Thanks." Garet tried to sound casual but was afraid she just sounded edgy.

She tipped the large soda cup in Candi's direction and leaned against the door with her butt to push through the exit. So much for keeping a low profile in Shadetree, Georgia.

❖

Tess's home was cozy and warmly decorated, the sort of place that made you want to settle in and draw or read a book. She could easily visualize lounging with a cup of coffee in front of the old brick fireplace on a chilly morning.

"This is a great house." Garet looked around the living room.

"Thanks. You can drop your bag anywhere."

Tess started to walk to the kitchen and Garet followed. She left her messenger bag on the floor at the end of the couch. Tess took plates from the cupboard and placed them on the table near the pizza box.

"The house belongs to my aunt. It was built in 1912, I think. Or maybe it was 1915."

The living room and kitchen had narrow, well-traveled hardwood floors, dark from age and sun exposure. White wainscoting halfway up the walls trimmed with chair railing ringed the kitchen. A set of stairs bordered the wall of the living room, near the front door, that angled up to a second floor. Garet waited for June to settle into a chair on her knees before she sat down. Tess served them each pizza and then cautioned June to wait a second for the cheese to cool. Garet understood June's urgency. Pizza was her favorite food and it was hard not to fold the piece and take a huge bite. But she was acutely aware that she should set a good example for June. It wasn't as if she was at her apartment alone, eating in front of the TV.

Actually, she'd expected them to eat the pizza and watch the movie at the same time. But maybe a little kid and a messy cheese pizza didn't mix well with an upholstered sofa. Probably safer to keep red sauce and greasy fingers in the kitchen.

"Can I get you something to drink?" Tess was standing in the open fridge. She looked over at Garet.

"Sure." She watched June blow on her pizza to hurry the cooling process.

"I have iced tea, a sparkling water…"

"Iced tea would be great."

Tess poured them both a glass and returned to the table.

"So, June, I hear we're about to watch one of your favorite movies."

June nodded. She'd just taken a big bite.

"How many times have you seen it?" Garet sampled her slice. It was very good. Normally she'd have gotten a few more toppings, but at Tess's request, she'd kept it simple. It turned out a cheese pizza was better than she remembered.

June swallowed before answering. "Maybe twenty times."

"Twenty times might be an exaggeration, don't you think?" Tess quirked an eyebrow.

June shrugged and took another bite.

"Well, you must be an expert then." Garet nodded and tried to sound serious. "That'll come in handy if I have any follow-up questions."

"You're funny." June grinned.

"What makes you say that?" Garet was curious.

"Grown-ups never ask kids for help."

"Well, maybe they should." Garet took a sip and peered at June over the rim of her glass. "Kids know stuff. Am I right?"

June nodded enthusiastically.

"Don't encourage her." Tess smiled. "We recently had a very serious debate about how animal crackers are not for animals."

June giggled.

"I think there's a story here that I missed out on." Garet looked from Tess to June and back.

"I'll fill you in later. For now, eat." Tess pointed at June. "Or it'll be bedtime before we get to watch the movie."

Tess blushed at the mention of bedtime. Garet tried her best not to read into it.

CHAPTER NINETEEN

Tess started the movie and the three of them sat on the sofa with June in the middle. The relaxed coziness of it all made Tess realize how rarely she did this sort of thing. The only two people who came over to watch movies were her mother and Charlotte. And now, Garet was here, someone she hardly knew, and yet, who seemed so familiar at the same time. It was odd to note the comfort of Garet's presence while still attempting to retain professional distance.

June raced to her room while the title sequence scrolled across the screen to retrieve Chester. The rainbow-horned narwhal was imperative for the viewing. June lay between Garet and Tess with her chin resting on the stuffed toy.

As Dorothy Gale and Toto skipped through the scruffy Kansas farm, cast in black and white, Tess found herself more often than not watching Garet instead of the movie. June, on the other hand, was riveted to the screen. Something about how six-year-olds watched TV was mesmerizing. Wide-eyed and in complete awe of all the colorful images that now filled the screen as Dorothy and Toto made their way along the yellow brick road.

Dorothy and her companions survived the poppy field and had just reached the gates of the Emerald City when Tess's phone buzzed. Charlotte's name flashed on the screen.

"Sorry, I need to get this call. Do you mind if we pause the movie?"

"Sure, no problem." Garet shifted so that she was leaning forward.

June blinked up at her as if she were coming out of a trance.

Tess held the remote in one hand and her phone in the other as she stood up. "Hello." She motioned that she was taking the call in the kitchen. "Charlotte, how are you? I'm so glad you called."

"Mama will probably be on the phone forever." June sighed and flopped off the couch so that she was sitting on the floor with her legs stretched beneath the coffee table.

"Well, what should we do then…I mean, forever is a long time."

"I have crayons." June's eyes widened and a big smile lit up her face.

For anyone else, that might have been a funny thing to say. But for Garet, there wasn't anything that brought more joy than a fresh box of crayons. She even loved the way they smelled.

"Crayons are one of my favorite things."

June ran out of the room and returned with a jumbo box of crayons and some white construction paper, along with an odd sampling of coloring books. Garet repositioned herself on the floor next to June.

"What's that?" June asked.

Her sketchbook had fallen out of her satchel enough for the spiral bound edge to show.

"Oh, that's my sketchbook."

"Can I see it?"

"Sure." Garet stretched for the book and then opened it on the coffee table.

June stood up, her hand was on Garet's shoulder as she fidgeted and studied each page.

"That's a bear." June pointed.

"Yes, that's a bear and this is the tree he lives in." Garet slowly turned pages as she talked.

"What's the story?"

"This little stray kitten shows up on the doorstep of a fastidious bear and the kitten turns the bear's world upside down."

"What is fastidust?"

"Oh, it just means that the bear has a very orderly, calm life and likes things that way."

She turned a few more pages. There was a night scene in the forest. The white kitten was surrounded by darkness.

"Is the kitten lost?" There was concern in June's question.

Garet loved the way kids got invested in stories.

"Yes, but don't worry. This story has a happy ending."

June was quiet for a minute. Then she settled back onto the floor and started to color. It seemed she'd moved on from the story. But then she spoke.

"I think you're the kitten."

"What?" The statement caught Garet by surprise.

"You're the lost kitten." June's expression was painfully sincere.

"No, I'm not." Garet didn't mean to sound defensive but was afraid she did.

"And my mom is the bear."

Garet's mouth hung open. She was about to argue when Tess returned from the kitchen.

"Hey, what are you two up to in here?"

"Coloring." June didn't look up.

Tess felt she'd interrupted some serious discussion. Garet had the oddest expression. There were crayons and paper all over the coffee table. How long had she been on the phone? It seemed only a few moments, but given the scene of comfortable chaos in the living room you'd have thought she'd been gone for an hour.

"Hey, June Bug, maybe we should finish the movie a different night." Tess sat at the edge of the couch and watched over June's shoulder. She was working very busily with a light blue crayon.

"Nooooo." June was not happy about relinquishing the day.

"It's bedtime for you, and I'm sure Garet has things to do also."

"But Mama, we only just now started coloring." June scowled. "Besides, I'm not sleepy. I want Garet to stay over."

Oh, dear. Now Tess was the one yelling no inside her head.

"June, it's bedtime." Tess stood and waited for June. "I don't want to have an argument in front of our guest. We'll finish the movie another time."

If it was possible to sigh grumpily, June did exactly that.

"Why do I have a bedtime and you don't? It's not fair." As a parent, Tess was mildly embarrassed that her six-year-old was essentially fighting her about bedtime in front of Garet.

"I'm kinda sleepy too." Garet made a big show of fake yawning. "I probably should get going." She leaned over where June was still seated with her legs tucked beneath the coffee table. "Hey, we'll finish coloring next time, okay?"

June nodded and reluctantly accepted Tess's hand.

"Thanks for everything. It was…nice." Garet sounded as if she was bothered by something and was trying to hide it.

"Is everything all right?"

"Oh, sure, I think I'm just tired." Garet shoved her sketchbook into her bag and stood up.

Tess had given her an opening to leave and it seemed she couldn't depart fast enough. Maybe she was annoyed that they hadn't finished the movie. It was Tess's idea that they watch it in the first place so that they could begin preparing a production plan for the play.

"I'm sorry about cutting the movie short—"

"Oh, no, really, it's not a problem."

Now she was sure that Garet was distracted, but for the life of her, she couldn't decipher by what.

They were both standing now and she followed Garet to the door.

"Well, thank you again for dinner and the movie." Garet partially turned.

"Wait, I forgot to give you money for the pizza." Tess was about to go in search of her wallet, but Garet stopped her.

"That's not necessary." Garet smiled. Although, her smile was tinted with melancholy. "It was my treat." Garet shifted her weight from one foot to the other and shoved her hands in her pockets. "Consider it a peace offering for probably being the least experienced substitute teacher you've probably ever met."

Garet got bonus points for acknowledging the truth, even when it didn't paint her in the best light.

"Hey, we're all beginners at some point in our careers, right?" Tess touched Garet's arm. The gesture was meant to be friendly, but her nervous system had other ideas. The tingle that traveled from her fingers up her arm surprised her.

Garet stared down at Tess's fingers. Had Garet felt the same little jolt of electricity? There was an awkward moment when neither of them spoke. Tess withdrew, folding her arms across her chest and averting her eyes.

"Well, I should get going." She tipped her head in June's direction. "Someone is getting sleepy."

Tess glanced over, catching June mid-yawn.

"I'll see you tomorrow." Garet opened the door.

"See you tomorrow." Tess stood in the open doorway watching her leave. "Thanks again for the pizza."

She waited until Garet backed out of the drive and pulled away before closing the door. She'd had to fight the strongest urge to draw Garet into a hug. A completely unprofessional impulse and one she knew she should avoid.

"Come on, June. Time for bed." Tess started to gather the crayons and put them away.

June yawned again as Tess followed her upstairs to the bathroom. Ten minutes later, teeth were brushed and June was snuggled under the covers in her favorite Disney princess pajamas, with Chester tucked in beside her.

"Did you have a nice time tonight?" Whatever scene she'd interrupted between Garet and June still nagged at her. She hoped June would volunteer some part of their conversation.

"Uh-huh." June nodded.

"What did you two talk about while I was on the phone?" She sat on the edge of the bed.

"Her art book."

"You mean sketchbook?"

"It's more of a story book, I think." June rubbed her eyes sleepily. "It's a story about a fasted-toes bear and a lost kitten." June stared up at her. "What's fasted-toes mean?"

"Do you mean fastidious?" Tess tried not to laugh.

"Yeah, that's what I meant."

"It means that somebody likes things the way they like them, I suppose. A person who is very tidy and exact. They prefer things to be accurate, orderly, and they probably don't like for things to change."

"Oh." June had a thoughtful expression. "I told Garet she's the kitten."

"You did?"

"And you're the bear." June rolled onto her side. "Good night, Mama." Her words were muffled by the pillow.

Tess sat for a moment, stunned by June's assessment. As if in slow motion, she reached to switch off the bedside lamp. She tenderly kissed June's cheek.

"Good night, sweetheart."

She left the bedroom door ajar and returned to the kitchen to make a cup of tea. As was her habit, she stood at the window over the sink, staring into the glassy darkness while she waited for it to steep. June's comment stayed with her. She couldn't quite shake it.

Was she too set in her ways? Was she overly meticulous? Possibly.

And what about Garet?

Garet did have that look of practiced innocence. Maybe it wasn't simply an act, maybe it was for real. But thinking of Garet as a lost kitten seemed like a stretch.

Tess set the used tea bag in a saucer near the sink and took a sip. Still too hot. She turned off the lights and held the warm cup in both hands as she slowly climbed the stairs to her bedroom.

CHAPTER TWENTY

Garet sat staring at the blank sheet of drawing paper on her slant board. She held the pencil in her teeth as she riffled through her sketchbook for inspiration. The thumbnails were finished and now that she was reading over them she wondered what she'd been thinking. The story sagged in the middle and the stakes needed to be higher near the end.

The digital clock on the stove told her it was only nine o'clock. The night was young; she had plenty of hours to get some good solid work done.

Oh, who am I kidding?

She tossed the pencil on the counter and covered her face with her hands and sighed loudly. What the hell? Why was work so hard all of a sudden? This was what she did. She was used to working at night. She'd scarf a bowl of some super sweet children's cereal and then use the sugar rush to channel her inner kid onto the page.

Think, think, think.

No, just relax. *Don't* overthink the story.

Slumping to the slant board, she rested her forehead on her arm.

Spending the evening at Tess's had been a complete and utter distraction. She couldn't focus. June's comment about her being cast as the lost kitten also didn't sit well. What did a kid know anyway? She wasn't lost. She knew exactly what she was doing.

Didn't she?

A reality check, that's what Garet needed.

She reached for her phone and texted Lane.

Hey, what are you up to?

A few seconds later, Lane responded. *I'm watching TV at your apartment.*

Garet dialed Lane's number. She didn't feel like texting. She needed an actual conversation with someone who knew her well enough to offer some perspective.

"Hi, how is my favorite substitute teacher?" Lane was in a chipper mood.

"Struggling to get anything that even resembles progress done on my book."

"Oh, wait, is teaching kids more taxing than you expected?" Lane's question oozed sarcasm.

"Ha ha, very funny." Garet flopped onto the sofa. "You're not going to believe who I share a classroom with." She knew Lane would be mad that she'd waited so long to share the news about Tess.

"Who?"

"Mandolin girl."

"Shut the fuck up." Lane was obviously surprised, and she was a very hard person to surprise. "And you're just now telling me this?"

"Yeah, her name is Tess Hill. I think I'm still kinda in shock about it myself." Garet sighed and pinched the bridge of her nose.

"Okay, aside from this being the best news ever, I sense there's a complication?"

"No, not really." Unless having an attraction to someone who clearly wasn't interested in you was considered a complication.

"Why am I not convinced?" She could almost hear Lane's body language shift over the phone. She had Lane's full attention. "There's no way you don't want to ask her out. Only, now that would be super awkward, wouldn't it, because she's a coworker."

"And she has a kid."

There was a moment of silence.

"So, what are you gonna do about it?" asked Lane.

"I don't know. That's why I called you."

Lane laughed and then was quiet. Garet could almost hear the gears turning in Lane's head. Or maybe that was the whirring of machinery in her own brain.

"What's the kid like?"

"She's cute. Her name is June, she's six. She's actually one of my art students."

"Adorable." Lane, again with the sarcasm.

"I was over at Tess's place for dinner tonight and—"

"Wait, you were at her house? Okay, back up, I think you buried the lede here."

Garet took a breath and started over.

"Tess invited me to her place to watch *The Wizard of Oz* because we have to help the kids produce a play for the fall festival and I couldn't remember how the story went…" She trailed off. "Are you laughing? I can hear you laughing. This isn't funny."

"Except to everyone who isn't you."

"Listen, I need your opinion about something."

"Ask her out."

"No, not about that." Garet had been stretched out on the couch. She sat up. "Tonight, Tess left the room and I was showing June the sketches for my current book."

"And?"

"And when I told her the story, she said I was the lost kitten."

Lane didn't try to hide her laughter this time.

"Why is that so funny?"

"Because…" Lane tried to sound serious, but the amusement was still there. "Because you *are* the lost kitten." She took a drink of something. "Who is this kid? She's a psychic genius."

Oh no, was this one of those defining moments? One of those moments when you were happily going along with your life only to discover that you have no idea who you are. She exhaled loudly.

"Garet, are you still there?"

"Yes, I'm still here." Garet switched the phone to her other ear. "And if you start calling me Kitten I'm gonna drive to Atlanta and kick your ass."

Lane laughed. "I'm so scared right now."

"I don't get it." Garet genuinely meant that. "Why am I the lost kitten?"

"Okay, listen." Lane suddenly sounded sincere. "It's not a bad thing."

"How is being compared to a scared, lost kitten not a bad thing?"

"The kitten in your story isn't sad...she's a playful, easily distracted kitten in search of a home."

Lane got major points for having paid attention at some point when Garet hashed out the script for her new book.

"You think I'm in search of a home?"

"Yeah, sort of." Lane paused. "Maybe not an actual house... not a literal structure, but definitely a place where you feel accepted for who you are."

Garet didn't know how to respond. The knot in her stomach seemed to support Lane's assessment.

"Listen, Garet. You're this playful, sensitive, authentic person...and none of the women you've dated have seen those parts of you. And until you meet someone who sees you—the *real* you— it's not going to work. You'll just keep searching."

She knew Lane was right on some level. There was a deeper part of her that longed to be understood. And until she found that, she was lost.

CHAPTER TWENTY-ONE

The morning flew by. Maybe Tess had decided to take pity on Garet, a fledgling teacher. Because when the kids started to get wound up or started talking over her, Tess stepped in with grown-up, *teacher authority* and shut them down. Garet was grateful. Having the assist from Tess made the whole experience a whole lot less stressful.

But still, Tess's aloof professionalism left her wondering if any attraction between them was completely one-sided. Garet would come to that conclusion and yet, there would be moments of definite connection between them—the brush of a light touch as she bent to help Tess with a fallen music stand, the lingering gazes from across the room, and Tess's attentive demeanor while Garet was at the front of the class talking to the students. She was sure she wasn't imagining those things, but maybe she was reading too much into something that was simply friendly attention.

When the lunch hour arrived, Garet decided to brave the cafeteria.

Two minutes after she stepped foot in the fluorescent lit cavernous din of noise, she regretted her decision. The telltale hint of bleach wafted from the aging linoleum floor and mingled with something familiar—oh yeah, bad lunchroom pizza.

The room, the smells, the noise, all sent a childhood memory zooming to the front of the line inside her head. She immediately relived that gut punch feeling of fear and uncertainty of being the new kid when her folks first moved to Macon. The lunchroom was the most intimidating space for a new kid in school. An entirely different set of social rules were at play when the multi-grade herd descended into one big room for the noon meal. A chill ran up the back of her neck and she decided right then to turn and flee. She spun and almost face-planted right into Riley.

"Oh, sorry." Garet was in no mood to talk to the star athlete of the teaching squad.

"It's Garet, right?" Riley planted her feet in a wide stance and crossed her arms as if to block Garet's escape.

"Yeah, Garet." She was trapped into a moment of unwanted friendliness. "And you're Riley."

"Good recall." Riley grinned.

Garet was fairly certain Riley was used to women remembering her name.

"Hey, listen, I'm glad I ran into you." Riley braced her hands on her hips and grew seriously focused, as if she were on a field coaching. "Since you'll be here for the fall festival I thought you might want to join the teacher's team for the autumn 5K race."

"What?"

"The teachers form a team and run the race for donations. Then we donate the money to the local library. You know, supporting literacy and all that." Riley arched one eyebrow. "You run, right?"

"Um, no, actually I don't." Running long distances for fun was a personal sort of torture that she wanted no part of—ever.

"Hmm, I'd have figured you for the sporty type." Riley punched Garet's shoulder.

Ow. But she wasn't about to let Riley know it hurt.

"Yeah, sorry to disappoint you." Then her mood brightened. "Besides, I'll probably be too busy working on the play for the festival with Tess."

Bingo. Riley's smile evaporated. Garet almost felt guilty for rubbing it in. Almost.

"That'll probably take up most of my extra time, because we'll be working on stuff after school, you know, at night."

"I forgot about the play." Riley made a feeble attempt at regrouping.

"But, hey, thanks for thinking of me." She waved as she made her escape.

Riley remained rooted in place as the double doors swung closed behind her.

Note to self: avoid the cafeteria at all costs.

The peanut butter sandwich would have to sustain her for the afternoon. Tomorrow she'd plan better and bring more snacks, because there was no way she was venturing back to the lunchroom. Surely one of the perks of adulthood was the ability to avoid meals and the social torture of time in the cafeteria.

❖

The afternoon sped by for Tess. She'd decided to assist Garet with the children, which made all the classes run smoother. A few days of mild chaos had more than made her point, and Garet had been big enough to admit she was a newbie, in over her head.

She sat along the wall watching Garet finish up with the last class of the day. Garet's methods for conveying information to students were good, she almost seemed like a natural teacher. As was the case with many new teachers, it was the discipline that took training to master.

They'd only finished half the movie the previous evening. June had pestered her during breakfast to watch the rest of the movie tonight. It was Friday so maybe this was the best time to finish it. Preparations for the play needed to kick into high gear next week in order to get everything ready for the festival, which was only a few weeks away.

The bell rang and students filed past her. She joined Garet in the afternoon reorganization of chairs, so that they could start fresh on Monday.

"Thanks for all your help today." Garet smiled. "With you offering backup they might actually learn some things about art."

"I think you have some natural talent as a teacher." She remembered how hard it was to start as a new teacher. A little encouragement went a long way.

"You really think so?" Garet's expression brightened.

"I really do." Tess took a seat at one of the tables and organized art supplies—pencils, rulers, and erasers. "What do you do for work, Garet?"

June's description of Garet's book made her want to hear more, but firsthand, from Garet.

"You mean, when I'm not distracting young minds with art lessons?" Garet laughed.

"Yes. What do you do in the real world?"

"I write and draw graphic novels for children."

"Really?" Tess stopped organizing and looked up. "What are the titles?"

"Let's see...*Raven Builds a House, Marty Moose's Big Day Out, If Cars Could Fly, The Cave of Infinite Color*—"

"Oh, my gosh." Tess's heart sped up. "I loved *The Cave of Infinite Color*. Actually, I've read all of your books." That was impossible wasn't it? Wouldn't she have noticed the author's name? She must have read *Raven Builds a House* a thousand times to June at bedtime. It was the sweetest story about what exactly makes a place a home.

She stared at Garet as if she was seeing her for the very first time.

"I write them under a pen name." Garet answered her unasked question. "Elizabeth Allen. My middle name is Elizabeth." She seemed bashful talking about her work, as if her secret identity had been suddenly revealed.

"Garet, you're very talented."

"So, you really liked *The Cave of Infinite Color*?" Garet ignored the compliment.

"I did." Tess visualized the pages of the book in her head. "This may sound strange, but the way you wrote about color in the book is the way I think about music. I would describe that book as lyrical."

"Wow, thank you." Garet shoved her hands in her pockets. "That might be the best compliment I've ever gotten."

Tess's cheeks warmed. She hadn't meant to be such a fangirl, but this revelation about Garet's work had completely taken her by surprise.

"Why take a teaching position? I mean, if that isn't too personal. Your books are very popular."

"The way it works is you get half of the advance up front and then the rest trickles in as you meet certain benchmarks...you know, pencils, inks, and finally the color. The books take several months to produce, sometimes over a year." Garet sat down near Tess, resting her elbows on the table. "Usually, I take freelance art jobs to supplement until the book is finished, but this time I thought I might try one three-month job."

"Teaching isn't an easy temporary thing to do."

"No kidding." Garet laughed, a genuine, warm your heart kind of laugh. "I wrongly assumed that teaching would be easy, and over by three o'clock each day, leaving plenty of time to work on my book in the evenings."

"Your story made quite an impression on June."

"Did it?" Garet smiled. "She's an adorable kid, by the way." Garet swept her fingers through her hair and sighed. "I mean, that was the other part of this whole teaching thing. I wanted to spend some time with kids. I thought it might make me a better storyteller, you know, if I spent some time with my audience."

"I'm not sure how you'd improve your stories. They're so good." She couldn't help the compliment. Garet's books were that good.

Garet blushed and averted her eyes.

"Listen, June was hoping we could finish watching the movie tonight if you're available." Now that she was getting a glimpse of who Garet really was she wanted to know more.

"Sure."

"I mean, if you don't need to work this evening."

"I was thinking of taking tonight off anyway. I'm kinda stuck at the moment. I can work over the weekend."

"Great." Tess stood up just as June skipped into the room.

"Did you ask Garet to come over yet?" June wrapped her thin arms around Tess's waist. She looked up at Tess first and then at Garet. "Did she ask you yet?"

Garet laughed.

"And what if I hadn't asked her?" She playfully frowned at June. "What have we said about polite invitations?"

"Not to blurt things out…but I—"

"June Bug."

"I'm sorry." June tempered her enthusiasm. "Can we please ask Garet to watch the movie tonight?"

"Yes, we can." Tess lightly caressed June's back with her hand, then turned to Garet. "How about I make dinner since you brought pizza last time?"

"Sure—"

"Spaghetti! Let's have spaghetti!" June bounced up and down, the tiny, sparkly backpack jostled on her narrow shoulders with each tiny jump.

Tess shook her head.

"Garet, how do you feel about spaghetti?"

"Next to pizza, it's my favorite." Garet's eyes fairly sparkled.

"You and June are a match made in heaven." Once again, her mouth got ahead of her brain. She shouldn't have said that out loud. But Garet didn't seem to mind.

Garet retrieved her leather messenger bag while Tess gathered her things. June reached for Garet's hand and started to tug her toward the door before Tess could intervene. There was nothing she could do but follow them. June and Garet hand-in-hand was a very normal, friendly thing but it made Tess's stomach flip over and then drop suddenly, as if she'd just ridden the biggest roller coaster at the state fair. Only this was no imaginary thrill ride, this was very real. A woman whose work she admired, who she found attractive in all the right ways, was holding her daughter's hand, and joining them for dinner. No, this wasn't a thrill ride, but it was just as scary.

Tess turned off the lights, closed the door, and trailed behind them down the corridor toward the parking lot. The afternoon sun glowed through the double door at the end of the hallway. The rays of sunlight cast Garet and June in silhouette, with a starburst highlighting their joined hands. Her breath caught in her throat. The visual of June and Garet holding on to each other unexpectedly caused her to feel anxious, protective, and exhilarated all at the same time.

CHAPTER TWENTY-TWO

G aret was touched by Tess's offer of a spaghetti dinner, which she knew was nothing fancy. But still, the notion of a home cooked meal warmed her insides in a way she hadn't expected. She lounged at the table with a glass of iced tea while Tess stirred the sauce. The pasta was almost ready. She'd offered to help, but the kitchen was small so she didn't blame Tess for turning her down. This old house had what she'd heard referred to as an eat-in kitchen. Meaning, the space in the kitchen for the stove and sink were on the small side and there was just enough open floor space along one wall for a table.

She tried to avoid the trappings of a butch-femme relationship, not because she didn't enjoy some of them, but because she didn't want to be that predictable. Garet wasn't a fan of "roles" or clichés, but dang, she had to admit that watching Tess cook was incredibly sexy. Why was that? What was it about a woman in the kitchen, preparing food, that made her insides go all mushy?

Maybe it was that her mother had liked to cook, and her grandmother before that. And there was something about feeding people that conveyed nurturing. If you cooked for someone then you cared about them, right?

Not that spaghetti was a complicated, fancy dish. It was actually something even Garet could make without screwing it up. But it was just nice to feel fussed over, even a little bit. Garet liked the feeling she was having at the moment. She was in Tess's warm kitchen sipping sweet tea and trying not to stare. Lane had been right, of course. Tess had a very cute figure. Garet would venture as far as to describe Tess as adorably sexy. She was sexy in that sweet way that happens when a woman *doesn't seem to have any clue of how sexy she is.*

Tess drained the pasta and called for June. There was no response.

"I could go find her," Garet offered.

"If you don't mind." Tess measured servings onto three plates. "She's probably in her room at the top of the stairs."

Garet trotted up the steps. She hadn't been upstairs. She wondered which door led to Tess's room. The soft sound of June's voice seeped from the partially open doorway at the top of the stairs. She knocked softly and peeked inside.

June sat cross-legged on the floor surrounded by an array of Barbies on horseback and even a pink convertible. She didn't look away from her toys until Garet spoke.

"Hey there, your mom asked me to come get you for supper."

"Okay."

"The spaghetti is ready and we wouldn't want it to get cold."

June nodded. The reminder that spaghetti was on the menu seemed to spark a bit of enthusiasm.

"This is a nice room." Garet surveyed the cluttered coziness of June's room as June stepped past her.

"Thank you."

Chester the Narwhal was in the place of honor on June's bed. Other stuffed animals were piled in the window seat. Pink was the primary color of the room. Being in June's room made her want to ask a million questions. Who was June's father? Did she know him? Did she miss him? Had it been hard for Tess as a single parent?

June took her hand and tugged. She'd lingered, lost in thought.

"Sorry."

"You came to get me for dinner, remember?"

"Right." Garet laughed. "Thank goodness you were here to remind me."

The table was already set when they returned to the kitchen. Dinner was a casual affair. More than once, Tess had to assist June with the unruly pasta.

"She loves spaghetti but hasn't quite mastered it yet." Tess used her fork to return some runaway pasta to June's plate.

"That's why I cheat and cut mine up." Garet made a big show of cutting up her spaghetti with a knife. "See? Now it's all short pieces." Garet shoved a forkful in her mouth.

"I want to cut mine up too, Mama."

Uh-oh, now she'd started something and she couldn't tell if Tess approved of this breach of etiquette or not. She was fairly sure that Emily Post had written at some point that cutting up spaghetti with a knife was akin to slurping drinks with a straw, but she'd made a habit of doing both.

"Here, let me help you. If that's okay with your mom." Garet hesitated, her utensils hovered over June's plate as she waited for the green light from Tess. Tess nodded. Garet reached over and made quick work of June's noodles, which were now short enough to scoop up with a spoon or fork.

"This is great." June beamed.

"Don't talk with your mouth full." Tess shook her head.

"Sorry."

"So, June, what did you learn in school today?" Garet somehow thought it might be easier at the moment to make small talk with June than with Tess. She and Tess had connected on some slightly deeper level earlier. They'd had some sort of breakthrough, when they talked about her books. That breakthrough was making her feel nervous around Tess. Kid topics seemed safer.

"Miss Larkin read us a book."

Garet remembered meeting Anna Larkin her first day. She'd been the friendliest of the teacher's lounge crew. It made sense that she taught first grade; she'd had a playful air about her.

"What was the book about?" Apparently, first graders didn't embellish while eating spaghetti.

"The Lorax and how he talked for the trees. You know, because trees don't have mouths."

"Oh, *The Lorax*, that's one of my favorite books." Garet smiled. "Did Miss Larkin show you the illustrations? I always thought those trees looked like cotton candy."

June nodded because her mouth was full.

"Do you read books every day in class?" Garet really had no idea what happened in first grade. She'd experienced it herself, obviously, but that seemed like a million years ago. And now she couldn't even recall her teacher's name. Wait, Goodwin, Mrs. Goodwin was her name.

"Not every day." June looked reflective. "We're learning to sit still, but we're not very good at it yet."

Tess laughed, causing her to cough because she'd just taken a sip of her sweet tea.

"It's good to be able to assess your own skills at something." Garet nodded.

"What does assess mean?" June's fork was midair.

"It just means to know when you're good at something and when you're not." Tess joined the conversation.

Garet appreciated the assist since she wasn't sure how complex the definition should be.

"I'm not very good at sitting still." June returned her attention to her supper.

Garet couldn't help laughing.

The supper dishes were left to soak in the sink while they watched the second half of the movie. Garet worried that the flying monkeys might scare June, but she seemed completely entertained instead.

The seating arrangement was the same as the previous viewing. With Garet and Tess at each end of the sofa and June in the middle. She was so small that she was able to lie across the cushion perpendicularly with elbows out, with her chin propped on her hands, and her knees bent so that her feet fidgeted at the back of the couch. Garet wondered if when left alone, June treated the couch as a jungle gym.

Every time she glanced over at Tess, Garet got this funny little twitch in her stomach. She was trying to focus on Judy Garland, and her discovery that there was no place like home, but it was becoming more difficult to care about what was on the small screen the longer they sat together on the couch. No more than four feet separated them, and yet, Garet felt as if they were worlds apart.

As if on cue, June yawned just as *The end* appeared on screen. "Come on, sweetie, time for bed." Tess patted June on the back.

"I'm not sleepy." June groaned and rolled onto her side.

"No fussing." Tess stood and held her hand out to June. "It's already a half hour past your bedtime."

"I should probably go." Garet got up also. She didn't really want to leave, but it seemed like the polite thing to do.

"Oh, do you have to leave?"

The question surprised her.

"Um, no…"

"I thought we could have some tea." Tess hesitated. "And maybe talk about the play a little if you're not too tired."

"Sure." Garet's heart did a little tap dance, but she tried not to show her excitement.

"I'll just be a few minutes." Tess followed June toward the stairs. "Make yourself at home."

Tess glanced back as she climbed the stairs. Garet smiled as she sat back down. June waved and Garet waved back. June seemed unusually slow with her bedtime routine. She was clearly tired and sleepy but fighting it.

June kicked her way under the covers and dropped to her pillow. Tess pulled the quilt up to June's chin, making sure she was snug.

"Can Garet stay over?" June asked.

"What?"

"Can she stay over? She could borrow my sleeping bag and then we could have pancakes in the morning." June rubbed her eyes with the heels of her hands.

"I think Garet needs to go home and work on her novel." Tess was struggling to respond to June's request. She'd never suggested anyone sleep over before, and the brief thought of it sent Tess's heart rate into overdrive.

"Well, sometime." June yawned and hugged Chester. "You'll ask her sometime, right?"

"We'll see, sweetheart." She kissed June's forehead. "Go to sleep now."

CHAPTER TWENTY-THREE

Tess descended the stairs enjoying the view. Garet looked up from her cozy slouched position on the sofa. Garet sat up as Tess drew near.

"Are you still up for tea?" Tess wasn't sure because Garet looked as sleepy as June. She wondered if Garet had been staying up late to work on her drawings for the book.

"Yes, a cup of tea sounds great."

Garet followed her to the kitchen and hovered while Tess put on hot water. Was Garet nervous?

"Um, let's see, I have chamomile, and..." Tess searched the cabinet near the stove. "Raspberry and mint."

"Chamomile sounds good." Garet studied the chaotic array of photos and June's artwork stuck to the front of the fridge with magnets. "These are good. June's got quite an artistic talent for her age." Garet gently moved the corner of one drawing in order to see the one beneath it.

"You think so?" Tess poured water into two mugs and added tea bags.

"Yes, definitely." Garet accepted one of the cups. "Oh, thanks."

Tess took a seat at the table and Garet joined her. She reached over and switched off the glaring overhead light, leaving only the small light over the sink. They sat quietly. Tess dunked her tea bag a few times as if that would rush the steeping process.

"Where do you keep your music stuff?"

"Excuse me?"

"I just thought you'd have instruments all over the house or at least a piano."

"The spare bedroom upstairs is sort of my music room." Tess offered sugar to Garet, but she declined. "Expensive musical instruments and six-year-olds don't mix well."

"Oh, right...I can see how that might be hazardous." Garet sipped her tea. "You play beautifully. I never really got the chance to tell you that."

"Thank you." Compliments made her a little uncomfortable.

"I don't really care for bluegrass music."

"Ouch."

"Sorry, I mean, I didn't really care for bluegrass until I heard you play." Garet paused. Her expression was so sincere that it was almost painful. "When you perform, you have this way of playing... it touches you without needing to know anything about the music."

"That's a very kind thing to say, thank you."

"I'm not very good at critiquing music. I'm sorry if that sounded..."

"No, don't worry about it." Tess instinctively placed her hand over Garet's where it rested on the table. She realized what she'd done and pulled back. "Music either speaks to you or it doesn't. It's not supposed to be academic."

"I suppose it's like art in that way."

"Funny you say that." Tess relaxed against the back of her chair. "When we work on a particular arrangement for the band I always think of it as painting with sound. The song begins to have layers and texture." Tess was visualizing a performance in her head. "The most fun part of being in a band with great players is to hear what else they bring to the song. Everyone gets the chords and then we work together in rehearsal to sort out the parts. You write the song and then take it to the group and it comes back as this exciting new thing. That's the beauty of collaboration. I love working with other people who are good at what they do."

"So, you not only perform, but you write songs too? You're so talented." Garet's compliment was understated, but genuine.

"I only really play once a month with the guys. I'm not sure I'd consider myself a performer."

"I admire anyone who can get up on a stage and play music. It's not like I have to draw with an audience. If I did, I'd be in real trouble."

"I guess I see your point."

"And why the mandolin?"

"When you're in a band and you're arranging things, every instrument occupies a particular range. When we first started playing together in high school we already had guitar and bass. I wanted to contribute something different. The mandolin has a higher sound. It occupies a higher frequency." Tess focused on Garet. "I suppose I prefer the altitude."

Garet laughed. "This is the most interesting conversation about music I've ever had."

They were quiet for the moment. The ancient grandfather clock on the mantel chimed. It was getting later, yet somehow she wasn't tired. Talking with Garet felt...nice.

"So, how long have you lived in Shadetree?" Garet slouched in her chair and toyed with the little paper tag attached to the string of the tea bag.

"We moved here when I was about to start the ninth grade. Music ended up being the way I made friends in a new school." She thought of her parents. "My dad was the county fire chief." Tess sipped her tea. Why did her throat feel suddenly so dry? "My mom grew up here, but she'd gone away to college and then met my dad. His first job was in Virginia, but Mom always wanted to move back to Shadetree."

Tess allowed her eyes to lose focus as she thought back. "My mother worked a job she never really loved as an office manager for a bank. We'd drive down here at least once a month to stay with my grandparents. I can still see the change in her expression the moment she walked into my grandmother's kitchen. She was home." She paused, picturing the scene in her head. "Years dropped away and she was a girl again sitting at the table, sampling an apple from the bowl in the center of the table."

"That's a nice memory." Garet's words were soft.

Tess smiled at Garet, but then averted her eyes.

"I'm not sure I ever loved this place as much as she did, but I loved the way it made her feel. Her love of home was contagious."

"And you and June?"

"I suppose when I needed a safe place, this was where I came."

Tess was sure Garet wanted to ask more questions about June and exactly how all that had happened. They were already in choppy waters. This was the sort of intimate, get-to-know-you talk that led to other things. Tess needed to change the subject. She wanted to know more about Garet anyway.

"After you finish your book, then what next?"

"Well, it's due to my editor by early December." Garet looked as if she was doing a math problem in her head. "I'll be teaching until Christmas break and I had planned to head back to Atlanta after that. I have a friend subletting my apartment. Oh, yeah, you met Lane at brunch that day. She's staying in my place until I move back."

Right.

Temporary.

Garet was only temporary. And temporary was something Tess definitely was *not* looking for. Tess needed to remember this. For Garet, the whole teaching thing was just a part-time job, a brief sidestep before going back to her *real* life.

Garet sensed the shift immediately. As if a cold draft had blown through the house, slamming doors as it traveled through. Whatever warmth had sparked between them had cooled. Even Tess's body language had changed. Tess gripped the tea cup in both hands and wouldn't make eye contact with Garet.

What had she said to upset Tess? Was it talking about work that had killed the mood?

"It's getting late...I should probably get going." But she hoped Tess would ask her to stay.

"Of course." Tess stood and carried her cup to the sink. "We can work on the plans for the play Monday." She turned and smiled thinly. "I'm tired too."

Okay, that seemed like code for *you should leave*. Garet couldn't help feeling disappointed. It seemed they'd made some progress toward becoming friends, maybe even something more, and then everything stalled.

It was probably just as well. She needed to stay focused on her work. That's why she was here. Garet shouldered her bag and trudged to the door. She reached for the handle but turned.

"Hey, thank you for tonight." She held the shoulder strap of her bag with one hand and shoved her other hand in her pocket. "Everything was...really nice."

"It was a pleasure." Tess said the words, but it didn't sound as if she meant them. "June enjoys your company."

"She's a great kid." That was the truth. There was no mention of whether Tess enjoyed her company, however, and that was a bit disappointing.

There was an awkward moment that seemed to last for ten. Garet considered kissing Tess on the cheek, or giving her a hug, or—nothing seemed right. Tess was standing apart from her so that she'd have had to make a big move to do either. In the end she just shrugged it off and opened the door.

"Have a good night." Garet didn't look back as she walked to her car.

CHAPTER TWENTY-FOUR

Tess couldn't quite shake her melancholy vibe. Saturday was usually fun day. She and June would start the day with pancakes and then the sugar rush would help her get through the morning chores of dishes and laundry. But the day was a little overcast, just like her mood.

Today was her last day to help Mark at the music store for the season. She'd planned to work a few hours to help him out and then the rest of her weekends between now and the end of November would be spent getting the production ready for the fall festival.

"Mom, we're here." Tess announced their arrival so as not to surprise her mother.

She needn't have called out because June sprinted to the kitchen the minute she unlocked the door. The smell of baked goods wafted through the house.

"Hi, sweetheart." Her mother looked up. She was using a rolling pin to flatten and spread cookie dough on the marble countertop, dusted with flour. "Do you want to cut the shapes?" She turned to June who'd already perched herself on a stool at the counter.

"Yes!" June reached for the cookie cutter shapes. There was a star, a flower, a dinosaur, and basic circles of different sizes.

"June, please go wash your hands before you start helping Grandma bake, okay?" Tess watched June trot toward the bathroom and then turned back to her mother. "I'm glad we had an early lunch if you two are going to make sugar cookies."

"Well, I was outside earlier and it looked like rain so I thought June might like to make cookies." Her mother gave the dough a couple more passes with the rolling pin.

"I won't be long today. I told Mark I could only work a half shift." Tess held the stool to stabilize it as June returned to her perch.

"Which shape should we make?" June turned to her with a bright expression.

"I was always fond of star-shaped cookies." Tess brushed June's hair off her forehead. "I think you might need a haircut, June Bug."

"I like stars too. Let's make stars." June ignored the comment about a haircut and positioned herself to use the cookie cutter.

"How are things at school going without Charlotte?" After June pressed the shape into the dough, her mother scooped up the fragile cookie with a spatula and placed it on the baking sheet.

"Not too bad."

"You know, I met Garet briefly when I picked up June the other day."

That had been days ago and her mother was just now mentioning it. That seemed odd. Was her mother waiting for her to reveal something? Usually she was more forthright.

"Garet Allen seemed very nice."

"She is." Tess wondered how long the encounter had lasted, surely not long.

"I really like her," June chimed in without looking up from her cookie making.

"We invited Garet over to watch *The Wizard of Oz*." Tess felt weird revealing this to her mom. It wasn't as if they'd had a date or anything, so why did she mind sharing?

"She came over twice." June waited for more dough to be rolled out. "Once we had pizza, and then we had spaghetti."

"We split the movie up so that June didn't stay up too late." Her mother arched an eyebrow. Now Tess worried she'd made the movie watching sound like more than it was. "You said you thought she was nice...how much of a conversation did you have with Garet?"

"Oh, it was brief." Her mother shifted to allow June to press more star shapes. "But I've heard a little more from Hildy."

Oh no, the gossip mill had begun. Tess hadn't thought to ask where Garet had rented a place. She should have guessed that it might have been Hildy Green's cottage. It wasn't like Shadetree had very many rental options. There weren't really any apartment buildings. More likely granny units or garage apartments, or even off-season cabin rentals.

"What did Hildy say?" She didn't want to seem too curious about Garet, but she couldn't help asking.

"Hildy said that Garet stays up late working and is a gracious neighbor." She paused. "Hildy also described Garet as very nice looking, but that part I knew from meeting her myself."

Tess's cheeks warmed. She was sure she was blushing. Having her mother comment on Garet's looks was a bridge too far. She'd come out to her parents in college. Despite her small town, southern upbringing, Tess's mother had taken the revelation in stride. She supposed once your parents came to terms with a pregnancy out of wedlock, then everything else was simply about degrees.

She leaned into the open fridge to cool off, pretending to search for a drink.

"Do you mind if I take a Coke with me?" She didn't turn around.

"Sure, I think there's a can in the door." Her mother was focused on June. "Don't rush. Make sure to press down good so that you don't lose any part of the star."

"All right, well, you two have fun. And save me some cookies." Tess retrieved her bag and made tracks for the door.

Ten minutes later, Tess had parked down the street from the music shop. She sat in the car while she sucked down the soda she'd swiped from her mother's fridge. She didn't normally drink soft drinks, but the carbonation, sugar, and caffeine had been just what she needed at the moment.

The shop was fairly quiet. Tess stowed her purse behind the counter and waited for Mark to finish ringing up a customer for some sheet music. The bell over the door dinged loudly as the customer exited.

"Are you okay?" Mark asked.

"Yes, why?" Tess blinked.

"You jumped when the bell over the door dinged."

"Oh, I was thinking of…something…"

"How's Charlotte doing?" He was riffling through receipts and didn't look at her.

"She's doing fine."

"Tim was in here yesterday buying guitar strings."

"He was?"

"Yeah, he said he was planning to start playing again." Mark braced one hand on the counter and glanced over. "I was thinking, sure, man, whatever you say. But there's no way he's gonna have any free time with a new baby in the house."

Mark had three kids, so he knew from experience, just like Tess did, that children have a gift for making free time evaporate.

"He'll figure it out." But Tess worried that he might not.

❖

Garet tried to focus. She'd struggled the better part of the day to work on the spreads for her book. Her story consisted of twelve spreads, which would end up being a thirty-two-page storybook. That meant twenty-four separate paintings, each a finished piece painted on nine-by-twelve-inch illustration board. She'd sketched the layouts on Bristol board first, working out the general design for each spread and then used tracing paper to transfer the basic layout to the illustration board, which was too thick to use with a light box.

When finished, every pen stroke, every expression on the face of each character would be intimately personal, and yet, she never let on. If asked about her work she'd always strive to appear remotely interested in what critics said about her books, when in fact the slightest criticism cut right to her heart.

This was the fun part, figuring everything out, bringing the story to life with images. This was when things started to come together. Normally, after a day of drawing she'd feel energized and optimistic, but by early afternoon she was drained and needed a break.

Creating art usually settled her, grounded her. But she was becoming vaguely aware of a growing restlessness, of things as they were no longer being quite enough. Garet had given this notion a voice inside her head the morning she'd left Atlanta. Seated across from Lane, listening to Lane talk about her newest crush. The moment had crystalized in her memory. Wasn't she ready for a change? Wasn't Garet ready for things to be different? She was tired of repeating the same patterns over and over. Didn't she want more from life?

What did *more* look like? She wasn't sure.

Garet had only finished two of the spreads when her phone pinged with a text from Lane. She'd been struggling at the slant board all day and the drawings looked like it. Sometimes if you couldn't get in the zone it was best to walk away and take a break. If you were tired, the work ended up looking labored and stiff, not good.

What's up? Garet texted back.

Do you still need a bike? I could bring one up tomorrow.

That'd be great. Garet paused to think. If she did a bit more work in the morning, then she could hang with Lane in the evening and not feel guilty. *If you come up late in the day, I'll get us pizza and beer.*

Sounds like a plan.

Garet set aside the phone and reviewed the drawings in front of her. Her phone pinged again.

Gears or no gears?

What?

The bike. Single speed cruiser or gears?

Is a cruiser with gears an option? Garet knew Lane had a small fleet of bikes, but she couldn't recall what each one looked like.

Old school with gears. Got it.

Text me when you're on the road and I'll order the food.

See you tomorrow, friend.

Maybe talking to Lane would help. Garet was spinning around inside her own head with no sounding board. The only two friends she'd made in Shadetree were Tess and June. She couldn't talk to them. First off, she was rarely alone with Tess long enough to have a deep conversation. Then there was June, and, well, she was too honest. Garet laughed, thinking back to the first day of teaching when June told her she wasn't very good at it. June had also been the one to tell Garet that she was the lost kitten in her own story. It had taken her days to shake that comment. Maybe she still hadn't. What did June mean by that? What did a kid know about that sort of thing anyway? Especially a kid living such a charmed life as June.

Garet sighed and rotated on her chair.

Coffee. Maybe more coffee would improve her focus.

She ground enough beans for one cup and waited for the water to boil. Making pour-over had a Zen quality to it. There was no way to rush the process. You had to wait for the water to do its work. Garet set the filter and holder aside and sipped. This was a good cup of coffee. She added just the briefest dash of cream and returned to her temporary workstation.

Sometimes it was good to walk away from the drawings because when you came back to them the mistakes seemed obvious. She reworked the first page so that the bear's expression was neutral rather than annoyed. The annoyance would come later when the kitten upset the bear's orderly world.

Garet sipped the coffee as she stared into space, not focusing on anything.

Was June right? Was she the kitten? Was she upsetting Tess's orderly world?

She suspected no one was allowed enough access to bring anything disorderly into Tess's world. Tess's life was structured and controlled. Not in a bad way, but orderly nonetheless. Garet's life was not orderly. She existed from book to book; everything else was temporary. Everything else was in servitude to her art.

CHAPTER TWENTY-FIVE

It rained late on Saturday so that Sunday morning everything was damp. Every leaf and blade of grass was heavy with droplets from the overnight showers. The sky was still active. Small clusters of clouds swept past overhead allowing intermittent sun exposure. The temp was crisp and the sun was brightly white against the blue patches when they appeared. Garet decided to take a stroll along the river path to get a little blood circulation going before she spent the better part of the day hunched over the drawing board, and before it started to rain again. Dark clouds along the distant ridgeline suggested a thunderstorm might be in the near future. But she was certain there was plenty of time for a walk before the dark clouds reached Shadetree.

Turning left onto Front Street, Garet ambled at a leisurely pace down to the old train depot now brewery. It was closed, of course, but the Riverside Café was packed. Garet thought of the first time she'd eaten there, the second time she'd seen Tess. Things could have gone so easily if she'd only gotten Tess's number that day… if she hadn't ended up working with Tess at the school. Dating Tess just wasn't meant to be.

But that was a strange thought. It didn't make sense. Normally, if things so easily came into Garet's life, then that meant something. She'd assumed they were supposed to meet for some reason. But in this case, as far as Tess was concerned, fate was obviously only toying with her.

Water droplets like miniature crystal balls amplified and reflected the Sun's rays, giving the leaves a sparkly sheen. When a light breeze kicked up, the drops splashed down like rain. A drop hit her on the back of the neck. She turned up the collar of her denim jacket.

As the path transitioned to woods along the river, Garet slowed down. Having spent the previous day drawing an imaginary woodland scene, she was now focused on every tiny detail along the trail. Moss so bright green that it was practically chartreuse covered rocks half buried in dead leaves. The contrast of the rough brown leaf debris made the delicate moss almost luminous. And the same splash of green was painted all around the trunk of a nearby poplar tree. Overhead, the leaves were shifting into their autumn wardrobe. And the faintest scent of wood smoke from someone's chimney danced with the breeze.

All these small details sent her back to her childhood in the small Georgia town of Brunswick, closer to the coast. The place her family lived before Macon, near her grandparents. Unpaved roads that were more sand than dirt lined with large stands of long leaf pines. There was also the smell of the marsh at low tide with a scent that existed nowhere else. The nights were warm, the sun set late in summer. The lightning bugs danced at dusk in the shadows. She never saw lightning bugs in Atlanta.

Standing at the edge of the river, she realized she didn't spend much time in the woods any more. As an adult, she'd drawn upon her childhood experiences for the illustrations of her books. It was almost as if she'd forgotten the joy of tuning in to the small things in the wild. The details one could only notice by personally experiencing them. Simply finding a photo of something online for reference wasn't the same as experiencing the world the thing lived in—the texture, the smell, and the small habitats that existed around every stone.

A scuttling, rustling sound caught her attention. She'd been following the trail very near the river, and on rocks just off the path, she spotted a salamander. She knelt down, but not so close as to scare the creature away. Garet didn't have her sketchbook, but she was pretty good at committing visual details to memory and transferring them to a drawing later.

Dampness soaked through her jeans as she knelt to get a closer look. The salamander twitched as if considering whether to flee, but then froze. His dark skin glistened with moisture and each toe flared out into a rounded shape.

"What are you looking at?"

Garet flinched and the tiny creature bolted. Somehow June had managed to be standing only a few feet away and Garet hadn't heard her approach. June tiptoed closer, but there was nothing to see. Tess wasn't far behind June, holding the leash of a scruffy medium sized dog.

"I was watching a salamander." Garet stood and brushed damp dirt from her knee. There was a big, wet circle on her pants.

"Is it still there?" June was right next to her now.

"No, he darted away." Garet held up her hand in greeting to Tess. "Hi."

"Hi." Tess smiled.

"I didn't know you guys had a dog." This pup looked like a slightly larger version of Dorothy's famous dog, Toto.

"We don't. This is Richard. He belongs to our neighbors." Tess looked down at the dog who'd obediently taken a seat near her foot. "We offered to bring him along for a walk."

Tess had been totally surprised to see Garet on the trail. First of all, Garet hadn't seemed the outdoorsy sort. Or if she did have outdoorsy inclinations, not the sort that would happen before noon. For some reason, Tess had assumed Garet wasn't a morning person. Not that it was super early, but still. Maybe she should stop making assumptions where Garet was concerned. Because she'd been mistaken on a few counts.

She'd discovered that Garet was someone whose work she quite admired. Garet's books showed depth, insight, and sensitivity. Why would she assume that the woman who created those stories didn't share the same traits?

Had living in a small town for too long made Tess judgmental? No, it wasn't that. She'd merely made a snap assessment of Garet based on the first day they shared the classroom. It was hardly fair to judge someone centered solely upon their very first day on the job.

"I'm glad I bumped into you." Garet smiled down at June. "I mean, both of you."

"Why?" asked June.

"Well, it's more fun to walk with friends isn't it?"

Had Garet put special emphasis on the word *friend*? Were they friends? Tess tried not to read into Garet's attentive gaze. God, she was all over the place. One minute annoyed by Garet, the next moment finding her irresistibly adorable. Maybe she should just try to stop thinking so much.

"Please join us." Richard tugged at the leash. June skipped ahead and Richard wanted to follow. She mirrored Garet's slow, easy gait as they continued down the path. Beside them, the river rippled softly, a soothing sound. Sunlight bounced off the water's surface every time it broke through the clouds, sending sharp strands of light bursting through the leaves of the trees along the bank.

"June, don't get too close to the water." Tess was nervous every time June climbed on rocks along the edge. One misstep and she'd tumble into the river.

The wind suddenly picked up and a large drop landed on top of her head, and then another.

"Uh-oh." Garet was looking up. "I thought the rain would hold off longer, but I think I might have been wrong."

Tess had insisted that June wear a jacket, but the one she was wearing wasn't exactly rain proof.

"June, we should head home. It's starting to rain."

As soon as the word *rain* escaped her lips, a dark cloud settled overhead and a downpour ensued. Garet started to head back up the trail, but it occurred to Tess that Garet was pretty far from Hildy's place. Too far to avoid getting drenched.

"You should come with us." Tess motioned for Garet to follow them. "Our place is closer."

"How did you know where I live?" Garet had a puzzled expression as she turned back.

"Oh, my mother and Hildy are friends." Tess had given herself away. But it wasn't as if she'd been snooping to find out this information. It had simply dropped into her lap thanks to the Shadetree gossip circle.

"Well, if you don't mind." Garet fell in step beside her.

"The house is not far. We can cut through right there." Tess pointed to a break in the trees where a side trail was visible.

The large drops were more numerous now and the wind increased. June ran ahead of them as they picked up their pace. Tess's sneakers had very little traction so that when she made a turn too quickly her right foot went right out from under her. Strong hands under each arm caught her, stopping her backward fall. She sank into Garet's chest until she could regain her footing. She'd dropped the leash, but Richard trotted back to check on her.

"I've got you." Garet's words were kind and sure.

"Thank you." She could feel the warmth of Garet's skin, their faces were so close.

Garet shyly released her and stepped back. The rain was coming down in sheets now so they resumed their speedy retreat to Tess's.

They cut across the lush, soggy backyard of her neighbor's house and angled for the front porch, which had a short overhang. June trotted up the front steps, Garet stood to the side to allow her to follow June through the door. Once inside, Richard shook, misting the entryway. June had fared the best in her favorite red rubber boots and water-resistant windbreaker. Garet's denim jacket was dark at the shoulders and her sopping hair fell into her eyes. She brushed it back. Tess hung her soaked cotton jacket on a peg near the door and then offered to take Garet's.

With the rain, the temperature had dropped. Garet cupped her hands and blew on them. Tess shivered too.

"Maybe we should build a fire." Tess helped June out of her boots so that she wouldn't track mud into the house.

"I could do that if you tell me where the firewood is." Garet briskly rubbed her hands together.

"On the back porch." Tess pointed toward the kitchen. "Kindling and matches are in a wooden bucket near the hearth."

"I'm on it."

Tess watched as Garet slipped her shoes off and padded through the kitchen in sock feet. It all seemed so unexpectedly familiar, so normal, and the recognition of that made Tess's stomach just the least bit unsettled.

CHAPTER TWENTY-SIX

G aret stoked the fire and added another dry piece of wood. She waited a moment for it to catch and then replaced the screen to keep embers from popping out. There were dark spots on the aged hardwood floor around the fire already, but she didn't want to be responsible for adding more.

"Wow, the rain is really coming down." Thunder rumbled in the distance.

"Here you go."

Tess handed her a mug of hot cocoa with a cluster of tiny marshmallows on top. June had opted for a juice box and animal crackers which she'd asked to take to her room. The kid seemed unfazed by the chilly downpour. Maybe young children ran hot because they were always in motion. Tess relented but followed June upstairs to make sure she would not feed any of the cookies to Richard. It seemed as if there was some backstory there, but Garet didn't press for details. She took a seat on the sofa watching the flames lick the dry logs.

The dull murmur of raindrops on the roof and the crackling of the fire were sounds that soothed her. She closed her eyes and sank against the high-backed sofa. The cushion shifted signaling Tess's return. Garet blinked and straightened her posture. It was possible she'd allowed herself to become too comfortable, but there was something about Tess that made her feel welcomed and cozy.

"You're fine." Tess smiled. "It's that kind of lazy day."

Tess propped her sock feet on the coffee table next to a haphazard stack of coloring books. She'd changed into a fresh shirt while she was upstairs. Garet's jacket had kept her mostly dry, except for her hair and her jeans, which were fairly soaked all down the front.

"Oh, dang, I just realized that maybe I shouldn't be sitting on your couch." She quickly stood.

"No, don't worry about this sofa. There's nothing you could do to it that June hasn't already done." Tess looked up at her. "But I should have offered you something dry to put on. I probably have some sweatpants that would fit you."

Garet considered the danger of becoming one step cozier in close proximity to Tess.

"I'll get them for you."

Before she could formulate a response, Tess was climbing the stairs. Garet tasted the hot chocolate. It was so damn good. She couldn't remember the last time she'd had hot cocoa.

Her phone vibrated in her pocket and she checked the screen. There was a text from Lane.

Hey, man, got held up. I'll be a little late delivering the bike.

That was a lucky break. Especially since she'd completely forgotten Lane was driving up. This was great news. Now she could hang out at Tess's a little longer.

No worries.

She considered telling Lane where she was.

I'm at Tess's place waiting out a thunderstorm.

Three dots indicated Lane was typing, in all likelihood some sarcastic response.

Then I'll def take my time, punctuated with a smiling emoji.

Hmm, no sarcasm. That was unusual. That made her nervous.

"Is something wrong?" Tess crossed the room from the stairs.

"Oh, no, just my friend Lane." Garet placed her phone on the coffee table facedown. "She's loaning me a bicycle and was going to drive it up later."

"I stole these from my brother, Nathan, at some point." Tess held classic gray sweats out to her. "I think they'll fit if you want to try them."

Garet was relieved to receive the well-worn University of Georgia sweatpants instead of yoga pants or something that she'd look ridiculous in. She was fairly sure she had the exact same pair.

"There's a half-bath off the kitchen if you'd like to change." Tess gave her jeans an up-and-down look. "I was going to suggest that I could throw those in the dryer, but maybe I should wash them first."

Garet remembered the knee, stained with dirt.

"That's too much trouble...I can wash them later."

"It's no trouble, really. They'll be done by the time you leave."

Garet calculated wash and dry cycle times in her head. This sounded promising. She left the room to change and then sheepishly handed the rolled up jeans to Tess. While Tess retreated to the laundry room, Garet tended the fire. There was a nice blaze now and it spread warmth and light throughout the storm-darkened room. She leaned close to the window near the fireplace to examine the sky. The dark, churning clouds didn't seem to be moving out any time soon.

She returned to the sofa and finished off the hot cocoa. Tess sat next to her. There remained between them a respectable distance of open space, but that didn't keep the air from tingling with some sort of electrical current. This whole situation was surreal and heavenly at the same time. Garet had the strongest urge to reach for Tess, to touch her. Instead, she set the empty mug on the table and shoved her hands under her legs to keep them from wandering.

"This is nice." Tess relaxed against the cushions. "I love rainy days."

"I guess I do too, but maybe for different reasons."

"What do you mean?"

"Well, as a kid, I always loved rainy days because they gave me an excuse to stay indoors and draw. My parents always wanted me and my brothers to stay outside and play as much as possible." Garet paused, thinking back. "That worked great for my brothers, they were super athletic, but I was never really into sports." Garet laughed.

"What's funny?"

"I was just realizing that maybe my mom simply wanted the house to herself."

"I'm sure that was it." Tess smiled.

They were quiet. Distant thunder rumbled and then a strong wind pelted large drops against the windows. Outside, leaves swirled past, but inside the firelight danced warmly and the muscles in Garet's shoulders began to relax.

"How many brothers do you have?" Tess asked while staring into the fire.

"Two, both older. We're not that close." There were lots of reasons why and she didn't want to go into them and ruin the mood. "You know, adulthood...We all let things get in the way of staying in touch."

"Yes, we do. My brother travels for work, and he has kids too." Tess paused. "Life is too busy."

"Yeah." If anyone had said that to Garet a month ago she'd have disagreed, but something was shifting for her. She was beginning to realize that the pace of her life in Atlanta was a bit too much. She was thirty-two, tired of the starting-over of the dating scene, and generally feeling like she just wanted more from life—all of life, not just the parts that related to her career.

Tess sensed Garet's mood shift. Garet leaned forward and rested her elbows on her knees as if she were wrestling with some deep thought, or possibly arguing with herself about something. This whole situation was very cozy, almost intimate, and Tess had a strong desire to reach out and touch Garet. To place her hand on Garet's shoulder to soothe whatever was troubling her. But it was as if the space between them on the sofa was impassable, a barrier of some unknowable danger.

"What are you thinking about?"

Garet turned to look at her. A still damp tendril of dark hair fell across one eye and she brushed it aside.

"Life, I guess."

Before Tess could respond, the washer chimed. She'd put Garet's jeans on a quick wash cycle because she wasn't sure how long she'd be able to stay. She left the room for a moment, with Garet's comment still hanging in the air.

In the laundry room, she tugged the jeans free and tossed them in the dryer. She braced her hands on the dryer and took a deep breath. This was ridiculous. She was attracted to Garet. They were both adults. She should ask Garet out. Yes, they worked together, but this was a short-term situation. Maybe she'd been thinking about this all wrong. Maybe the fact that Garet was only here temporarily was a good thing. There would be fewer consequences, no chance of falling for real, and more chance of simply having a fling.

Tess took another deep breath and stared at the shelf full of washing detergent and fabric softener. Was she capable of having a fling? She wasn't quite sure.

When she returned to the living room, Garet was standing near the fire. In the dimly lit room, the orange glow of the flames warmly lit the contours of her face. The scene triggered a surge of emotions that scared her and she had the sudden urge to flee.

"I'm just going to run upstairs and check on June." She chose the safety of a diversion.

Tess stepped softly at the top of the stairs. There was no noise from June's room. When she leaned through the door she saw that June was on the bed asleep with Richard curled up next to her. She pulled the door closed and tiptoed back downstairs.

"What are June and Richard up to?"

"They're both asleep." She joined Garet by the hearth.

She watched the fire dance as if it were the most interesting thing in the room. Garet's nearness caused a tingling sensation to rise from deep inside. She looked up, meeting Garet's gaze and then she did something she rarely did, she gave in to her desire.

Tess filled her fingers with the short hair at the back of Garet's head and drew her down until their lips met. Garet smelled like fresh air and vanilla. Her lips were soft, warm, and undemanding. The warmth of Garet's palms seeped through the thin fabric of her blouse as Garet stepped closer. She slid her palm down Garet's arm from her shoulder as she gently explored Garet's lips with hers.

After a minute or maybe ten, she broke the kiss and rested her forehead against Garet's shoulder. What did she want to happen next? Garet laid her chin on Tess's hair and tenderly stroked Tess's back. Everywhere Garet's body connected with Tess's was electrified. Garet had awakened something in Tess and she didn't know what that meant exactly, but she knew what she wanted right now—more.

She stepped out of Garet's embrace and tugged her toward the sofa. Tess sat down and Garet dropped next to her. This time there was no space between them. Garet gently stroked her face with her fingertips.

"You are so beautiful." Garet pressed Tess's fingers to her lips and kissed them. "I've wanted to kiss you."

"Then kiss me now." Tess held Garet's face in her hands.

Garet's mouth on hers was igniting a full-body hormone rush. The place between her legs throbbed and she angled toward Garet's body, hoping to telegraph the nonverbal need to be touched. Garet was respectfully restraining herself, keeping her hands in safe places, or maybe she wasn't feeling the same intensity that Tess was feeling right now. She was frustrated by her attempt to get closer to Garet in the awkward side by side position they'd assumed on the sofa.

Tess shifted so that she was partially reclined and Garet repositioned next to her. She wanted Garet to drive but wasn't sure how to let Garet know without just coming out and saying it.

Garet was trying to go slow, to savor this unexpected turn of events. Her brain was trying to catch up with the fact that Tess had kissed her. Tess Hill had dragged her to the sofa to make out. She suddenly felt as inept as a high schooler trying to get to second base. This wasn't just any woman, Tess was special. She didn't want to make the wrong move, or move too fast and blow the whole thing.

Tess arched against her. Her stomach muscles twitched as Tess's fingers slipped past the hem of her T-shirt. Her senses exploded. She felt Tess's hands on her back now, under her shirt. Tess's mouth was hot and demanding. Garet's fingers were on the top button of Tess's blouse—

"Mama, I'm hungry."

Garet lurched up, wedging herself against the far side of the sofa. She crossed her legs and brusquely swept her fingers through her hair. She'd reacted so quickly that she'd almost launched herself completely off the couch. Beside her, Tess smoothed down her shirt and then her hair. She was on her feet now, in an attempt to intercept June.

Thankfully, June seemed oblivious to what she'd almost seen. She was sleepily rubbing both eyes with the heels of her palms. Richard trailed behind her.

"Come on, sweetie. We'll find something for you." Tess smiled thinly back at Garet as if to say *sorry*, as she ushered June to the kitchen.

Oh, man, that was close.

Garet sighed and let her head fall back against the couch. Would things have escalated between them if June hadn't surprised them? Most definitely. Garet was consumed, she wanted more of Tess. *Damn.* That was an unexpected complication to *just being friends.*

After a few minutes, Tess returned, leaving June in the kitchen.

"I'm sorry." Tess looked defeated.

"It's okay." Garet really meant it.

"This is my life." Tess covered her face with her hands.

"Hey, let me take you out...for real." Garet touched her arm. "Please."

Tess smiled. "Really?"

"That can't possibly be a serious question." Garet wanted to kiss Tess again, and again. She should probably leave. "Should I go? I should go." Garet was about to stand, but Tess stopped her with a hand on her thigh.

"I don't want you to go," Tess whispered.

Garet didn't really want to leave either.

"Mama, can we watch a movie?" June was back.

As if on cue, her phone buzzed on the tabletop. Lane was on her way.

"That's my friend Lane. I should get home."

"Your jeans probably aren't dry yet."

Garet stood and so did Tess.

"Maybe you could just keep them, until I see you again?" Garet was serious about taking Tess on a date. "That is if you don't mind if I wear these home."

The rain had dialed down to barely more than a drizzle so she figured she could just walk home and still have time to shower and change before Lane arrived.

"Okay, then." Tess stroked June's hair as she sat down between where they were standing, next to the sofa. June was focused on some jaunty cartoon show that Garet hadn't seen before.

"I'll call you later." Garet almost leaned in to give Tess a quick kiss on the cheek but stopped herself. The kid factor was really throwing off her game, what little game she had.

CHAPTER TWENTY-SEVEN

Within forty-five minutes, Garet was back at her place, showered, and in dry clothes. The twenty-minute walk home in a chilly drizzle was just the thing to cool her off. Leaving Tess's the way she had, she'd literally felt as if she might spontaneously burst into flames.

Garet searched through an oversized duffel bag until she found her favorite sweatshirt. The cottage was furnished with a dresser in the bedroom, but only half her stuff had ended up in the drawers. It seemed old habits were hard to overcome. She pulled the sweatshirt over her head and then finger-combed her damp hair into some semblance of order. Next on her agenda, coffee. Just then she caught a glimpse of Lane's pickup truck pulling into the driveway. Scratch coffee, maybe she and Lane could go somewhere and get beers and food. She wondered if the brewery was open by now. The place had been closed earlier, but maybe they opened in the afternoon since it was Sunday. She opened the door and waved at Lane.

"Hey, thanks for driving the bike out to me." Garet stood in the doorway.

"No problem. The highway was clear, hardly any traffic." Lane wheeled the mountain bike up to the front of the cottage. She leaned it against the wall under a narrow overhang. "You mentioned car problems. What's up with your car?"

"Some days it starts right up, some days it takes several tries."

"Too bad you drove the blue beast all the way out to rural middle-of-nowhere, otherwise you could swing by the shop and I'd have someone take a look at it."

"Yeah, I wish I'd thought of that sooner." It was pretty handy to have a friend who owned a garage. If it hadn't been for Lane, the Volvo probably would have thrown in the towel long ago. "Maybe I should bring this inside." Shadetree seemed like a fairly safe little town, but she didn't want Lane's bike getting stolen on her watch. Bikes were too easy to roll away.

"Yeah, probably a good idea." Lane wheeled the bicycle to Garet and after handing it off, followed her inside.

"This was the simplest ride you had?" Not that Garet wasn't grateful, but this looked like a high-end bike.

"It's not that nice. Don't worry, you can't hurt it."

"Don't jinx me, man."

"Oh, I brought you a helmet too. I'll go grab it." Lane jogged back out to her truck. She returned and handed the helmet to Garet with a flourish, as if she were a king bestowing knighthood. "Don't ride without it."

"Yes, Mother." Garet reached for her phone. "Hey, want to grab a beer and maybe a burger?"

"Sure."

"Just give me a sec. I'm checking to see if the brewery is open." The voice mail message confirmed that they were open for dinner on Sundays. "They're open. Do you mind driving? I'd say we could walk, but I've already gotten caught once today in the rain."

"Is that how you ended up at Tess's?"

"Yes…that's a longer story which requires beer." Garet ushered Lane to the door.

Lane's truck was a little beat-up. Unlike her Mustang, which no one drove but her, other mechanics at the garage drove it for work related errands. As a result, the cab of the truck looked more like a dorm room. To-go cups from 7-Eleven littered the floorboard on the passenger side, and the center of the bench seat had a console piled with a random assortment of hoodies and one Atlanta United beanie.

"This truck is a mess." Garet kicked the cups and trash aside as she climbed in.

"Yeah, I need to have one of the guys take it and have it detailed." Lane put her arm on the edge of the seat as she rotated to back out of the driveway. "But then that would last about forty-eight hours before it was a wreck again. Most people just treat their cars like a walk-in-closet."

"Or, apparently, a dumpster." Garet opened a rumpled KFC bag to discover a half-eaten biscuit inside.

"Don't think I don't know what this is about." Lane grinned.

"What?"

"This whole discussion about car care and maintenance is an obvious stall tactic."

Garet laughed. "Beer first, then talking, okay?"

"I can't wait to hear all about it."

❖

"Your food will be up soon." The waiter delivered two draft beers.

Garet tasted hers. It was good. They'd decided to try the local brew, and she'd not been disappointed.

"Okay, so we've ordered food and now we have beer." Lane rested her elbows on the table. "I think I've been more than patient. You can't just text me that you're at sexy-mandolin-girl's house on a rainy afternoon and then leave me hanging."

Garet drew curvy lines in the condensation of her glass.

"It was nice."

Lane sipped her beer, waiting for more.

"I'd gone for a walk and bumped into Tess and her daughter, June. It started to rain and we were closer to her house than mine."

"Sooo, it was just proximity and nothing more."

"I thought that too, until she kissed me." Garet couldn't help smiling. Thinking of the kiss warmed her insides. She took another swig of beer to cool down.

"Wait, *she* kissed you?"

"I wasn't going to make a move. But ever since we realized we were going to be working together she's been giving me signal after signal to back off."

"Until today. Until she kissed you."

"Yeah." Garet sat back in the booth as the waiter delivered her burger and a mountain of fries. She glanced up at him. "Thanks."

"Y'all need anything else?" He waited until they both shook their heads.

"Okay, finish the story." Lane ate some fries, two at a time.

"We started making out and just when things were…well, you know…June came downstairs. And that was that."

"The kid interrupted you two?" Lane had a bite of burger in her cheek like she was a chipmunk storing up for winter. She chewed and swallowed. "Did she see anything that she'll need therapy for later?"

"No, no, nothing like that. We had our clothes on. I mean, my jeans were in the dryer, but I'd borrowed—"

"Wait, back up, Tess got you out of your pants?" Lane dabbed at her lips with her napkin. She had a serious expression, as if in preparation to cross-examine a witness to a crime. "For someone who writes stories for a living, you suck at telling stories."

"Unlike *you*, not everything that happens to me has sexual subtext."

"Or does it?" Lane pointed her index finger at Garet like an imaginary gun and cocked one eyebrow.

"No, it doesn't. I got caught in the rain, my jeans were soaked. Tess offered to wash and dry them. The kiss had nothing to do with me losing my pants…or vise-versa."

"All right, all right, calm down." Lane laughed.

"I am calm." Who was she kidding? "No. I'm not calm at all."

"I know you're not. I can see it on your face every time you say her name." Lane paused. "Say her name."

"No."

"Come on, say it."

"Tess." Her heart rate increased.

"See what I mean?"

Lane was right. Simply saying Tess's name kicked her nervous system into overdrive.

"It doesn't matter." Garet shook her head.

"What do you mean it doesn't matter?"

"I'm only here for three months, and she's got a kid, and…" She trailed off. Garet was about to say, it was complicated. But that sounded so lame.

"The timeline thing isn't such a big deal, but the kid thing, that's huge." Lane wasn't joking any longer; she sounded suddenly serious. "Any relationship with Tess, right out of the gate, is a relationship with two people."

"I know." If they decided to see each other it would never be just Tess and her. June would always be there. And anything she did that affected Tess would also have an impact on June.

The whole situation seemed too enormous to get her head around. Amazing, heart-stopping first kiss aside, Garet wasn't sure if she could handle dating Tess. Not because of Tess. Tess was an adult and a grown-up. She knew the risks of a relationship. Garet visualized the disappointment on Jillian's face at the end of their big breakup scene. It was one thing to experience that as an adult, but quite another to deal with a breakup as a kid.

She remembered the feeling well.

Her parents split when she was thirteen. It was a truly terrible, awful time.

Her brothers had stayed with her dad in Brunswick and she'd moved to Macon with her mom.

The thought of putting June through anything remotely similar would break her heart.

Who was she kidding. They'd kissed once and she'd already time traveled through a relationship all the way to divorce…and they hadn't even been on a first date yet.

Uh-oh. Garet was struck like lightning by the memory that she'd pretty much already asked Tess out. *Stop. Think.*

Garet had started this whole temporary job thing to earn some money, but also to learn something, about children and possibly about herself. Since she'd taken the first step and traveled way outside her comfort zone, she was obligated to pay attention rather than run away at the first hint of uncertainty. A sense of calm settled over her. She decided to at least stay in one place long enough to fully experience what was truly there. New experiences were scary, but not necessarily bad. What was the harm of one date?

"Hey, where'd you just go?" Lane studied her from across the table.

"Nowhere, sorry." Garet smiled. "Should we have another beer?"

She was starting to relax, starting to feel better about the entire situation. There was no need to get ahead of herself. Nothing had really happened, so nothing could go too wrong. Garet settled against the cushioned booth and sampled her fries.

CHAPTER TWENTY-EIGHT

Tess and June walked Richard home. Tess's neighbor Betty greeted them at the door.

"I was afraid you'd gotten caught in the rain." Betty held the door open for them to enter.

"We did." Tess unclipped Richard's leash. "I let him lie near the fire to dry. I hope we didn't keep him too long."

"Heavens no. Ray's been watching football all afternoon, so Richard would never have gotten a walk. He's watching the Georgia Bulldogs' game day review on the SEC Network. Wild horses couldn't tear him away, let alone a scruffy little mutt."

"Go Dawgs." Tess wasn't much of a sports fan, but she could fake it when required.

"Exactly." Betty nodded knowingly. "Say, June. I made some cupcakes yesterday just for fun. Would you like one?" Betty was talking to June but then turned to Tess. "If that's all right with your mother. I was going to make some tea also. Can you visit for a spell?"

"I really need to check on Charlotte. She had her baby a few days ago."

"Oh, I didn't realize." Betty's eyes lit up.

"Yes, ma'am, a little boy. She named him Tucker."

"Mama, can I stay and have cupcakes?" June held her hand and tugged.

"Cupcake, singular." Tess held up her index finger to signify only *one*.

"June can keep me company while you visit with Charlotte."

"Are you sure?"

"Oh, yes, absolutely." Betty extended her hand for June to grasp. "Let's have some afternoon dessert."

"Thank you, Betty. And, June, mind your manners." June looked back and nodded.

Tess let herself out and crossed the soggy lawn between the two houses. Once inside she texted Charlotte.

Can I come by for a visit?

Charlotte responded right away.

Yes! Tucker is down for a nap. Come NOW!

On my way.

Tess remembered what that was like. As a parent you learned to relish those kid-free moments to chat or hang out with adults. Charlotte was probably starved for *friend time*.

Hmm, starved, that was a good idea.

She decided to stop along the way and pick up a treat for Charlotte. Having a new infant made even small things like popping out to the grocery store to satisfy a craving much harder. Seeing Charlotte and stopping by the store would hopefully keep her from thinking about *the* kiss.

Too late.

Now that she'd thought about it she couldn't un-think about it. Tess took a deep breath as she backed the Subaru out of the driveway. Her cheeks flamed hotly simply thinking of Garet's lips touching hers. How were they ever going to go back to just being coworkers? This was a terrible complication that she did *not* need.

The market was oddly deserted, likely a result of the ballgame. Everyone had probably loaded up on food and snacks before kickoff. Tess headed for the freezer case and grabbed a pint of Charlotte's favorite Ben and Jerry's, Cherry Garcia.

"Hi, Tess."

"Hi, Melinda." Melinda scanned the ice cream at the checkout. Her daughter, Tammy, had been one of Tess's students, but she'd graduated three years earlier. "How is Tammy?"

"She's doing great. You're so sweet to ask after her."

Tammy was very kind and likeable, just like her mother.

"What's the student play gonna be this year?"

Tess didn't want to linger so long that the ice cream would melt, but good manners required at least a brief chat. Besides, she genuinely liked Melinda. They weren't close friends, but it was always nice to see her at the market and Tess enjoyed hearing that her former students were doing well with life after high school. So many young local women married right out of high school and stayed in town, but Tammy had a head for math and had been attending Georgia Tech in Atlanta, undoubtedly not an easy transition from Shadetree.

"The kids picked *The Wizard of Oz* this year." Tess angled for the door.

"Oh, that's one of my favorites. I'll be there with bells on."

The students sold tickets for the play to raise money for the school library. Almost everyone in Shadetree bought a ticket or two, even if they didn't attend.

"Great to see you, Melinda…Oh—" Tess spun toward the exit and collided into Riley Caldwell like an unmovable brick wall. "Sorry."

"No need to apologize." Riley grinned. "It's good to take care of those cravings." Riley's gaze was focused on the chilly pint of Cherry Garcia between them, or possibly Tess's breasts.

"This is for Charlotte." She raised the frosty container as she pushed through the double glass doors of the grocery. The last thing she was in the mood for right now was flirtation from Riley.

The drive to Charlotte and Tim's took only five minutes. They lived in a duplex at the edge of town. Tim's pickup wasn't in the driveway. That meant she could really find out how things were going. Tess didn't want to ring the bell and risk waking the baby. The door was unlocked so she called softly from the threshold through the partially open doorway.

"Charlotte, it's just me."

"Come in, come in." Charlotte kept her voice down. She motioned excitedly with her hand.

The minute Tess stepped inside, Charlotte swept her up in a hug.

"Oh, my God, *you* are my hero." Charlotte's eyes widened.

"I thought you might need this." She handed the pint to Charlotte.

"You know me so well." Charlotte scurried to the kitchen. She was still in her pajamas and robe. "I'll grab two spoons."

"None for me, thanks." Tess surveyed the cheerful chaos of the living room but didn't sit down.

"I'm not getting fat by myself." Charlotte held out a spoon to her as if it were a weapon.

"As you wish." Tess laughed and scooped a taste for herself. The brief discussion with Melinda and the ride over had given the creamy dessert just the right amount of time to thaw without being overly melted.

"Okay, sit...tell me everything." Charlotte dropped at one end of the sofa and tucked her feet under a floral throw pillow.

"Well, first off, I miss you every day."

"Same." Charlotte took a bite and rolled her eyes. "Why does this taste so good?"

Tess was glad she'd thought of it rather than showing up empty-handed.

"Where's Tim?"

"He got called in to work."

Tim was a welder in an auto body shop about a half hour away.

"He's been missing some shifts so I think he felt like he had to go in, even though it's the weekend." Charlotte offered Tess the pint.

"All right, twist my arm." She helped herself to one more spoonful.

"How is my replacement?" Charlotte set the pint on the nearby coffee table. "I've been sort of dying to call you and find out how classes are going, but then Tucker will get fussy and I'll completely forget what I was going to ask, or who I was going to call. I totally get the whole *baby brain* thing now. That shit is real." Charlotte shook her head.

"Don't scare me by saying something like *replacement*." Tess shuddered. "Let's call her your temporary substitute. Her name is Garet Allen, and she's...fine."

"Fine?" Charlotte scrunched her nose and scowled. "Okay, there's something you're not telling me."

"June and I bumped into her today when we were out on a walk and then it started raining…so I invited her to come back to our house to dry off. I made hot chocolate. She built a fire, and while June was taking a nap, we…kissed." All the words tumbled out.

Charlotte was silent, but her wide-eyed expression spoke volumes.

"I know, I know. We're coworkers. We have a professional relationship. I shouldn't have kissed her."

"Um, that's not what I was thinking."

"It wasn't?"

"No." Charlotte hugged the pillow to her chest. "I was thinking, yay!"

"You were?"

"Tess, you haven't been attracted to anyone in, well, forever." Charlotte grinned. "Tell me more. What's she like?"

"She's really cute." Saying things out loud helped her settle. Charlotte wasn't judging her, she genuinely cared about Tess's happiness. "She has short dark hair, intense blue eyes, and when she's not substitute teaching, which she barely has any experience at, by the way, she writes children's books."

"Wow, she's a published author?"

"You've seen her books. She writes under a pen name, Elizabeth Allen."

"Shut up." Charlotte blinked. "She's, like, famous." And then she frowned. "Oh, great, how am I gonna go back to my students after they've been in class with her?"

"Please, are you kidding? The kids love you." Tess patted Charlotte's leg.

The baby monitor on the coffee table came to life. Tucker cried. Charlotte shot off the couch, scooping up the pint of melted ice cream as she went.

"Hold that thought. Let me put this in the freezer and I'll be right back."

Tess took a deep breath and closed her eyes. It was nice to talk things over with Charlotte. This was exactly what she needed, a sounding board.

A few moments later, Charlotte returned with a bundle in a blue blanket.

"Do you want to hold him?"

"I'd love to." Tess supported his head against the crook of her arm, allowing his tiny body to rest in her lap. He gripped her finger and looked up at her with huge, searching brown eyes. The weight of him in her arms, the sweet smell of his skin, his vulnerability—everything came rushing back. She remembered how scared she'd been after June was born. Being a parent was such an enormous responsibility.

Was she about to screw things up for June?

Her vision blurred as tears gathered around her lashes. An unwanted tear rolled slowly down her cheek. And then another.

"Hey, what's going on?" Charlotte scooted closer on the sofa.

"I have this perfect bubble, you know. June and I are good. What if adding another person ruins it all? What if things don't work out and June ends up getting hurt?"

"Tess, sweetheart, slow down. You've gotten yourself to the end before even starting anything. What if things went well? Did you consider that option?" Charlotte put her arm around Tess and scooched closer. "You're allowed to have a life too."

"I'm sorry. I don't know why I'm crying." Tess wiped at the tears.

"Because you're scared." Charlotte kissed the top of her head. "But it's okay to let someone in."

Was Tess really so frightened that she'd deliberately choose to remain walled off? Would she opt for isolation within some fortress of self, hiding behind the demands of motherhood, rather than even try? Or would she choose to wade into that treacherous unknown between self and possibility? Tess drew a jagged breath. At some point, if she gave in to her desire she would have to brave the intricate paths of her own heart to see where they might lead. Maybe the risk was too great.

Tess imagined herself at the precipice of a brittle cliff, the edge of which crumbled a little more each time she was with Garet. What would happen if she truly fell?

CHAPTER TWENTY-NINE

Garet parked and followed the stream of students through the main school entrance. This wasn't her first day in the classroom, but all the nerves from that first day were back. They'd set up shop in the pit of her stomach and were causing a big ruckus, threatening to upend that one piece of dry toast she'd managed to choke down for breakfast.

The beers with Lane had helped distract her the previous evening. But after Lane left, when she was alone with her thoughts, well, things spiraled. She and Tess not only had to work together for a few more weeks, they had to co-produce a children's play. That kiss, regardless of how perfect it had been, was probably going to ruin everything. Garet was simultaneously excited and dreaded seeing Tess in class.

Tess was already in the room, rearranging chairs for the first period when she arrived. Butterflies swarmed in her stomach. She tried to act cool but figured she was failing miserably. June's statement that she was the lost kitten seemed uncannily prophetic, because that's exactly how she felt at the moment—lost and needy, two very unattractive qualities in her opinion. But Tess's smile was warm and kind. She'd feared getting the brush-off, but that hadn't been the case at all.

"Good morning." Tess stopped moving chairs and gave Garet her full attention.

"Good morning." The butterflies calmed down just a little.

"I thought maybe we could use our free period this morning to work out some details for the play." Tess retrieved a spiral notebook from her bag. "Since you don't know the kids as well as I do yet, I took the liberty of assigning some roles. Is that okay?"

Garet was relieved to talk about something other than what had happened the previous day. It seemed they were going to ignore the fact that they'd kissed, for now, which was fine with Garet. Denial was a very comfortable option at the moment.

"Thanks for doing that." Garet dropped her bag on the nearest chair and took a seat across from Tess.

"These are the kids that I know want to work on backdrops." Tess tore out a page and handed it to her. "And June is one of them. I hope that's okay."

"Absolutely." Garet pretended to care about the names on the list when all she really wanted to do was reach for Tess's hand.

"She saw me working on the list this morning and would not relent until I agreed." Tess was less sure than usual, almost shy. "I know she's younger than the other students working on backdrops, but she wants to spend more time with you..." The words grew softer and sort of trailed off, and from Tess's expression, Garet wondered if she was actually talking about June, or herself.

"You know, I knew I wanted to be an artist by the time I was seven. She might be a little younger than that, but maybe she just knows."

"I think she actually wants to be the Jane Goodall of narwhals."

Garet remembered the stuffed narwhal with the rainbow horn that June held while they watched the movie.

"The unicorn of the sea."

"Funny, that's exactly what June says."

They locked eyes for a moment, until Tess returned her focus to the notebook on the table in front of her.

"I selected Lucinda for the part of Dorothy. She's in tenth grade. I thought it would be best to have one of the older students take the lead since several of the songs require the singer to be able to reach different octaves."

"So, should I try to create backgrounds for every scene?" Garet was excited by the idea of working with Tess on this joint, creative project.

"Not every scene. Normally, we try to do a lot with a little. You'll see why once you attempt to get the kids to stay focused and actually finish their assigned tasks."

Tess the teacher was back. The morning's first encounter, which was the smallest bit more intimate, had passed and professional distance had returned in its place. Maybe that was for the best. Professionalism would be required in order for Garet to function and actually focus on teaching. Tess's mouth, her lips, were completely mesmerizing if Garet gave in to the urge to focus solely on her.

The collar of Tess's blouse was open in such a way that it highlighted the silky curve of her neck. The deep blue color strikingly contrasted against the creamy vee of her décolleté. The light from the windows created soft patterns of shadow and light along the glimpse of collarbone revealed by her open collared shirt. Her layered hair fell past her shoulders in a casual feathery way.

"Garet, are you listening?"

"Sorry." She'd been building an image in her head of all the tiny details that were Tess and completely zoning out.

"I was saying that some of this work counts as class time, so not all of it needs to be done after school, but for the larger pieces you might need to paint those in the parking lot. You know, when it's not raining."

With the mention of rain, her mind instantly took another field trip. She reimagined lounging on the sofa, with Tess in her arms, unguarded and receptive. This was going to be a very long day.

❖

For Tess, the hours dragged by, except for those moments when she allowed her mind to drift back to the previous day's rainy afternoon with Garet. In those instances, seated at the back of the room, time accelerated and she'd jolt back to reality having missed a half hour of Garet's class time.

Things between them had gone more smoothly than expected. Garet had been professional and considerate. There'd been no mention of the kiss or what had almost transpired on her sofa. Thank God things hadn't gone any further or she'd have never been able to face Garet. That being said, there was enough unspoken tension between them that she knew they needed to talk, just not at work. When asked, her mother had offered to take June Saturday evening. Tess had used the excuse that she and Garet needed to spend time working out the details of the performance, but she suspected that her mother saw right through the ruse. Her mother had insisted that June plan to spend the night, which only made Tess's situation more tenuous. Could she tear herself away from Garet without the curfew of June's bedtime? She wasn't so sure.

The final bell rang, and as the last student left the classroom Tess decided now was the time to ask Garet about Saturday night. If she knew there was a plan for them to talk, one-on-one, then maybe she'd be able to regain her focus for the rest of the week. Perhaps that was wishful thinking.

Garet was gathering her things. Now was the time. They'd spent all day in the same classroom, why was she so nervous?

"Nice teaching today." Despite the fact that she'd zoned out for part of it, the segments she'd heard had been smart and thoughtful.

"Thanks."

Garet stopped fussing with her stuff and smiled at Tess. She had a great smile.

"Listen…"

"Uh-oh, that sounds serious." Garet's smile faded.

"No, it's not, or maybe it is." She was digging a hole for herself. "My mom offered to babysit Saturday and I just thought it might be good if we got together. You know, just the two of us."

"Sure." Garet's expression brightened.

"I mean, to talk."

"Oh, right…talking is good." But Garet's disappointment was obvious.

"What happened yesterday…"

"Yes?"

"That was very out of character for me, and I didn't want it to make things uncomfortable at work."

"Yeah, I totally understand."

"So, we're okay, right?"

"Oh, yes, absolutely." Was Garet upset? Garet seemed upset. "Well, I should get going. I've got some illustration work to catch up on."

"Your second job."

"Exactly." Garet smiled thinly. "Those pages don't draw themselves."

Tess watched Garet walk away. She lingered in the quiet for a moment. Somehow, the conversation left her with a deep sadness she hadn't expected. Garet had acted as if she'd been given the brush-off, but that hadn't been Tess's intention at all. Or was it? Had she become so practiced at avoiding romantic entanglements that she gave off that vibe without even meaning to? Well, at least there was a plan for them to get together Saturday. She could explain things better then. She had an entire week to figure out what she wanted to say.

CHAPTER THIRTY

Garet checked with the two students currently working on trees. She added a bit of brown to the plastic tub between them. One-ply plywood elements of different scenes were strewn all over the end of the parking lot farthest from the building. The shop class had followed her drawings really well. She'd done a schematic on grid paper for the Emerald City, the apple orchard where the travelers got pelted by talking trees, the corner of the house that fell from the sky, and of course, the yellow brick road winding through rolling hills of poppies. The backdrop area of the parking lot was roped off using sawhorses to ensure no one accidentally drove over one of the masterpieces in progress. Each section lay on the concrete, with details marked using a super fat Sharpie marker. Now came the fun part—painting the colors.

The scale of the backgrounds was larger than anything Garet normally worked on, which made the entire project a bit of an adventure. She was figuring everything out the same as the kids.

"Hey, Anthony, try and get some of the green on the leaves instead of the black top." Luckily, they were using water based acrylic paint so not too much damage could happen…she hoped.

She was slowly making the rounds, visiting each station to make sure everyone had enough paint, and mostly to make sure everyone was having fun.

The last backdrop she checked on was the one she'd been painting with June, the yellow brick road.

"Whoa, what happened to the road?" Garet studied the meandering trail of yellow.

"It was too straight." June was on her knees in an area of fresh paint. She talked with her hand, the one holding the brush, and little dollops of yellow paint flew everywhere. "Going straight is no fun."

"Yeah, I get that." Garet smothered a laugh. "Maybe you should put the brush down while we discuss this." She gently took the sloppy, dripping brush from June's hand and dropped it into the water bucket.

"You don't like it?" June stood beside her looking down at the chaotic masterpiece.

"Oh, yes, I like it." Garet pondered how best to redirect June's artistic enthusiasm. "I mean, I love it, but the yellow brick road probably shouldn't be so curvy that no one can follow it. Do you know what I mean?"

"Yeah…maybe I put in too many turns." June rubbed her forehead, leaving a big swath of yellow paint.

"Here's the good news." Garet rested her hand on June's shoulder. "Yellow is a light color so if we let this dry for a few minutes we can go over it with dark green and take out a few of the switchbacks."

"What's a switchback?"

"See those? Where the road doubles back on itself? Those are called switchbacks."

"Oh."

"Want to help me mix some green while we wait?"

June nodded. Garet picked up a blue canister to stir into some of the yellow in a separate plastic container.

"See, if we put less blue the green is bright and if we add more blue it gets darker."

"Can I do it?" June's eyes widened.

"Sure. Hold it right here." She tried to assist June so that some of the blue actually ended up in the tub, but she was only partially successful. A bit of blue splashed on Garet's sneakers. Oh well, she was due for a new pair anyway.

"Sorry!" June was worried by her mistake.

"It's okay." Garet smiled. "These Chucks look so worn out that I think a splash of blue actually improves them."

June grinned, showing the gap between her teeth.

Garet demonstrated how to stir the colors together.

"Okay, you mix this really well while I go check on the others. And when I come back we'll paint some grass."

❖

Tess clapped her hands and approached the stage.

"That was great. Let's do that number one more time from the top." She turned her focus to Gail, seated at the upright piano. "Do you have time for one more run through?"

Gail nodded.

Gail normally taught tenth grade, but she was also the pianist at her church and loved helping Tess with the music for the fall play each year. Tess couldn't imagine trying to play piano herself and direct the kids at the same time.

Tess took a seat near the center of the tenth row. The auditorium seated about two-hundred and had decent acoustics. The wooden folding seats weren't the most comfortable, but the space was definitely serviceable for a school production.

Strains of "If I Only Had the Nerve" filled the air, and she couldn't help smiling. Was she the cowardly lion in this scenario? Possibly. She found that she was equal parts drawn to Garet and afraid to get too close at the same time. Maybe it had been too long since she'd dated anyone. So long that she'd forgotten how it all worked. Was she supposed to be aloof? Or was it better to seem eager? That didn't feel right.

Dating didn't used to be so complicated. Did it?

Wait, she'd thought the word *dating*. Was that what they were doing? Or more accurately, not doing. They'd been tiptoeing around each other all week. She was afraid to say too much and clearly, so was Garet. They talked about school and the students and the production. They talked about everything except the kiss. Maybe the kiss had been a fluke. She'd been the one to initiate the kiss, and now she was unsure if Garet had kissed her back.

Stop thinking that way. Of course, Garet kissed her back. That's how they ended up groping each other like hormonal adolescents on the sofa, right before June came downstairs. Tess covered her face and shook her head. That was too close for comfort.

Her phone buzzed in her pocket just as the last refrain concluded. She stood and glanced at her phone as she walked toward the stage.

The text from Garet read, *How's it going in there? I think we need you outside.*

Wrapping up now. I'll be right out.

"That's enough for today. Thanks, everyone, you're doing a great job." Tess stood near the stage. "This will be the last group rehearsal for this week. Please practice learning your parts of the songs over the weekend so we can pick up with everything next week."

"When do we get to start practicing with the sets?" Lucinda, cast to play Dorothy, was taking the production very seriously.

"We'll have the sets in place by the end of next week." Tess clapped her hands. "Great work! This year's show is going to be a hit."

"Do you need me tomorrow?" Gail was packing up her sheet music. The piano was on the main level, near the first row, close to the stage.

"No. Thanks, Gail. I'm going to let the kids have tomorrow off." It was hard enough to get them to focus on regular days, but on Friday everyone was too distracted by the end of the week.

"Sounds good." Gail smiled and shouldered her oversized purse. "I'll plan to be here Monday then."

Tess texted Garet that she was on her way. She waited for the last of the students to exit and then turned the lights off and closed the double doors. She dropped her phone in her bag and was looking for her keys so she didn't see Garet and June until she was right on top of them.

Tess blinked at the sight that greeted her on the breezeway.

June looked as if she'd gotten in a fight with a bucket of yellow paint and lost. There were splotches of green too, but yellow was everywhere. Clumps of paint were in her hair, across her face, on her clothes, even her red rubber boots hadn't come through unscathed.

"We had a little trouble with the yellow brick road." Garet smiled sheepishly, her hand rested on June's shoulder.

"It looks amazing!" June's face lit up with a broad toothless grin.

Tess started laughing and then they were all laughing. And the laughter felt good.

CHAPTER THIRTY-ONE

Garet swept her fingers through her hair one more time as she checked her look in the mirror. She'd gotten just the right amount of controlled messiness with the gel, so that her hair was stylish without looking forced. For a moment she'd even considered ironing the front of her favorite blue flannel shirt where it'd gotten all scrunched in the dryer, but that seemed like overkill. This was a casual get-together-to-talk sort of outing. Trying too hard only meant she was getting her hopes up, inevitably to be dashed over dinner. She schooled herself and tried to lower her expectations.

Rather than eat at a restaurant in Shadetree, Tess had suggested they take a picnic somewhere. Garet assumed Tess's strategy was to avoid small town, nosy patrons, and she was on board with that plan. There were only two real options for dinner in town, and inevitably both would be crowded with locals on a Saturday evening.

Tess had offered to pick her up, said she had a nice spot in mind.

Garet watched at the window for Tess's car. This was to be more of a late lunch than dinner, or perhaps could be considered an early-bird dinner. By Garet's calculations, unless they were driving far, they'd probably eat around six. Was Tess nervous to be out after dark? If they were back before dark did that make it less of a date?

She'd been so anxious for Saturday to arrive that she'd worried that the days would drag, but instead, the week had zipped past. Between classes, painting backdrops after school, and working on her illustrations at night, there'd been hardly any time left to lag. That was a good thing, considering every moment her brain was free to roam on its own, it returned to thoughts of Tess.

The light green Subaru turned into the driveway, and Garet grabbed her denim jacket and a small messenger bag containing an extra sweater and a bottle of wine. The temp all day had been mild, but autumn weather could shift if the wind picked up so an extra layer seemed like a good idea. She hadn't asked Tess about the wine, but it was bad form to allow Tess to bring everything for their outing.

"Hey." Garet spoke through the open passenger door before climbing in.

"Hi." Tess waited for her to fasten her seat belt before backing out.

Hildy waved from the front yard as they turned onto the main road. So much for secret getaways.

"Seems like perfect weather for a picnic." A comment about the weather. The ultimate in boring small talk. "Where are we going?"

Tess was heading away from town to the north. Garet hadn't really explored much outside of Shadetree.

"There's this spot along the river that I like. Only locals know about it." Tess turned to her and smiled. "It's not far."

Tess was wearing a green crew neck sweater over a T-shirt and jeans. Casual picnic attire, which made Garet feel better about not ironing her flannel shirt.

True to her word, Tess turned on a side road less then fifteen minutes after leaving Garet's place. Tess parked in a turnout alongside the gravel road. Nothing marked this place except what looked like a deer trail near where they'd parked. Tess reached for a basket, but Garet stopped her.

"Hey, let me get that." Garet put the strap of her own bag over her head so that the strap cut across her chest.

She was feeling so strangely aware of every little thing. She wanted to be chivalrous, but not too chivalrous. There was a cushion of space between them that neither had breached until she reached for the handle of the basket and their fingers touched. For Garet, the brief contact was like a match strike. She was too warm and had the urge to lose the flannel shirt and wear only the T-shirt she had on underneath. She took a deep breath and tried to relax.

Tess started down the narrow wooded path and Garet followed. After a few moments, it opened onto a small clearing next to the river. A collection of huge granite boulders formed a natural dam that caused the river to slow, creating a rather large pond.

"This is a great swimming hole in the summer." Tess unrolled a quilt that looked handmade and motioned for Garet to sit down. "When the weather is warm this spot is packed."

"I'll bet." Garet set the basket on the quilt between them.

Leaves rustled overhead as if to call attention to their vibrant color. Yellow poplars and red oaks blended together in a beautiful autumn display. In contrast, the tree trunks seemed grayer without the green to pull forth the usual brown highlights of the bark. And then there was the air. Garet believed each season had a particular smell and fall was her favorite. There was a crispness, a clarity that existed once humidity traveled south for the winter.

"What are you thinking about?" Tess's voice was like a caress.

"The way the air smells."

"I always notice that too." Tess was serving food onto two plates. "I hope you like what I brought. I apologize for not checking with you first."

"I'm sure I'll love whatever you have. I mean, I'm sure I'll like it." They made eye contact as she accepted the offered plate. Green was a good color for Tess. It brought out the little flecks of amber in her irises.

Tess had made finger sandwiches and potato salad, with garnishes of olives and almonds to choose from. There was also a small platter of different cheeses along with an assortment of crackers. There was one covered dish left in the basket, possibly dessert. The first sandwich was ham. She consumed it in two bites, and then remembered the wine. She opened up the flap of her messenger bag and searched for the bottle opener, then held up the wine in Tess's direction.

"I brought this in case we wanted to open it." But there was only one problem. "Although, I just realized I forgot to bring glasses."

"I have some." Tess held up two plastic cups. "I brought them for water, but we can use them for wine instead."

"Perfect."

Tess watched Garet open the wine. She couldn't help focusing on Garet's hands as she worked the cork free from the bottle. Her mouth was suddenly as dry as the desert. Maybe wine was a dangerous idea. But it was too late to turn back now.

"I haven't had this one before, but I'm a sucker for a good label design." Garet poured the red wine with a playful expression.

Tess sipped. It was very nice with the cheese. She let it sit on her tongue before swallowing, savoring the breadth of the flavor.

"I think the backdrops are coming along nicely." Garet sampled the wine. "A few of the kids have potential as artists. You've got some good performers too. I snuck into the auditorium one day and watched a bit of the rehearsal."

"You did? I didn't see you."

"That means my stealth skills are improving." Garet's lips were slightly redder from the wine, making them look highly kissable.

"What?"

"Nothing." Tess returned her attention to the river.

She'd told Garet that they should talk and now that they were here, that was the last thing she wanted to do. To her credit, Garet hadn't pressed for anything. She'd been friendly and professional and not the least bit flirtatious all week. So much so that Tess wondered if getting interrupted by June during their big make out session a week earlier had completely scared her off. Frankly, Garet's polite distance was beginning to make her crazy. She hugged her knees to her chest and watched the slow swirl of the water; the cool blue gray of the October sky had strokes of orange from the late afternoon sun reflected on its gently rippled surface.

"Garet, I know I said I wanted to get together and talk, but to be honest, I don't know what to say." She didn't look at Garet.

"Yeah, I know that feeling well." Garet was braced against one arm, with her long legs out in front of her. "Sometimes talking is overrated." She took a sip of her wine.

Tess had brought more food than they could possibly eat. Garet's half-finished plate was on the quilt next to her and Tess had barely touched her food. Something about Garet's nearness was chasing her appetite away. A risky scenario given how good the wine tasted.

Was it possible for someone to make you feel excited and soothed at the same time? Because that's how she'd been feeling all week around Garet.

To top off everything else, she'd chosen the *most* unsexy outfit for their outing and now, regretted it.

"I'm not sure what I thought would happen when we came out here." Tess placed her palm on her forehead and closed her eyes.

"I tried not to think about it." Garet's lips were suddenly very close to her ear. "I didn't want to get my hopes up." She brushed Tess's hair aside and lightly kissed her neck. "Is this okay?"

The whispered question drew Tess back from wherever she'd gone. She moaned softly and nodded. Garet kissed her neck again and chills raced down her arm. So much for talking. Tess rotated so that they faced each other. Garet kissed her, slowly at first, but then passionately. She allowed Garet to invade her personal space. Garet braced with one arm as she lowered Tess to the quilt. Garet's hand slid up the front of her sweater and lingered over her breast. Tess wrapped her arms around Garet's neck. Garet's leg was between hers now and Garet was partially on top of her, although still supporting her weight on one elbow.

Garet stopped kissing her and nuzzled her neck. Garet was so warm and she smelled delicious and Tess wanted to just give in to it all. But Garet seemed cautious. Garet brushed the back of her fingers tenderly along the contour of Tess's cheek. Tess pressed Garet's fingers to her lips and kissed them. Then she sucked two of Garet's fingers into her mouth, swirling her tongue around them. Garet's expression darkened and her cheeks flamed. Garet slowly withdrew her fingers and set upon Tess with intensity. Garet's full weight was on top of her as Garet applied pressure using her thigh between Tess's legs as Garet kissed her deeply, passionately. She arched against Garet, whose hand was inside her sweater moving upward.

"Wait." Tess broke the kiss. "Stop." She was breathless and the words came out raspy.

"I'm sorry." Garet raised up, pulling away. "I'm sorry, I just thought—"

"No, it's not that." Tess reached for Garet's hand. "I want you, I mean, I want this." Tess sat up. "I'm… I feel too out in the open here. Can we go somewhere?"

"Yes, I'd like that." Garet visibly relaxed.

"Can we go to your place?" She wasn't sure she wanted to be at her house. Even if intellectually she knew June wasn't going to come home and surprise them, there was evidence of June everywhere. For this one night, Tess wanted to be out of her element. In some strange way she hoped a different environment would help her focus on figuring out how she truly felt about exploring a dating scenario with Garet. At least, that was her hope.

CHAPTER THIRTY-TWO

Garet's body hummed, practically vibrated, in the passenger seat as Tess drove back to town. The picnic had been quickly relocated to the tiny kitchen in the cottage. The basket of food had been abandoned on the counter near the sink, the only open space away from her drawing board. Tess was standing in the living room, which technically was still part of the kitchen. She looked nervous, or possibly unsure.

"Sorry, this is all the glassware I have." Garet handed her wine in a coffee cup.

"This is totally fine."

"Are you talking about my glassware...or being here?"

"I'm not sure." Tess sampled her drink.

"Do you want to sit down?"

"Maybe." Tess smiled. "Sorry, is my unease making you uncomfortable?"

"No, I just want you to be okay." She took the cup from Tess's hand and set it next to hers on the coffee table. "Come here." She drew Tess close and held her.

"This feels good." Tess's words were muffled against her shoulder.

"Tess, we don't have to do anything tonight. We don't even have to talk. I'm happy simply getting a chance to be close to you like this." She closed her eyes when she sensed Tess relax against her. "Being near you but not with you this whole week was making me crazy."

"Me too."

"You hide it well." Garet laughed softly.

"So do you." Tess angled her face up and kissed Garet lightly. "Let's stop hiding for a little while."

"Okay."

Tess unfastened the buttons of Garet's shirt and started kissing her neck. Tess's exploration was tentative, measured, and Garet stood quietly, with her palms resting on Tess's hips, unmoving, even though a fire was beginning to roar deep down inside.

"I haven't done this...been with anyone in a long time." Tess slipped her hands inside Garet's shirt and slid it off her shoulders and down her arms.

Tess slid her fingers up Garet's exposed arms until she reached the short sleeves of her undershirt. All the tiny hairs along the way stood at attention. She wasn't sure what her response should be to Tess's confession, so she didn't say anything.

"Would you mind taking the lead?" Tess met her gaze.

What did Tess mean by that? Garet needed to be sure.

"I'll take the lead wherever you want this to go." She caressed Tess's face.

"How about the bedroom?"

"Really?" Garet was worried this was all a dream and at any moment she'd jolt awake and Tess would be gone, a figment of her overactive imagination.

"Yes, really." Tess drew her down until their lips met.

The signals all week from Tess put space between them, but this was a different Tess. The way Tess moved her body against Garet's signaled that things were about to head in a very unexpected direction. Garet broke the kiss, grasped Tess's hand, and led her toward the bed.

"I'm sorry it's a little messy in here." She hadn't expected company. The disheveled sheets were a rumpled mess. She made a swift move to toss them aside.

Tess lifted the hem of her sweater to pull it over her head and Garet helped. Tess's hair crackled with static and they both laughed. The form-fitting T-shirt was next, leaving Tess facing Garet in only her bra and jeans. Tess began to unfasten the button of her jeans, but Garet stopped her.

"I want to do that."

Tess blushed and averted her eyes. She tried to tame her hair by smoothing it with her hands. Garet swept her T-shirt off, her jog bra followed, and then she stepped closer to Tess. The light in the room was dim and growing dark as the sun sank beneath the western ridge, but she didn't mind. Garet almost preferred feeling her way through things. Besides, there was enough ambient light from the living room to highlight the curve of Tess's breasts and the soft roundness of her stomach at the top of her jeans. Tess had a beautiful body.

She tenderly kissed Tess's shoulders as she worked to release the fasteners of the bra. Garet slid the straps down Tess's arms and let the satin garment fall to the floor. Tess's nipples grazed hers as they kissed, turning up the flame that was already beginning to rage.

Tess closed her eyes for a moment, savoring Garet's closeness. When she opened them Garet was kneeling in front of her. Garet feathered kisses across her stomach as she tugged Tess's jeans over her hips and off. She'd lost her shoes somewhere between the living room and the bedroom and couldn't have pinpointed when exactly she'd lost them. Garet moved to the bed and Tess followed. She snuggled close to Garet, resting her head in the little hollow space of Garet's shoulder.

She was wearing only her panties but she wasn't cold. Garet's chest against hers was warm, flushed. Garet was barefoot and still in her faded jeans with the top button teasingly undone.

Garet shifted, hovered above her as if she was strategizing her next move.

Tess had not dressed for sex. She'd worn a wool pullover and everyday panties, not the sexy underwear you'd choose for a first encounter. Her brain and her subconscious were clearly at odds with each other. She had not in any way mentally prepared herself for sex with Garet, yet here she was.

She squeezed her eyes shut when she felt Garet's fingers slip beneath the elastic of her underwear and slide them slowly off. Garet's breath, her lips, were warm against Tess's skin. She shivered, not from cold, but rather anticipation.

"You're cold." Garet covered Tess's body with hers.

"No, I'm warm." The fabric of Garet's jeans brushed her sex, and electricity shot through her core.

Garet rolled off her and shucked out of her pants and boxer shorts. Tess savored the view. Garet's body was lean, but solid. The muscles in her stomach tightened as she took Garet in. Her shoulders were broad and her slender arms flexed with toned muscle. She would have stared at Garet's nude form all night, but Garet was on top of her again, insinuating her hips between Tess's legs. She relaxed and opened herself to Garet. If she was going to do this, if she was truly going to allow this to happen, then she wasn't going to hold back.

Garet explored the contours of her body with her mouth and hands. Tess was on fire. Garet was going to make her come and all they'd done so far was kiss.

Garet had avoided the place between her legs with deliberate precision, which made her ache even more to be touched there.

Garet sucked and teased her nipple, holding it for an instant between her teeth. Then Garet kissed her, deeply. She was practically in a trance, under Garet's spell, the thrall of her gifted touch.

"Is this still okay?" Garet searched her face for the answer.

"Yes…"

"What about this?"

Garet's fingers were between her legs, stroking, teasingly tormenting her.

"That's good too." Her response was breathy as she fought for air.

"Tess, you're so beautiful." Garet slipped her fingers inside. "I've wanted to make love to you…tell me if this feels…"

"That's good…Don't stop." She dug her fingers into Garet's ass as Garet pumped inside her.

She wasn't even sure how Garet was doing what she was doing. Somehow, she was inside and at the same time stroking her clit with her thumb, and she was coming undone. She rocked beneath Garet, with only one crystalized thought: *more.* That precipice she'd been so worried would drop away was crumbling beneath her. She was careening over the razor-sharp edge of it with only one thing to hold on to: Garet.

Every muscle in her body contracted, and she clung to Garet so tightly she feared Garet might not be able to breathe. Garet held her until the tremors subsided. Her head dropped to the pillow, her forehead damp with sweat. Her bones seemed to have lost the ability to support her limbs. A blissful daze washed over her.

Garet was propped on one elbow beside her. Garet's lips caressed her shoulder. At some point Garet tugged the blanket over them, although Tess had no sense of being cold.

Tess had the most serene expression. Moonlight seeped in through a gap in the drapes casting the room in a cool blue hue. She wondered if Tess was asleep. Her breathing was so deep and slow and her body pressed against Garet's was so relaxed. She rested her palm on the slight curve of Tess's lower stomach, that sexy contour of a woman's body just above the dark curls. In her opinion one of the sexiest parts of female anatomy. But this wasn't just any woman lying beside her, this was Tess. Garet took a moment to examine the weight of that.

She hadn't come when they made love and she didn't mind. Pleasing Tess had been her sole focus. Garet was sure that Tess rarely put her needs first. She wanted to upend that paradigm so she'd completely focused on reading every subtle signal from Tess's body, which was the stuff of fantasy—supple and responsive and gorgeous.

Beside her, Tess stirred. She turned and smiled without opening her eyes.

"Hi." Tess angled just enough to kiss her.

"Hi." Tess's grin was contagious. The place between her legs ached. She was getting turned on lying next to Tess—the warmth of her skin, the curve of her hip against Garet's center.

"You're pretty good at this." Tess pressed Garet's fingers to her mouth and kissed them.

"I'm glad you think so." Tess had no idea how sexy she was, which made her even more alluring. Garet fought the urge to roll on top of her and take her again.

"I'm sorry I dropped off there." Tess adjusted on the pillow to make eye contact. "I didn't want you to think that I'd fallen asleep. I just needed a minute." Tess draped her leg across Garet and then caressed the center of Garet's chest with her fingertips. "I feel like I received all the attention and now it's your turn."

Just the suggestion of making love again made her insides twitch and contract, until Garet thought she might climax without Tess even touching her.

"What would feel good to you?" Tess's question was barely more than a whisper.

Garet rolled on top of Tess. She guided Tess's fingers until Tess slid them inside. Garet inhaled sharply, closing her eyes for a few seconds to savor the sensation of Tess's fingers inside. She braced on one arm and held Tess's thigh against her ribs. She kissed Tess as she slowly rode Tess's hand and when she was very close, slid her fingers into Tess. They were inside each other now, an infinite loop of intimate contact. She pressed into Tess, moving on top of her. The orgasm was rising higher, drawing closer, with every rocking motion. Tess gripped her shoulder, she sensed they were climbing together but it was hard to pinpoint Tess's arousal as her own climax took hold.

She'd never been so attracted to someone and cared about them so much at the same time. These two realizations combined into an intoxicating cocktail and she was drunk on it. She could no longer discern where her body stopped and Tess's started, where her need ended and Tess's began.

Her body tensed, every fiber of every muscle taut and straining. She pressed her open mouth into the pillow and it swallowed her cry. Her arms trembled. She sank on top of Tess with her full weight. Garet's mind was fuzzy, her senses spinning.

"Are you okay?" Tess tenderly kissed her cheek.

Unable to speak, all she could do was nod. She'd never experienced anything as intense and wasn't sure what that meant, except that she was in real trouble. Just looking at Tess's sweet face made her heart hurt.

She kissed Tess, and then drew her close until Tess settled her head on Garet's shoulder.

Garet stared at the ceiling. She had no sense of her own body or of space or time. All she knew was that Tess was with her. Out of nowhere, a deep longing threatened to pull her under. She fought against it, encircling the warmth of Tess's body in her arms.

CHAPTER THIRTY-THREE

Tess woke feeling too warm and thirsty and, for a split second, confused by her surroundings. The room was dark. She was unsure of the time. Garet was asleep beside her. Her stomach did a summersault at the sight of Garet's bare shoulder and back, exposed above the covering. Garet was on her side, facing away from Tess.

They'd made love. She'd had sex with Garet.

Breathe, just breathe.

June was with her grandmother, she and Garet were adults, and everything was fine.

Everything is fine.

She formed the thought a second time to convince herself. Having no other confirmation that this was actually the case. Tess sat up and swept her fingers through her hair. She'd fallen asleep, naked, in Garet's arms. A very pleasant position to be in, but then the far too familiar sense of guilt crept into her thoughts. She'd left June with her grandmother to have sex with Garet. Had her subconscious known all along that this was her agenda?

Tess quietly left the bed and searched in the dark for clothing. Garet's discarded flannel shirt seemed the coziest choice. She partially buttoned it and walked to the kitchen. The shirt was obviously a favorite of Garet's. The fabric had been washed and worn to the point of ultimate softness.

Luckily, a lamp in the living room had been left on so she wasn't searching for a light switch in utter darkness. She checked the fridge for something cold and discovered a bottle of sparkling water. She was about to drink directly from the bottle but stopped herself. Had she regressed to college dorm life after one romp in bed? She took a glass from the dish drainer near the sink and filled it.

She leaned against the counter's edge and sipped. She realized that Garet had drawings and sketches strewn all over the adjacent countertop. Curiosity got the better of her and she rounded the island to take a closer look. There were rough character sketches and other typed pages with story notes. Taped to the slant board was a heavier illustration board with the beginnings of a finished ink drawing. This was like getting a glimpse behind the wizard's green velvet curtain to witness the magic firsthand.

After a few more minutes, she returned to bed. She tried to slip under the covers as stealthily as possible, but Garet stirred, rolling over onto her back, rubbing her eyes.

"What time is it?" Garet covered a yawn with her hand.

"I'm not sure. Late, I think." Garet's small breasts and her long torso were on full display as moonlight cut a swath across where she lay. Tess tried not to stare. "I was thirsty so I got up and served myself. I hope you don't mind."

Garet reached for the glass and took a few sips.

"Thank you."

Tess set the nearly empty glass on the bedside table and snuggled down next to Garet. Garet's arm was beneath Tess's head with her forearm draped across Tess's shoulder. Tess held Garet's hand in hers, entwining their fingers.

"I hope you won't judge me, because I'm not the sort of woman who usually has sex on a first date."

Garet grinned and rotated to kiss her temple.

"Well, first off, the judge's score is in and you ranked very high."

Tess swatted at Garet, landing a soft blow to her leg beneath the blanket.

"And secondly, I don't think this was a first date."

"Oh, really?" Tess wasn't so sure.

"By my count this is like our fourth date."

"Not that I question your math, but I'd like to hear exactly how you came up with that number." Tess released Garet's hand and rolled onto her side, draping her arm across Garet's midsection.

"Twice we had dinner at your house to watch the movie, that's two…and then the hot chocolate day…that's three."

"Oh, I forgot to give you your jeans back." Tess had been so distracted by picnic preparations that she'd neglected to bring them.

"Tonight, makes four." Garet sounded very satisfied with her reasoning.

"I'm feeling better already." She squeezed Garet lightly. "Okay, just so we're clear, I'm also not the sort of girl who has sex on a fourth date either."

Garet laughed. A genuine laugh. The kind of laugh that warmed the room, the kind of laugh that she knew could chase shadows away and lift your heart when you needed to be lifted.

They lay quietly for a few moments. Garet stroked her hair softly and she rested her palm at the center of Garet's chest.

"I couldn't help noticing your drawings in the kitchen. They are really beautiful."

"Thank you."

"How do you write your stories?"

Garet didn't answer right away.

"I've always believed that stories were found rather than written."

"I'm not sure you can tell such good stories without feeling much more than you reveal, Garet Allen." Tess was moved by Garet's modesty, but knew that there was a depth to Garet she hadn't quite reached. That would likely take more than four dates.

Garet started. "Oh, I just realized how late it is. You probably need to get home to June."

"June is staying all night with her grandmother." Tess found Garet's concern endearing, but misplaced. "If June were at home I'd have left hours ago."

"Oh, yeah…Right." Garet relaxed again.

"She actually won't be home until early afternoon because we're playing at the café tomorrow."

"Wow, is it the third Sunday already?"

"Yes." Tess raised up on one elbow so that she could see Garet's face. "Will you come listen to us play?"

"Absolutely." Garet kissed her.

Tess sank back to Garet's shoulder. After a little while, the slow rise and fall of Garet's chest told Tess that she was asleep. Tess's body fairly tingled, despite her effort to drift off. She knew sleep would elude her. This was all too real and too scary. This might be more than she had expected to feel about someone she barely knew.

❖

Garet handed Tess a cup of coffee as she stepped from the bathroom. Tess was dressed and about to leave, but Garet wasn't quite ready to give her up. She knew they'd meet at the café shortly, but still, morning-after nervousness was something to savor over breakfast, or at the very least, coffee.

"Thank you, this will help." Tess held the cup with both hands and sipped.

"You don't have to leave right away do you?" Garet leaned against the fridge.

"Actually, I should go home and shower and maybe run through a couple of the songs before I need to be at the café." Tess downed half the coffee and put the mug in the sink. "And maybe it'd be good if my car wasn't parked in your driveway while everyone is driving past on their way to church."

"Sorry, I didn't even think of that." Garet had momentarily forgotten the hazards of living in a small town and trying to have a private life.

"I'll see you soon." Tess kissed her sweetly, gathered her purse, the basket, and walked to the door. She turned at the last moment. "Garet?"

"Yes?"

"Last night was perfect."

"Yeah, it was." Her stomach knotted at the thought of it. "Hey, Tess?"

With her hair just a little mussed and her cheeks flushed, Tess looked even more beautiful if that was possible. She paused with her hand on the door.

"If you need to *talk* again, you know, just let me know."

Tess laughed. "Thanks, I'll keep that in mind."

And then Tess was gone. The cottage seemed emptier than before. She stood at the window and sipped her coffee, watching Tess drive away. She needed to shower and change. It seemed she wasn't going to do much work today. It was just as well that she'd gotten a little ahead of schedule because there was no way she'd be able to focus on anything today but Tess.

Garet picked up her phone and flopped on the couch to check headlines while she waited for the caffeine to kick in. As she scrolled, a text came through from Lane asking how the evening with Tess had gone. She wasn't quite ready to talk to anyone about what had happened the previous night, not even Lane.

Garet set her phone aside and headed for the shower.

CHAPTER THIRTY-FOUR

Mark already had the amps set up by the time Tess arrived at the café. She'd done her best to get ready quickly, but she found that her mind kept wandering. She couldn't seem to stay on task. The shower felt too good and she'd lingered until the hot water gave out. The sensitivity of her skin was heightened, and it tingled from Garet's remembered touch. If she hadn't already committed to play at the café she'd probably still be in bed with Garet.

She focused on preparation. Tess stowed the case at the back of the small stage. The guys in the band bantered about their various Saturday night adventures, but she didn't join in. Her evening was something she didn't want to share. Especially not with a bunch of guys she'd known since high school.

Her instrument was finicky this morning and she struggled to tune it. Mandolins were fussy instruments in general, and she was clearly having a hard time focusing. As she tuned the mandolin, she kept glancing up hoping to see Garet. Finally, she saw Garet at the door waiting to be seated. She waved and a huge smile lit up Garet's face. Just the sight of Garet caused butterflies to swarm in her stomach.

"Do I know her? She looks familiar." Mark looked up just in time to notice her waving.

"She's filling in for Charlotte. She came by the shop one day." Tess tried to sound nonchalant but feared that she'd failed. Mark knew her too well. He cocked an eyebrow as if to ask, *and what else*? "I'll introduce you." She shook her head and grinned.

They played at the café once a month. These were the guys she'd performed with since they were teenagers. She shouldn't have been nervous at all, but today she felt even more vulnerable than usual on stage, as if Garet could see past all her defenses, as if Garet could see everything about her. Not for the first time, she was grateful that all she had to do was focus on her mandolin. If she'd had to sing, her voice would have given too much away.

Garet took a table one row back from the stage and didn't try to hide the fact that she was completely focused on Tess. Every time they locked gazes the entire room dropped away. Tess had moments where she felt lightheaded, and at one point, sat for one song on a stool, rather than standing. Sitting down helped ground her.

Garet was wearing the same gray hoodie she'd worn the first day they'd met. Under the hoodie she had on a rumpled white oxford shirt, with paint splattered jeans. Garet was so damn good-looking. And she was so casual about it, as if she was unaware of how attractive she was, which only served to turn up the volume on Tess's infatuation.

Mark was crooning their arrangement of "At Last," by Etta James. The song made Tess want to leave the stage and slow dance with Garet in front of God and everyone else. She closed her eyes and allowed her imagination to go there instead. With her eyes closed, sensations of Garet's hands on her body threatened to overwhelm her. She opened her eyes and stared at the floor for a moment to get her head in the right space.

How was any of this going to work?

How would she share a classroom with Garet after the way they'd been with each other? She couldn't unknow the weight of Garet's body covering hers. Or the way Garet's lips felt on her skin, her tongue, and her strong fingers. Tess listed off the things she would be unable to forget and possibly unable to get over.

And the worst part was, she wanted all of it and more.

Garet could hardly take her eyes off Tess. There was some sort of transformation that happened when Tess played music. She was already beautiful, but when she played it was as if she practically glowed. It was as if another dimension of Tess's personality rose to the surface. No, that wasn't quite right. It was more that her smile became more brilliant, her expression radiant. It was joy, that's what it was. When Tess played music, joy was the by-product. Her love of the instrument, her friendship with the other musicians on stage, and the energy she shared with the audience, it was all magnetic. If you saw Tess play music you'd want to know her, you'd want to be granted access to her inner circle.

Garet had the strongest urge to rush the stage and sweep Tess up into her arms. She wanted to spend the afternoon in bed, and the night, and the next morning. She'd never been so completely and utterly captivated by someone before. There was a risk that she might lose control of her feelings altogether. They were running way out in front of her brain, refusing to listen to any sound reasoning about the reality of the situation. There was another person involved in this equation, a person Garet genuinely cared about—June.

"Okay, hon, here ya go." Candi blocked her view for a minute as she delivered Garet's breakfast order.

"Thank you." Garet was starving. All she'd had was coffee.

"I guess I know why you're here this morning." Candi winked. "Don't worry, your secret is safe with me." She touched Garet's shoulder as she left the table.

Candi was on to her. First the pizza takeout and the call from Tess about a lemonade for June. Now she was here going all fangirl over Tess. And hadn't she declared not so long ago that she didn't even care for bluegrass? Oh, how the mighty had fallen.

Tess laughed at something the lead singer said and touched his arm. The band was taking a break and the guy followed her to the table. Garet recognized him from the music store. She abandoned her scrambled eggs and stood as they approached.

"Hi, Garet." Tess's hand was on the guy's shoulder. "I wanted to introduce you to my good friend Mark. You met him briefly at the music store, which he actually owns."

"Hi." Mark extended his hand and Garet shook it.

"Nice to meet you." Garet motioned to the empty chairs at her table. "Would you guys like to join me?"

"Thanks, but my wife is over there." He glanced toward a table near the windows. "But, thanks. And it was nice to see you again, Garet."

Tess took a seat as he walked away. The café was packed and noisy. The minute the music stopped the volume of random chatter increased. Tess braced on her elbows and leaned forward conspiratorially, offering Garet a tasteful yet tempting view of cleavage. Garet's throat was suddenly dry so she sipped water.

Tess was wearing a skirt and dark leggings with casual winter boots that almost came to her knees. The sweater had a deep V-neck and it looked as if she was wearing a camisole underneath. Tess's hair was up in a top knot, which only served to draw attention to the sensual curve of her elegant neck. Garet tried not to stare, but it was hopeless. She felt like a teenager who'd just discovered that sex with girls was amazing.

"Can I order something for you?"

"No, but maybe I'll steal a piece of your toast."

"Please, help yourself." Garet slid the small side plate piled with sourdough toast across the table. "Would you like some eggs too? The serving sizes here could feed a small army."

"Thank you. I think this is all I need." Tess put a dollop of strawberry preserves on a slice of toast. "For some reason, my appetite is a bit upended this morning."

"I wonder why?" Garet knew she was blushing.

"Are you okay? How are you feeling today, you know, about this?" It was noisy. Garet had to strain to hear Tess.

"I'm great. How are you?" Garet internally cringed. *I'm great. How are you?* Way to woo the woman of your dreams. She was blowing it. "The band sounds really great today…you sound great." She'd just said *great* three times in a row, but it was too late to retract. Why was she so nervous?

"Thank you." Tess took a sip of Garet's water. Sharing toast and water seemed more intimate than usual. "To be honest, I'm having a hard time focusing."

"Yeah, I'm having a hard time focusing too." Every single thing in the world paled in comparison to Tess. "Can I see you later?"

She didn't want to seem needy, but if she didn't get to spend time with Tess, like, soon, Garet thought she might lose it. Getting any drawing done today was going to be nearly hopeless.

"I'll have June."

Tess probably thought that was unappealing in some way, but it wasn't.

"I'd love to see June."

"Sunday nights we make macaroni and cheese for dinner. Would you like to join us?"

"Yes." She was afraid she sounded too eager, but she couldn't help it.

"Come over around five then. And listen, don't feel as if you have to stay for our second set. I know you have your book to finish."

Was she kidding? Garet wasn't leaving, not as long as Tess was performing. It was a certain kind of special treat to have an excuse to sit quietly and stare at Tess for as long as possible. Nope, she wasn't going anywhere.

CHAPTER THIRTY-FIVE

Tess folded a stack of June's tiny shirts and tucked them into the top drawer of her dresser. June was on the floor, surrounded by storybooks. The weather had shifted by early afternoon. A misting rain and a cold wind swept in from the north, keeping June indoors. She was lying on her stomach, kicking her sock covered feet at nothing as she turned the page.

June had been more excited than Tess expected by the news of Garet joining them for dinner. Tess was excited too, although at different times during the day it had been hard to distinguish excitement from fear. Both made her heart race and both feelings seemed appropriate for her current situation. She'd had incredible sex with a woman she couldn't stop thinking about and now she'd invited that woman over to join her and her six-year-old for macaroni and cheese. Now that she completed the thought it seemed completely absurd. Two incongruent worlds were about to collide at the dinner table.

Hadn't she just sat on Charlotte's sofa and gone on and on about how she and June had a perfect bubble and she didn't want to ruin it by adding another person? And then the first, the *very* first, time she was truly alone with Garet she slept with her.

Tess tried to rationalize, to give herself a break for doing something so irrationally impulsive. In her own defense she offered up exhibit A: she'd not had sex in at least four years, maybe five. Her body had been in withdrawal. The situation had been completely outside her control and beyond her ability to say no.

Exhibit B seemed more compelling and believable. Garet was only in Shadetree for another month and a half, maybe less. She was allowed to have a fling with another consenting adult, without proposing marriage or needing a U-Haul in typical lesbian fashion. Garet didn't strike her as the clingy, move-in-immediately type. She felt sure in her assumption that Garet was no more expecting this to turn into some long-term thing than she was. Granted, she'd never ever done a fling, but even more reason to give it a try, right?

So why was she so nervous?

Because deep down she knew Garet touched her in ways no one else had, and not simply in a physical way. It was as if at some point during their lovemaking the previous night a veil had been torn away and she could no longer hide behind it. On some level she suspected Garet knew that too.

Someone knocked at the door. Was it five o'clock already?

"I'll get it!" June launched off the floor and bounded down the stairs. "Mom, Garet is here!" she announced from the entryway.

"June, there's no need to yell." Tess focused on taking one step at a time even though she also had the impulse to bounce down the stairs and into Garet's arms. Instead, she opted for a polite greeting. "Hi, Garet."

"Hello, Tess." Garet's expression communicated so much more than merely hello. "I'm sorry, I think I'm a little early."

"That's no problem." The antique grandfather clock on the mantel said four forty-five. It seemed they were both trying to act reserved in front of June.

"Come on." June tugged at Garet's hand. "I told Mom that you and I could make dinner."

"You did?" Garet arched her eyebrows in surprise, or possibly alarm as she was towed past where Tess stood toward the kitchen.

"We get the box kind. It's easy." June was in charge. "I'll show you."

Garet looked over her shoulder at Tess as if to say, *help*. But how could Tess intervene? June was as excited as she was to see Garet.

"Okay, we need to boil the water first." June clanged pots in the cabinet until she found the one she was looking for.

Garet read the directions on the box out loud and assisted June with measurements. Garet casually leaned against the counter waiting for the water to boil. Tess had prepared a salad ahead of time and took the bowl out of the refrigerator so that she could add tomato slices. She also anticipated the next steps for June and set milk and butter out near the stove. The noodles needed at least ten or twelve minutes to cook which was more downtime than June could tolerate. She ran upstairs to retrieve a book.

"I'm sorry if this is too much. She really wanted you to help her cook." Tess touched Garet's arm. A tingling sensation traveled up her sleeve to the little hairs at the back of her neck from the simple contact between them.

"I'm enjoying this. Really." Garet smiled. "Thank you."

"For what?"

"For letting me come over."

"I—"

"Garet, you can read this to me later, okay?" June burst in. She handed Garet a book she'd authored.

Garet looked over at Tess. She seemed unsure how to respond to June's request.

"June, maybe you should ask Garet politely." She brushed her fingers through June's hair. "And did you know that Garet wrote this book?"

"You did?" June looked from Garet to the book and back with an astonished expression. "Why doesn't it have your name on it?" June furrowed her brows, not ready to accept this new information without proof of some kind.

"Well, it does have my name." Garet took *Marty Moose's Big Day Out* and turned it over. The book had been read at least a thousand times. The corners of some of the pages were bent and the hardcover was worn at the edges. "My middle name is Elizabeth. I just decided to use my middle name for the books."

June's eyes widened and she hopped excitedly, bracing one hand on the counter.

"Hey, I think this is ready to drain so we can add the cheese." Garet set the book aside, turned off the timer, and held on to June as she used a step stool to reach the stovetop.

Tess stood aside as Garet and June took turns adding ingredients. June began stirring, but then needed Garet to take over once the sauce began to thicken. For someone who admitted she had no real experience teaching kids and no children of her own, Garet had an easy rapport with June. She talked to June as a fully formed person, rather than dumbing things down to some false kid level. Tess never talked down to kids and disliked it when others did.

"Now we just need plates." Garet waited for June to respond.

"Up there, but I can't reach them." June pointed at one of the cabinets near Garet.

"Luckily, I can." Garet smiled as she handed the plates to June. "Do you want to hold them?"

"Maybe it's safer to put the plates on the table and then serve from the pot." Tess decided to weigh in before half the cheesy macaroni ended up on the kitchen floor.

"Good call." Garet grinned and followed June and the plates to the table.

❖

"Okay, June Bug...bedtime." June had been sitting at the kitchen table with Garet ever since dinner.

June kept making requests for Garet to draw different animals so that she could color them. Garet's hand must have been getting tired because she'd drawn at least thirty different cartoon figures. Crayons and sheets of white bond paper stolen from the upstairs printer were scattered all over the table.

"Just one more," June whined.

"You said that three drawings ago," Tess gently reminded her.

"Aww...I don't want to go to bed. I'm not sleepy."

When in fact, she was obviously tired, bordering on grumpy. June would run in high gear until that last possible moment and the minute she was in bed doze off immediately. Sometimes she only got half of a book read before June was sound asleep. It helped that she'd read the stories enough to know how they ended. That way June could fall asleep happy without missing out on how the book ended. There was comfort in returning to familiar stories.

"Hey, how about I read that book you wanted to hear." Garet propped her elbows on the edge of the table. "I mean, if that's okay with your mom." Garet glanced over to gauge Tess's reaction.

"Yes!" June reached for Garet's hand.

"Are you sure?" Tess worried that June was taking advantage of Garet's easygoing nature. Or that Garet was being extra nice to June as part of a tactic to win her over. She didn't really believe that. Garet's interest in June seemed sincere. In any case, it was working, Garet was winning her over. Tess was astonished at how quickly Garet had managed to do that.

"I'm sure."

"I'll clean up down here." Tess started to rinse dishes and put them in the dishwasher. She called after them. "June, don't forget to brush your teeth."

Garet waited for June to brush and rinse. Luckily, June had changed into pajamas after dinner in preparation for a lounging Sunday evening, so she was already dressed for bed. Kids were hilarious. June dove under the covers with her stuffed narwhal and expectantly waited for Garet to sit down.

"You can sit right here." June made room by scooting over a little. "That way I can see the pictures while you read."

This kid knew what she wanted and how to ask for it. Garet decided she should take lessons. Something happened to people between kiddom and adulthood. They learned how to mask their feelings. It was so refreshing to be with June. There was no pretense. She liked Garet and had no fear of letting her see that. She was open and trusting, and Garet could easily see why Tess hadn't dated in a while. How could you feel safe sharing your child with someone, while also trying to get to know them yourself? Garet could easily see how complicated and rife with pitfalls that would be. She felt lucky that Tess was sharing June with her, that Tess obviously trusted her enough to allow her to share an exchange as intimate as reading a bedtime story.

June snuggled close, resting her cheek on Garet's upper arm for maximum viewing angle. Something about June's closeness tugged at Garet's heart. She'd never really considered being a parent herself and under normal circumstances thought of children as a curiosity, something she didn't know a lot about from personal experience. But this was nice in a way she hadn't expected.

On one level, she liked June simply because of who she was in the process of becoming. On another level, she cared about June because of how precious she was to Tess. It would be easy for things to get complicated fairly quickly and the last thing in the world she'd want to do would be to upset June in some way.

"Why aren't you reading?"

June's question brought her back from the mental spiral.

"Sorry." Garet adjusted the angle of the book so that she could see it better. "Marty Moose had big plans for a big day out. The only problem was that Marty couldn't drive, partly because he had no thumbs, which made holding the steering wheel very difficult."

June yawned. The bed was cozy and warm, and June was snuggled close. Garet was afraid she was getting sleepy too. She'd pretty much been a bundle of nerves all day, and now that she had a full stomach and was in a lounging position, she realized how tired she was.

"Luckily, Marty's neighbor, Clover, drove a taxi. Clover loved to drive…"

Garet sensed June's body relax next to her. June was asleep and Garet was afraid if she moved she'd wake her up. She quietly closed the book and let it rest on her chest. She'd just lounge for a few more minutes to make sure June was completely asleep before she got up. Closing her eyes felt good. She took a deep cleansing breath and for the first time all day, genuinely relaxed.

CHAPTER THIRTY-SIX

Tess finished cleaning up the kitchen and decided to make a cup of herbal tea for herself and Garet. She poured the hot water and set the tea bags in to steep, but Garet still hadn't come back downstairs. She feared that if she didn't come to her rescue, June might have Garet reading a second story, possibly a third. June was a master of bedtime stall tactics.

When she reached the landing at the top of the steps she paused. No one was talking, which meant, no one was reading. She peeked inside to see that June and Garet were side by side on the bed, asleep. June was under the covers and Garet was on top, but they made a very cozy pair. The bedside lamp was on, but it was a low wattage bulb. The soft glow wouldn't be intrusive if you were already feeling sleepy.

Tess stood in the doorway and allowed her mind to truly take in the scene. Garet and June together like this seemed so normal. The recognition of that caused the knot in her stomach to tighten. June was already obviously getting attached to Garet. They'd been painting backdrops together and now they'd had two weekend coloring sessions. And it was all her fault. She'd let her guard down and let Garet in. She hoped like hell she knew what she was doing.

The important thing was to pay attention and be cautiously aware. She wasn't sure how Garet was feeling about anything, but from her perspective this, whatever this was, came with tremendous risks. Tess took a shaky breath and entered the room.

She put her hand on Garet's leg and squeezed. Her goal was to wake Garet but not June. Garet blinked and looked up, confused about where she was. Tess held her index finger to her lips, a sign for Garet to speak softly or not at all.

Garet glanced over at June, smiled, and nodded. Then she delicately rolled away from June and off the bed. She stretched and yawned. Tess took the storybook from her, switched off the lamp, and ushered Garet to the door.

"I'm sorry." Garet spoke softly once they were on the stairs. "I can't believe I dozed off like that."

"It happens to me sometimes too."

"Yeah, if someone would cuddle and read me a story at night maybe I'd sleep better." Garet grinned mischievously.

"I made us some tea." Tess invited Garet to sit at the kitchen table. She removed the tea bags and set one of the cups in front of Garet.

"Thank you." Garet reached for Tess's hand. The electricity between their joined hands was immediate. "This was a fun night for me. I hope it wasn't too much for you."

"What do you mean?"

"You know, spending last night together and then tonight." Garet sampled the tea. "I really just needed to see you again before we were in a professional setting. Otherwise this whole thing between us would seem like a dream."

"I think I understand what you're saying." Tess wondered if Garet expected to spend the night. She wasn't sure how she felt about that or how she'd respond if Garet suggested it.

But Garet didn't.

They were quiet. The tea warmed and settled her nervous insides. She reminded herself that she wasn't doing anything wrong, that there was nothing to feel guilty about. But she couldn't help wondering what would happen if June walked in and saw them holding hands, or worse, kissing. Which was what Tess longed to do. Garet's lips were soft and inviting and she couldn't help thinking of what they felt like on her mouth, on her skin.

"Should I go?"

Garet's question triggered some internal sense of urgency. Her desire for Garet to stay was astonishing in its suddenness.

"Do you want to leave?" Tess studied Garet's face.

"No." Garet caressed the back of Tess's hand. "I'd like to stay for as long as you'll let me."

It was true that in this situation, in this house, with her child asleep upstairs, Tess held the keys to everything. She could see by Garet's expression that whatever Tess felt was the right thing to do, the proper thing to do, that Garet would honor that and not fight it. At the moment, sitting across from Garet, she found no joy or triumph in being right, or perfect. What was right anyway? What did perfection even look like?

Tess decided there was too much light in the room. She continued to hold Garet's hand as she led her upstairs to her bedroom at the opposite end of the house from June's. Once inside the room, she softly closed the door and turned to face Garet, who was genuinely surprised by this turn of events.

"Just for a little while, okay?" Tess touched Garet's face. "I don't think it's a good idea for you to spend the night."

"Okay." Garet pressed Tess's palm to her lips. "Thank you."

"Stop thanking me." Tess smiled. "I want you to be here. My body doesn't know what this is yet between us, but it knows that I need you."

"I need you too."

Garet's fingers were at the back of her neck, Garet's other arm encircled her waist, drawing her firmly against Garet's body. They kissed long and languorously. They undressed each other in a frenzy and fell onto the bed. She had the sensation of moving through a heated dreamscape. Garet's hands on her body were the only thing keeping her from floating away, from disappearing into the darkness. Garet's sensual touch glowed incandescent against her penetrating need to be held, to be taken, to be seen. To be seen for herself alone, as a woman, apart from motherhood, apart from responsibility.

She clung to Garet, rising to meet her, their bodies feeding off each other. She'd fallen now so much further than expected, and had done it so quickly. The crumbling precipice she'd feared would give way was a distant vision. She'd fallen so far beyond it she could no longer see it.

Tess swallowed her cries, buried her face against Garet's neck as she came. But Garet didn't relent, she was so close. Tess rocked against her, coming again when Garet climaxed. She drew Garet's head to her shoulder and held her there.

"Just hold me." They hadn't spoken while they made love. Garet seemed able to read her body as if it was imprinted with braille, knowing intuitively what Tess needed and how. This was an unsettling discovery. Had she lost all power to resist Garet now?

Garet kissed her softly as she tightened her embrace.

CHAPTER THIRTY-SEVEN

Two weeks had passed since Garet spent the evening with Tess. The weekend of two blissful nearly sleepless nights had been followed by an extremely busy week of classes, play preparations, and late hours working on her book. She'd worked hard all week thinking they'd have the weekend to connect, but then June came down with some sort of bug. Tess spent the weekend at home taking care of her and didn't want Garet to catch it. They'd been able to talk a little on the phone, but having a sick kid underfoot was exhausting and not conducive for serious conversations.

Seeing Tess every day in class was like splendid torture. Garet couldn't wait for the day to begin, which was a new thing for her, since she wasn't really a morning person. She'd started making two coffees, and on the days that she didn't ride the bike to work, she delivered one to Tess. She worried that her attraction to Tess was obvious to everyone, including June.

The Volvo had been showing signs of revolt for weeks and had recently decided not to start at all. She wasn't sure if it was the battery or starter and hadn't had time to figure it out. Normally, Lane would tow it to her garage, work some magic, and get the Volvo back on the road. But Lane wasn't here, so Garet put off dealing with whatever mechanical issue was afoot. Luckily, she'd borrowed the mountain bike from Lane after she'd first arrived in Shadetree. And the temps had been perfect for riding through town to work—not too warm, not too cool. Beautiful autumn weather in the Deep South, dry and clear.

Garet and her team of assistants carried the backdrops for Kansas and Oz inside and she was in the final stages of installing them. Two-by-four struts had been necessary to ensure that the larger scenes wouldn't topple onto any children during the performance. Since this last phase of the installation required power tools, which the kids were not allowed to handle, Riley had offered to help. In an attempt to be a team player, Garet had accepted the offer, but an hour into the process was regretting it.

Apparently, Riley wasn't simply skilled at sports, she also knew everything there was to know about power tools. It wasn't that Garet's ego was tied up in any of this stuff. She'd decided early on to simply focus on supporting Tess and encouraging the students to have fun with the production. But spending the afternoon with a know-it-all jock was wearing thin. She didn't really need a lesson on how to use a hand drill and hadn't asked for one.

Garet had waited until Thursday to finish the supports for the backdrops. Friday night would be the performance, the night before the Saturday festival. Tess had advised not installing things until right before the show. That timing would provide less opportunity for things to get messed up. One year, the sets for *Anne of Green Gables* had been completely repainted with zombies by some seniors as a prank. Ever since, the stage got locked down the night before the performance.

"It looks like that's the last one." Riley surveyed the brace behind the Emerald City.

This was the largest set piece. Garet was on a ladder. She looked down at Riley from her perch, resting the hand drill on the small platform at the top of the ladder.

"Yeah, I think that's it." Garet handed the drill to Riley and climbed down. "Thanks for your help." It seemed like the right thing to say even if she wasn't feeling it.

They put the equipment back inside the large toolbox and locked it. The shop teacher had told her he'd come by and pick it up before the curtain opened. The last thing they needed was one more obstacle backstage. As it was, she was worried the kids might trip over the braces that extended behind each environmental prop. In fact, she pretty much expected it.

"So, you've got another month and then you're outta here, right?"

Riley's question caught her off guard.

"Yeah, I guess." Garet visualized the calendar in her head. "There's Thanksgiving break next week and then, almost three weeks after that before Christmas break." The time was going by faster than she expected.

Riley nodded and started toward the steps at the side of the stage.

"What?" Garet could tell there was something Riley wasn't saying.

"Oh, nothing." She turned to face Garet. Her expression seemed like a challenge. "It's just that Tess deserves someone who's here for the long term."

Garet's assumption that people knew they'd been seeing each other wasn't off base.

"I'm not sure you know what Tess needs." She didn't appreciate more unsolicited advice from Riley, especially not regarding Tess.

"Maybe." Riley nodded and quirked her mouth up into a half smile. "I care what happens to her. That's all I'm saying."

"I care about her too." Was it possible Riley really did have Tess's interests at heart? She was pretty sure Riley had a terrible crush on Tess so it was hard to hear anything from Riley without weighing it against that bit of context.

"I'm sure you do." Riley locked gazes with her. "Just treat her well."

"I plan to." Not that she owed Riley any sort of expectation.

As if on cue, Tess opened the wide auditorium door at the side of the stage. Light flooded the large room.

"Wow, this looks amazing." Tess's face lit up as she examined the sets on stage.

"Yeah, it really feels like Oz." Riley stood for a moment and then angled for the door Tess had just entered. "I'll see you two at the performance tomorrow. Good luck." Riley only really spoke to Tess, but that was okay.

Garet tried to imagine what it must feel like to have been attracted to Tess for all this time and then have some outsider swoop in and take her. That had to hurt. It wasn't her intention to hurt anyone, things with Tess had just happened. All of it seemed outside her control.

The door swished closed with a dull thud. They were alone on stage.

"Garet, the artwork is gorgeous." Tess beamed. "I can't thank you enough for working so hard with the children on these set pieces."

"It was more fun than I expected it to be." Garet shrugged and shoved her hands in her pockets so that she wouldn't be tempted to reach for Tess. They hadn't been able to be together for two weeks and she was afraid if she touched Tess she would lose control of her ability to stop. The school auditorium was no place to lose your cool.

"Was everything with Riley okay?" Tess grew more serious. "She seemed, I don't know, bothered by something."

"She wants to make sure I'm treating you well."

"Oh."

"Yeah."

"I guess we're more obvious than we think we are." Tess didn't sound upset about it which was a relief.

"Also, because Riley has a thing for you. But I'm sure you already knew that."

"Yes." Tess smiled thinly. "She's asked me out a few times, but…" Tess didn't finish the statement.

"But?" Garet wanted to know what came next.

"I'm just not attracted to her in the same way…plus, work romances are complicated."

"So I've heard." Garet smiled. She couldn't stand the distance any longer. She reached for Tess's hand and kissed it. "I miss you."

"I miss you too." Tess didn't pull away, but Garet could tell that even this small public display of affection on school grounds made her uncomfortable.

"Can I see you this weekend?" Garet was hopeful. The play would finally be over and they'd have some free time for the first time in days.

"I'd like that." Tess pulled away and crossed her arms, but her eyes held Garet and the connection warmed her heart. "Saturday is the festival. Would you like to go with June and me?"

"Sure."

"And then maybe June could stay with Mom Saturday night."

That sounded promising.

"My friend Lane is coming up to see the play Friday night. She'll probably stay over and hang out for a few hours at the festival."

"Oh, good, that will be fun. I'd like a chance to get to know her a little better." Tess paused. "Charlotte is going to try to attend the play also. I'd love for you to meet her."

Best friends meeting sounded serious, and for a split second, the idea of it made Garet nervous. She shook it off. Friends meeting friends was a good thing. Things were looking up. The weekend, beginning with the play Friday night, was going to be busy and stressful, but at the end of it would be time alone with Tess. She could make it through any gauntlet of obligation for that prize at the end.

CHAPTER THIRTY-EIGHT

Tess watched parents and audience members file in from stage left. She was partially hidden by the enormous curtain currently covering the set from view as she tried to keep an eye out for Charlotte. Garet's friend Lane had arrived early and was sitting in row five near the aisle. Tess wanted to introduce them so that they could sit together, since Lane was by herself.

She glanced over her shoulder to see Garet, working with June to ready the prop of the ruby slippers. At the moment when Dorothy's house lands on the Wicked Witch of the East, June would pull the striped stocking-clad legs out of sight. June was so excited to be allowed to help with props. She'd been grateful for Garet's patience throughout the preparation for this production, not only with June but the entire, sometimes distracted and fussy, cast. Managing the annual fall production was simultaneously one of the year's highlights and biggest headaches for Tess. It wasn't simply organizing the students to produce the play, it was also managing the expectations of the parents. Most were happy regardless of the outcome just to see their kids onstage. Others were more persnickety if their child didn't get the lead.

With Charlotte out of commission, Tess had enlisted Anna's and Mary's help with ticket sales and the collection of the funds. Their help was essential in keeping her sane.

Charlotte waved excitedly as she strolled down the aisle. Perfect timing. Tess hurried to intercept her. They fell into a friendly embrace.

"I'm so glad you made it." Tess held on to her for a moment.

"I wouldn't miss it." Charlotte beamed. "Tim is home with Tucker. It's good for them to have a little father and son bonding time without me around. Although, as you can imagine, it's hard for me to leave the baby even for an hour."

"I'd love to tell you that maternal worry eases as they get a little older, but it doesn't." Tess shook her head. "Hey, listen, I want to introduce you to someone." She took Charlotte's hand and guided her to the row where Lane was seated. Lane stood up when they arrived near her seat.

"Hi, Lane, this is my close friend Charlotte. She's the teacher Garet is filling in for." Tess turned to Charlotte. "Charlotte, this is Garet's good friend Lane from Atlanta."

They both said hello.

"I was thinking you guys could keep each other company since you're here alone."

"That'd be nice, thanks for joining me." Lane slid over one seat to allow Charlotte to sit along the aisle.

"It's so nice of you to drive out so far to support the kids." Charlotte took the seat.

"Well, the show is starting soon." She touched Charlotte's shoulder. "I'll see you after the show. Wish us luck."

"You don't need it!" Charlotte called after her.

The curtain was going up in five minutes, and backstage everything was chaos. Garet had happily allowed Tess to take charge, given the fact that she had much more experience putting on stage performances. But not everything about a children's production could be managed. You sort of just had to let things unfold and hope for the best, and most importantly, help the kids have fun.

"Are we ready for this?" She met up with Garet behind the Emerald City.

"I think we're as ready as we can be." June was standing next to Garet. She looked up at Garet and grinned.

Tess took a deep breath. June was so captivated by Garet that it made her nervous. But it was good for June to have other adults she looked up to, and Garet seemed to take June's adoration in stride. She didn't ignore it or minimize it, and for that, Tess was grateful.

"Gather around, everyone!" Tess waited for the kids to crowd nearer. "Okay, I'll announce the performance is beginning and you know, the usual stuff about turning phones off, etc." Tess clasped her hands in front of her chest as if she were about to burst into applause. "As soon as I return backstage, we'll open the curtains." Most of the children, who ranged in age from third to tenth grade, regarded her with nervous, wide-eyed expressions. "Hey, just remember, this is supposed to be fun. There are no perfect performances, that's the beauty of a live stage production. So, everyone relax...you've practiced and practiced...you know your lines and the songs. Let's go out there and have a great time." Tess looked over at Garet, who grinned back at her. They were in this together now, sink or swim.

Tess pushed through the curtains and the audience clapped loudly. She shielded her eyes from the intensity of the stage lights and glanced around the large audience. It seemed that every seat was filled. She appreciated how the community of Shadetree always supported the school in this way.

"Thank you all for coming. Please take a moment to turn off the ringer on your cell phone. Photos are okay, but please do not use a flash as it might distract the actors." Tess leaned closer to the microphone. "The program book contains the names of all cast members in tonight's production. Thank you to our orchestra, Gail Benson." The audience chuckled and applauded. She cast an outstretched hand in Gail's direction. Gail was a powerhouse, an orchestra of one. Gail took a small bow from the piano bench from stage right. "Tonight, we are excited to present our fall festival production of *The Wizard of Oz*."

The auditorium erupted with enthusiastic clapping.

"Thank you so much. Please enjoy the show." Tess bowed and slipped backstage.

Tess took a few moments to make sure everyone was in the proper spot for the opening scenes in Kansas. Garet had painted the farm and the road on a large canvas using only black and white. The canvas covered all the other sets and would be raised once Dorothy landed in Oz.

She looked for Garet, who had both hands on the ropes at the far end of the stage. She signaled for Garet to draw the curtain back. The crowd clapped again. It was really rewarding to put on a play for such appreciative parents.

The opening was all Lucinda, who belted "Over the Rainbow" with a stuffed dog in the crook of her arm. June had suggested they cast Richard in the role, and it had taken Tess almost a week to convince her that a stuffed dog would be better. She couldn't imagine Richard in the midst of this cacophony.

One of the most comical moments of the evening ended up being when Anthony ran across the stage carrying a tornado made from papier–mâché. He couldn't see where he was going and almost bumped into Lucinda as she ran for cover.

When Garet raised the black-and-white Kansas backdrop to reveal the brightly colored scenes of Oz, an appreciative gasp went up from the audience. Pride swelled in Tess's chest. Everything was coming together.

Scenes moved quickly. Partly because the kids were a little nervous and rushed their lines. Tess stood at the edge of the curtain to assist with forgotten lines and remind the young actors to speak loudly.

Garet watched Tess with sincere adoration. Tess was cool as a cucumber, completely unflappable, even when kids lost their place or props almost toppled. Garet tried her best to assist, but mostly just did what Tess told her to do. She was responsible for "special effects" and she'd promised June that she could assist. The most challenging test was going to be the scene with the flying monkeys.

She'd rigged two groups of monkeys, painted on foam core, with overhead ropes so that they could drop them down and swing them across the stage over the heads of the actors.

"Is it time?" June was giddy with anticipation.

"Almost." Garet was watching the scene to make sure they let the monkeys fly at the right moment. "Are you ready?"

June nodded.

"Okay, now!"

She tugged the ropes for both of them, and as soon as the foam core creatures dropped from above, she let June manage the thin nylon rope herself. June had such joy on her face, you'd have thought Garet had given her the keys to Santa's secret workshop.

"Okay, wait for them to swing across then tug again."

There was a simple pulley system to guide the monkeys over the stage and back. Dorothy and her sidekicks screamed and ran back and forth. The scarecrow lost one entire sleeve of straw in his frenzy at center stage. Garet wished she could have watched from the audience, who cheered and laughed.

"This is the most fun ever!" She felt June's tiny arms encircle her waist. She rested her palm on June's back.

"Yes, it is." Garet tousled June's hair.

The entire scene was hilarious and absurd and yet, Garet wasn't sure she'd experienced such perfect joy in...well, in forever. She took a moment to wipe away tears from laugher. Across the stage, Tess made eye contact and gave her an enthusiastic thumbs-up. She could tell Tess was happy. Pleasing Tess had become Garet's new obsession. The delighted expression on Tess's face lit Garet's entire world.

CHAPTER THIRTY-NINE

Garet tried to be as quiet as possible making coffee, but Lane stirred from her bed on the sofa. She raised up and squinted in Garet's direction.

"What time is it?" Lane dropped back to the pillow.

"It's almost nine." She set a cup for Lane on the coffee table and then took the chair opposite the sofa. "How'd you sleep?"

"Not bad." Lane half sat up so that she could sample the brew. Her hair stood up in odd places from how she'd slept. "How late did we stay up?"

"Pretty late."

"And how much of that bourbon is left?"

"Not much." Garet laughed.

"Ooh, don't laugh so loud. My head hurts." Lane slumped back against the sofa and closed her eyes.

Garet left briefly and returned with a bottle of Advil and a glass of water.

"Thank you."

After the play they'd stayed up late. There'd been so much to share with Lane. It seemed like so much had happened in the past two weeks, admittedly a lot of it only in her head since she'd really only seen Tess for that one dreamy weekend. But maybe the separation was good for Garet. She'd been forced to sharpen her other skills, like communication, in order to retain a sense of connection with Tess.

"What time are we meeting Tess?" Lane searched for her phone in the pocket of her jeans piled on the floor.

"We said we'd meet them at eleven, but if you need more time to wake up, just let me know and I'll text her."

"Eleven is good." Lane downed two Advil and finished the water. "A shower will do the trick. And maybe a warmup." She held up her mug.

"You've got it." Garet went to the kitchen to make another pour over. "I set out a towel for you."

"Thanks, man." Lane shuffled to the bathroom.

After a moment, Garet heard the shower. Garet was on pins and needles in anticipation of a day and night spent with Tess. She tried to temper her enthusiasm a bit so as not to come on too strong. But where Tess was concerned, more and more, she was beginning to realize that controlling her feelings was an illusion.

❖

Front Street and several downtown blocks were roped off as pedestrian only to allow for setup booths and eatery kiosks. The festival was already crowded when she and Lane arrived. Garet had suggested they walk from her place because she knew parking would be scarce. It was clear that the festival drew not only locals but tourists. The streets were packed.

It took a few minutes to connect with Tess and June. Tess had suggested they meet near the café, but the area was more crowded than Garet expected.

"Just relax, we'll find them." Lane patted her shoulder.

"Is it that obvious?" Garet scowled.

"Yeah, and I love it." Lane grinned. "I've never seen you like this, my friend. It's a good look for you."

"What look?"

"The look of love."

She was about to come back with something clever or deflect Lane's assessment, but Tess walked up at just that moment.

"Hi." Tess hugged Garet in a friendly manner, the sort of hug for far too public venues.

"Hi, Garet." June hugged her next. Kid hugs were different because of the height difference. She was never sure what was appropriate so she usually just patted June on the back while June hugged her around the waist.

"June, you remember Garet's friend Lane from the play last night?" Tess reintroduced them.

"Hi, June."

"Were the flying monkeys your favorite?" June launched right in.

"Well, actually, they were." Lane grinned.

"She can't stop talking about the monkeys." Tess smiled and shook her head. "Garet, I fear you may end up drawing some later for her to color."

"I'd be happy to."

"So, June, what's your favorite food at the festival?" Lane asked.

"Funnel cakes." June grinned, showing off the gap from her missing teeth.

"But not until we have some real food first, remember?" Tess stroked June's hair.

"Hot dogs!" June pointed toward a food truck.

"I love anyone who thinks hot dogs are real food." Lane adjusted her sunglasses with a smile.

"Hey, June, why don't we get hot dogs for everyone while your mom and Garet find a place for us to sit?" Lane lifted her dark glasses to make eye contact with Tess. "If that's okay with your mom."

"You don't have to buy us lunch." Tess pulled out her wallet.

"No, I insist. After such a great performance last night it's my treat."

"Did you see the flying monkeys? That was my favorite part. Mom said I could hang them in my room." June was holding Lane's hand as they walked toward the food truck.

"I hope she doesn't drive Lane crazy." Tess shook her head.

Garet was grateful to have a few minutes with Tess. They found an empty table and sat down. Garet texted Lane their location.

"You look beautiful today." Garet rested her elbows on the table and leaned forward a little.

"Thank you. You look pretty good yourself."

Tess's hair was down and it fluffed about her face in the light breeze. It was cool, but not cold. She was wearing a light jacket open at the front with a cotton blouse underneath. She had a scarf of some sheer fabric around her neck, but the creamy skin between the scarf and the open neck of her shirt was exposed. Garet longed to kiss that spot and a few others she couldn't stop thinking about.

She redirected her gaze when she realized Tess had caught her staring.

"Will I still get to see you tonight?" Garet didn't want to sound needy, but she couldn't help asking.

"If you still want to." Tess tucked an errant strand of hair behind her ear. "I made a plan to drop June off with my mother after the festival. And then, I could come to your place if that's okay?"

"That sounds perfect. I was thinking—"

"Hey, you two. Would you like to have your aura read?" Candi was dressed in something a person might wear to a Renaissance fair. Her outfit had a flowing skirt with a tight bodice that pushed her breasts up to the point that Garet feared they might escape. "It's for charity. All the money goes toward the Riverwalk beautification committee."

"Sure, how much?" Garet reached for her wallet in her back pocket.

"For five dollars I'll read for both of you."

Garet held up a five-dollar bill. Candi's bright pink nails contrasted sharply with the green brown as she snapped the money from Garet's fingers and tucked it into the basket she carried.

"Candi actually can read auras." Tess spoke to Garet.

"Now, don't talk for a minute and let me just get a good look at you." Candi squinted at them as if she were sizing them up. She looked them over long enough that Garet was beginning to get a little uncomfortable.

"Tess, as expected, your aura is pink colored. That means you love unconditionally. You're willing to love someone without expecting anything back from them." Candi took Tess's hand and squeezed it. "Hmm. She's a good one." That last statement she directed at Garet.

"Now, as for you." Candi turned to Garet. "Yours is lavender. Lavenders have the ability to transform their imaginings into works of art, which enhances the lives of others." She paused and leaned closer as if relaying some secret. "Outside their power, lavenders can feel a bit lost."

Lost? She wasn't lost.

"Hey, who's hungry?" Lane carried a tray loaded with hot dogs, fries, and drinks. June followed close on her heels with condiments and napkins. "Hey, I know you." Lane made eye contact with Candi.

"This is Candi. She works at the Riverside Café." Tess introduced them.

"Oh, yeah, right." Lane set the tray on the table and offered her hand. "I'm Lane."

"And her aura is definitely yellow." Candi pointed at Lane.

"What's she talking about?" Lane looked confused but intrigued.

"Candi is reading our auras." Garet watched with amusement as she sampled a fry.

"Yes, definitely yellow. Yellow is associated with freedom and joy, but in your case, I'd read it as a caution flag." Candi winked. She helped herself to a French fry and seductively took tiny bites of it until it was gone.

"A caution flag? That's perfect." Garet laughed.

"Y'all enjoy the festival." She spoke over her shoulder as she sashayed into the crowd.

Lane stood, watching her go. She was speechless, which Garet found enormously amusing. She was pretty sure Lane had met her match with Candi and that made Garet's day.

"Hi!" Charlotte walked up just as Lane was taking her seat.

"Hi." Tess stood and gave Charlotte a one-armed hug so as not to squeeze Tucker nestled in her arms. A stout, sandy-haired fellow in a faded red trucker hat, steering a stroller, followed on Charlotte's heels.

Garet had been introduced to Charlotte after the play. She assumed the guy must be Tucker's father.

"Charlotte, you met Garet and Lane last night." Tess recapped introductions. "This is Tim, Charlotte's boyfriend." Tess peeked inside the blue bundled blanket. "And this little guy is Tucker."

There were handshakes all around and Garet offered to find Charlotte and Tim chairs.

"No, we're gonna walk around until Tucker falls asleep." Charlotte waved Garet off. "You sit and eat before your fries get cold."

"You just missed getting your aura read by Candi." Tess didn't sit down right away.

"Oh, I already know mine is midnight blue because I need sleep!" Behind her Tim nodded in agreement and everyone laughed.

Chapter Forty

Lane headed back to Atlanta around four o'clock. Garet tidied up the cottage and took a shower to freshen up from a day of walking around booths, sampling lots of food, and having a generally great time. Despite the cool weather, the sky had been cloudless and she was fairly sure she'd gotten too much sun. Her nose and cheeks looked red after she'd showered.

She'd stocked up by picking up some to-go items from the market after leaving the festival. Tess had said she wouldn't be hungry after all the grazing they'd done, but Garet figured it'd be better to have some tasty bites on hand in case they got hungry later.

It took a few minutes of standing in front of her closet to figure out what to wear. It wasn't like she had tons of options because she hadn't brought that much stuff with her. A navy flannel shirt ended up winning. She pulled it on without a bra or T-shirt underneath. If she were lucky she wouldn't be wearing it for long. Her cheeks warmed at the thought of that as she closed the last button. She casually tucked the front of her shirt in and walked toward the living room. Headlights flooded through the front windows. A few seconds later, someone knocked at the door. She was so excited to see Tess that she considered skipping to the door but decided to try to play it cool.

"Hi."

Garet opened the door to see Tess and June on her doorstep.

"Hey, what a surprise." She hoped she didn't sound disappointed.

"My mom isn't feeling well tonight." The expression on Tess's face said she was disappointed too. "June and I were hoping you'd come to our house for dinner."

The hopeful look on June's face inspired Garet to rally.

"Sure, that'd be great." She motioned over her shoulder. "Let me just grab a jacket."

❖

Dinner ended up being a casual affair of breakfast for dinner, which Garet enjoyed quite a bit. Garet offered to do kitchen clean up while Tess got June into the bath. She finished the last of the dishes, and as she dried her hands on a nearby towel she paused to look at all the small things tacked to the front of the fridge. There were photos of June and her grandmother. A photo of another family that Garet assumed might be Tess's brother. There were various drawings by June. There was a narwhal, of course. And a drawing of two figures, one small and one large labeled June and Mom in blocky rough crayon lettering. There was also a drawing she'd done that June had colored. She felt honored to see something she'd had a hand in displayed with the family gallery of artifacts.

"I just put June to bed." Tess sounded tired.

"Perfect timing."

"You didn't have to do all the dishes." Tess glanced around the kitchen. "I'm sure we left some things from this morning in the sink too."

"It was fine." Garet hung the towel on a small hook near the sink. "Really, I was glad to do it." And she meant it. She liked being part of Tess's life, whatever that looked like, even if things sometimes didn't work out the way she thought they would. She figured with a kid you had to be flexible.

"I think I have some wine. Would you like a glass?" Tess disappeared into the pantry and came back with a bottle. "This is something I've had for a while. Charlotte gave it to me for my birthday, but I haven't opened it yet."

"Do you want me to open it?"

"Sure." Tess searched in a drawer and then handed a corkscrew to Garet.

"Are you sure you feel up to having company?" Garet worked the cork free and set it on the counter to allow the bottle to breathe for a few minutes. She didn't want to leave, but she also didn't want Tess to feel like she had to entertain someone if she was feeling beat. They'd had a pretty full day.

"I'm sorry, I must look tired if you're asking me that." Tess self-consciously swept her hands through her hair.

"No, not at all." Garet touched her face. "It's just...well, we had the play last night and the festival today...that's a lot of activity, that's all I meant."

"And you're my prize for getting through all of it." Tess took her hand and held on to it. "Let's take a glass of this in the living room. I think we both deserve some time to relax and enjoy the evening."

Tess poured two glasses of white wine and handed one to Garet. The lights in the living room were off. Garet had started a fire earlier, but it had burned down quite a bit. Only one small stick glowed red, but with no real flame.

"Why don't I put a little more wood on." Garet set the wine on the coffee table.

"That would be nice." Tess started toward the stairs. "While you do that I'll check on June."

Garet had a nice flame going again by the time Tess returned. She looked up from where she was kneeling near the hearth. She replaced the screen as she got to her feet.

"Everything okay?"

"Yes, she's sound asleep." Tess sipped her wine.

Garet dropped to the sofa. Sitting by the fire had sapped what little energy she had left leaving her a little sleepy. Tess didn't join her on the couch. She cocked her head and smiled at Garet.

"What?"

"Do you hear that?" Tess put down the glass and opened the window.

"Is that music from the festival?"

"It is. I think the live music lasts until at least ten."

Strains of some song she didn't recognize drifted in through the open window.

"How come your band didn't play?"

"I didn't think I could do it after the Friday night production. Plus, Mark has kids and they all wanted to play the games and stuff."

"That makes sense."

"Dance with me." Tess reached for Garet's hand.

Garet allowed herself to be tugged from her cozy spot on the sofa. Tess had turned off the light in the kitchen so the only light in the room was the warm orange glow of the fire and a bit of ambient light from the street. As if on cue, the live music wafting in switched to a slow song that she recognized, "At Last."

"This is a great song." Tess draped her arms around Garet's neck.

"Yeah, it is." Her hands were on Tess's hips as they swayed to the soft strains of music. "I think this might be *our* song."

"Really?"

"Yes, this is the second time I've heard it, and both times with you."

This probably was the best love song ever and she wondered if it were true. Were her lonely days finally over?

Tess looked up at Garet, focusing on her liquid eyes reflecting the firelight. She took a deep breath, breathing Garet in. She closed her eyes and rested her cheek on Garet's shoulder. She sank into Garet. This was nice. This was just what she needed, what she'd wanted all day. Just a few minutes alone with Garet.

The demands of the past two weeks had done a very good job of keeping them apart, and now that she had Garet in her arms all she wanted to do was cuddle up to her and stay there forever. Together, slow dancing in her small living room beside the crackling fire. This was pretty romantic, and intimate. She'd gradually, without overthinking it, been letting Garet into her world.

They danced through two more songs. Even when the pace of one song picked up their cadence remained slow, as if they were lost in their own tune. Tess had partially unbuttoned Garet's shirt so that she could press her lips to the sensitive skin she found there. Garet moaned softly and swept her hands up Tess's back before letting them slide back to her hips.

"Would you like to come upstairs?" Tess nuzzled against her neck.

"Yes."

Tess closed the window and quietly led Garet up the stairs and past June's bedroom. Once in her room, Tess closed the door. Garet waited in the center of the room. She joined Garet there and finished unfastening her shirt. Garet let it drop to the floor.

Tess feathered kisses on Garet's chest as Garet fumbled with the tiny buttons of her blouse.

"Here, let me help." Tess slipped the partially unbuttoned blouse over her head and tossed it on a chair.

Garet covered Tess's breast with her palm and kissed her.

Tess didn't want to do more standing up, not with the bed so close. She playfully pushed Garet backward onto the bed. Garet kicked her shoes off and Tess helped with her jeans, tugging them free and away before slipping out of her own. Garet's boxer shorts were next. And then Tess teasingly removed her panties while Garet watched. Then she crawled on the bed and straddled Garet.

This was the most aggressive she'd been with Garet, usually preferring Garet to take the lead. The expression on Garet's face told her that this turn of events might be unexpected, but she didn't seem unhappy about them.

"Is this okay?" Tess twisted her hair in her fingers, pulling to one side so that it didn't get in her way when she dipped down to kiss Garet.

"This is very okay." Garet's hands were on her thighs and she squeezed for emphasis.

"You can't spend the night." She almost hated herself for saying it, but she needed to be honest.

"I understand." Garet stroked Tess's arm. "I don't want to be a complication for June."

"You're not." Tess hesitated. "I just don't want her to be surprised by this." What was this anyway? Was this still only a fling? It didn't really feel that way from her perspective, but she and Garet hadn't discussed the future. Maybe they were both afraid to think about it.

Tess brushed her fingers through Garet's hair, lifting it from her forehead so that the moonlight from the bedroom window reflected in her eyes. Garet was so gorgeous that it made Tess's stomach ache, and other parts too. She was moving on top of Garet, getting very turned on. Garet slid her hand between them and stroked. Tess rose up just enough for Garet to slip inside. The sensation of being on top, with Garet inside her sent a shudder through her body. Who was she? Garet had tapped into some primal urge she'd allowed to lay dormant or that she'd chosen to ignore, and she wasn't sure which was true.

She was getting close but she wanted to switch positions. She slowly moved off Garet and onto the bed beside her. Garet read her desire without her saying a word. Garet was on top of her now, inside her again, bringing her to that sharp edge she'd feared, but now longed for.

Tess wrapped her arms around Garet's neck and hung on as tremors shook her body. She held Garet with her legs too in an attempt to get as close as possible. After a few minutes, her muscles became like rubber, sapped, and unable to move. Garet rolled onto her back beside Tess breathing hard. Had she come too? Tess was unsure. She'd lost her way, blinded by her own orgasm.

"Did you...?" She stroked Garet's chest.

Garet shook her head. "It doesn't matter. I only want to be close to you." She drew Tess to her and kissed her, deeply.

But that wasn't what Tess wanted. She wanted Garet to feel what she was feeling. She rolled on top of Garet and slid down her body until she reached that most sensitive place. And once there she used her tongue. Garet's fingers were in her hair. She sensed Garet's body grow taut as she worked with her tongue to send Garet higher.

She knew for certain when Garet came. Tess was learning the language of her lover's body. She wanted to be fluent in it, to know without asking what Garet needed.

"Tess." A breathless whisper.

She wanted Tess close. Tess slid up Garet's lean frame until their lips met. She kissed Garet passionately, deeply, and without reservation. Something between them had changed. Whatever emotional distance had separated them was no longer there. Tess sensed the absence of it. She searched Garet's face. What was happening?

"Tess, I'm in love with you."

She didn't know what to say. Was she in love with Garet? That was far too scary to consider. Rather than answer Garet, she kissed her, swallowing whatever words Garet had planned to say next. She didn't want to talk. She didn't want to promise things she couldn't deliver.

"Make love to me again." She held Garet's face in her hands.

Garet shifted Tess onto her back and kissed her deeply. Then as Tess had done, Garet slid down until her mouth was on Tess. Garet braced Tess's legs on her shoulders and used her tongue in ways Tess had only dared to imagine. The orgasm rose so fast that she cried out and quickly covered her mouth for fear she'd wake June. She writhed beneath Garet, who didn't relent until she crested with release.

She'd never had such a powerful reaction to someone.

She was spent, her body limp with the exhaustion only ecstasy could deliver.

Garet lay next to her. She snuggled close to Garet, drained but happy.

CHAPTER FORTY-ONE

Garet woke with a start. *Oh shit.* She'd fallen asleep and it was daylight. She was supposed to sneak out in the middle of the night, long before June woke up. Beside her, Tess began to stir.

"Tess, Tess, wake up," she whispered as she gently shook Tess.

"Hmm." Tess smiled sleepily and then recognition dawned. "We fell asleep." There was urgency in her statement.

"Yeah, I'm sorry." Garet sat up. "I don't know how that happened?"

"What time is it?" Tess searched for her phone.

"I'm not sure…early?"

"Mama?" The bedroom door was still closed, but June's voice was clear and close by.

Tess lurched out of bed and pulled on a robe.

"Just a minute, sweetie."

"Mama, can I watch cartoons before breakfast?"

"Yes, that's fine." Tess covered her face with her hands as she talked through the door. "I'll be right down."

I'm so sorry. Garet mouthed the words silently.

Tess shook her head as if to say it was okay. But was it?

"What do you want me to do?" Garet asked in a hushed voice as she attempted to tug her jeans on one entire leg at a time.

"Let me just think for a second." Tess chewed her lip and paced.

"There's no way I can leave without her seeing me." Especially if she was watching cartoons now in the living room.

Tess stopped pacing and faced her. The expression on her face was hard to decipher.

"It will be fine." She nodded as if trying to convince herself. "Yes, this will be fine." She hugged Garet and held on to her. "I'm sorry I made you feel as if you have to sneak around in order to see me."

"It's okay, I know you only want to protect June."

"But she's crazy about you. So, we'll just go downstairs and have breakfast like all of this is normal." She looked up at Garet. "It got late. You were tired. You slept over."

"Really?"

"Yes, that's all a six-year-old needs to know."

Garet took a deep breath, tried to channel internal calm, and followed Tess downstairs. June was cross-legged in front of the TV with Chester in her lap. She looked up and a grin immediately lit up her face.

"You're still here." It was more of an observation than a question.

"Good morning, June." Garet tried for nonchalant, but her heart was pounding. *Please let this be okay.* She worried, despite Tess's assurances. She didn't want to make things hard for either of them.

"Yes, it got late and I invited Garet to stay over." Tess kissed the top of June's head. "How about if I make pancakes for breakfast?"

Tess was the poster girl for parental Zen. Garet tried to follow her lead.

"Yes!" June approved of the suggestion. "Garet, you can watch cartoons with me." She jumped up and grabbed Garet's hand, then tugged her to the sofa.

Garet glanced over at Tess. It was impossible to know what she was thinking. June was wearing footy pajamas. She tucked her feet beneath her and half leaned against Garet.

"I'll bring you some coffee." Tess touched her shoulder on her way to the kitchen.

Once in the kitchen, Tess gripped the edge of the counter and exhaled. She'd been right, thank goodness. She'd treated Garet's presence as no big deal and June had gotten on board with that. But it was a big deal. She'd had affairs when June was much younger. This was the first time June had bonded with anyone she'd been involved with.

She placed her palm over her heart willing it to slow to a normal pace.

The coffee maker hummed and she mixed batter in a large bowl. It was a relief to have some task to focus on while she worked on mentally coming to terms with what had just happened. Before she poured batter into the pan, she carried a cup of coffee in to Garet.

The sight that greeted her stopped her in her tracks.

June was snuggled next to Garet. Garet had her arm around June while she excitedly explained the premise of the show. Tess lingered in the doorway taking in the endearing scene. A tear slid down her cheek. A tear of relief. Yes, relief. That's all it was and nothing more.

❖

It was almost noon by the time Garet made it back to her place. She showered and changed into fresh lounge pants and a T-shirt before making a large pot of coffee. There was a backlog of work she needed to address, and she needed maximum caffeine to make it happen.

She sat down facing her slant board, sipping coffee, and reflecting on the past seventy-two hours. So much had happened that it was hard to get her head around it all. The play had been a success. Tess had needed her and she'd come through. It was obvious that Tess was grateful. And then Lane had been in town. It was nerve-wracking to integrate friend circles, but she'd needed Lane to spend a little time with Tess and June. She was in bad need of an outside perspective. Lane had been more encouraging than she'd anticipated.

The date she and Tess had planned got completely derailed, but that ended up being okay. The only part of the entire weekend that she worried about was waking up at Tess's place. That had not been her intention and she feared that the entire episode put Tess in a stressful, awkward position. Garet needed to check in with Tess or she was going to be unable to focus. She reached for her phone and dialed.

"Hello." The sound of Tess's voice melted her insides.

"Hey." Garet closed her eyes, to better focus on the tone of Tess's voice. "How are you? I mean, is everything okay?"

"Yes, everything is okay." She could almost hear Tess smile through the phone. "That's not exactly how I wanted things to happen, but truly, everything is fine. June took the entire morning in stride. In fact, she wanted to know when you can sleep over again. Apparently, there are other cartoons that she feels compelled to share with you."

"I'm so glad." The tension in her shoulders released a little.

They were quiet for a few seconds.

"How are you spending the rest of your day?"

Garet tried to visualize where Tess was and what she was doing. She imagined her lounging on the couch with June coloring at the coffee table. The mental image made her smile.

"I've got some work to catch up on."

"I'm sorry." Tess paused. "I'm afraid the play and everything else has been too disruptive."

"You know, it's actually been really fun. I always shied away from the drama department in school, but now I'm thinking I missed out. Seeing the kids come together and really pull it off...well, that was pretty inspiring."

"Yes, every year I think it'll never come together and then somehow, miraculously, it does. It's fun to see the students really begin to own the production and put their whole heart into it. It's kind of magical."

"I'm not sure I could do that much work every year. I admire you and Charlotte for sure." Garet thought for a moment that it would be fun to come back next year just to watch the production for fun, when she didn't have to be backstage managing the chaos.

"I think your backdrop paintings were so beautiful that you made Charlotte a little nervous."

"Tell her not to worry. That job is hers." Garet laughed.

"Hey, Thanksgiving break is next week and with everything else that was going on, I forgot to ask you what you were doing?"

"I was planning to go to Lane's. Her family is in Atlanta and they put on a big spread every year." Garet sipped her coffee. "Besides, I need to go to my apartment and photograph some illustrations. I need to send two finished spreads to my editor in New York for a sales meeting in December."

"Oh."

"Yeah, I didn't bring my tripod or anything with me." She paused. "I guess I thought I'd be back in Atlanta more often. I didn't expect Shadetree to be so...hard to leave."

"I think I know what you're trying to say." There was some sort of scuffling sound on Tess's end. "Yes, you can take Richard to your room, but don't feed him."

Garet laughed.

"She just can't stand not feeding him animal crackers. I think he's actually gained weight."

"What do you do for the holiday?"

"We go to my Mom's. She and I share the cooking. My brother and his family won't be there this year. He's going to see his in-laws in Ohio."

They were quiet for a moment. Garet decided that talking with Tess wasn't helping with her general distraction. Hearing Tess's voice made her want to tug Tess through the phone and into her lap.

"I'll miss you." Tess's statement was soft, almost a whisper. She wondered if June was within earshot.

"I'll miss you too."

"But I'll see you in class tomorrow." Tess's voice brightened. "Good luck with your drawing session."

"Thanks. Until tomorrow."

"Good-bye."

Garet clicked off, feeling possibly more upended than before she'd called. The dark phone screen stared back at her like a small black hole of unsaid things. The first thing she'd thought of when she'd returned home and stood in the shower for too long, was that she'd told Tess she loved her. Overcome with a tidal surge of emotion, she'd professed her love to Tess and Tess hadn't said anything. What did that mean?

It wasn't that she expected Tess to feel exactly what she was feeling at the same time. Someone had to say it first. She'd considered mentioning it. Possibly apologizing for coming on too strong, but she hadn't. If she didn't mention it would Tess just ignore she'd said it? Maybe that was for the best. That thought didn't settle easily in the pit of her stomach. She was afraid in her most vulnerable state that she'd actually spoken the truth—she was in love with Tess. Now what?

CHAPTER FORTY-TWO

Tess helped June with her jacket and then searched around the living room for a missing glove. It was a cold day, despite the sunshine, and she didn't want June getting chilled during their walk.

It always seemed that the weeks between Thanksgiving and Christmas break zoomed by. The closer the days got to Christmas, the harder it was to get the kids to focus. The last two days of class would end up mostly focusing on projects that could be counted as cards or gifts for parents. It was Saturday and the end of the year was in sight. Tess didn't usually make a big deal out of New Year's, but somehow, this year seemed different. She and Garet had been seeing each other whenever possible, although, Tess still tried to shield June from as much of their budding romance as possible. With the holiday break looming it was hard not to think about the fact that Garet's tenure as Charlotte's substitute would be drawing to a close. Did Garet have plans to come back to Shadetree for Christmas? What about New Year's? It was odd how little they spoke of the future. Maybe they were both afraid to look that far ahead.

Tess worried that Garet's departure would be a big blow for June. They'd definitely developed a friendly rapport. There seemed to be genuine affection on Garet's part from June and for June, Garet had almost achieved hero status. She dreaded the moment when June discovered Garet was leaving.

If Tess were honest, she dreaded Garet's departure more than she cared to think about. For a whole bunch of reasons that had nothing to do with June.

Garet knocked as if on cue. June ran to open the door.

"Hi, June."

"Hi." June held the door open.

"June Bug, please invite Garet in," Tess called from the kitchen where the search continued for the missing glove. Finally, success. She was on her way to the living room and almost collided with Garet.

"Sorry." Garet caught Tess before they made contact.

"Hi." Tess felt flustered for some reason. "We were missing a glove, but I found it." She waved the tiny wool glove in the air. "June, put this on."

"It's nice, but cold. Are you sure you guys still want to go for a walk?" Garet asked.

"Yes, please." Tess reached for her coat on the rack near the door. "Some of us need to burn off a little energy." She tipped her head at June, who was hopping in place.

"Right. Got it." Garet smiled as she held the door.

June bolted out first, almost sliding on a patch of ice. Garet and Tess followed at a more reasonable pace.

"June, be careful of the ice!" June was making circles in the frosty dry grass with her boots.

"Wow, someone has a lot of energy this morning." Garet laughed.

"She's been like this all morning. Clearly, I'm a terrible parent and I need to lower her sugar intake."

"I personally think you're a great parent." Garet's hands were in her jacket pockets, but she gave Tess's shoulder a gentle bump.

Garet was wearing one of those denim jackets with the fleece lining, the collar was turned up against the cold. This wasn't the first time Tess thought Garet looked sexy in outdoor gear.

Tess had a shawl neck sweater under her coat, and she scrunched it up around her neck. She'd pulled her hair back while she was getting dressed to keep it out of her face. She removed the hair tie and let it fall around her ears for warmth.

"I love it when you do that." Garet grinned. "You have the best hair."

"Thank you." Tess's cheeks warmed despite the chill in the air.

They cut across the lawn and picked up the side trail that led to the River Trail. They'd barely stepped onto the trail when Tess's phone rang. It was her mother's number.

"Sorry, do you mind if I get this?"

"Not at all." Garet shook her head. "I'll walk ahead and catch up with June."

"Thanks." Tess accepted the call. "Hi, Mom, what's up?"

"Can you run to the bank with me? I'll pick you up."

"I'm on a walk with Garet and June. Can we go later, or on Monday?" Tess didn't really want to cut the walk short, but her mother's request sounded urgent.

"We need to go today. Mr. Jacobs sent me an email about these documents that need to be signed, but I forgot to check my email until just this morning. He's out on vacation until New Year's after today." She always forgot to check her email, let alone respond to it.

"Can't he email the documents to you?"

"I'd rather go to the bank." Her mother had a general distrust of email and the internet. "It relates to the mortgage, and since you're my power of attorney now you need to sign it too."

Tess wasn't convinced this was accurate, but it didn't seem as if her mother was going to be easily dissuaded.

"Hang on for a minute." Tess muted her phone and hurried to catch up.

Garet was farther along the trail with June.

"Hey, June Bug, grandma needs our help for a little while."

"Is everything okay?" Garet looked concerned.

"Oh, yeah, just some paperwork thing that has to be taken care of at the bank."

"I don't want to go." June wasn't happy about cutting the walk short.

"June, don't argue with me. We have to go."

"I want to stay with Garet," June whined and clung to Garet's hand.

"She can stay with me if that's all right with you," Garet tentatively offered.

"Yes! Yes! Yes!" June bounced around where they stood.

"Are you sure?" There would be less drama if she went to the bank without an unhappy child in tow.

"Yeah, we'll be fine." Garet nodded. "We'll walk slow and you can meet us at the café for hot chocolate when you're finished."

That plan almost sounded too reasonable.

"Okay, great." Tess checked her phone for the time. "This should only take about a half hour, forty-five minutes at the most." She unmuted the call. "Mom, I'm on my way. I'll meet you at the bank."

June ran ahead and Garet waved as she turned to follow her.

Tess stood for a moment watching them. It struck her that this was the first time she'd allowed someone she'd dated to care for June. She was trusting Garet with her precious little girl. They were in the woods, along the river's edge. Every protective impulse surged to the surface and she pushed it down. She was being ridiculous. Garet was attentive and June loved spending time with her. She was only leaving them for a half hour. Nothing was going to happen.

Tess repeated that to herself as she turned back toward the house to get her car.

Nothing was going to happen.

❖

"Hey, wait up," Garet called to June.

"Look at this." June was hunched over looking at the ground.

"Oh, yeah, it's like mini ice castles." The water in the topsoil had frozen and pushed up in little clumps of ice crystals.

June stepped on them. They made a very satisfying crunching sound.

Dead brown leaves edged with white frost also lay on the ground. The river wasn't frozen, but tiny ice ledges were visible among the rocks along the bank. The temp had definitely dropped overnight and hadn't risen much above the mid-thirties. This wasn't winter weather like you'd see in Minnesota or anything, this was Georgia, but obviously in the foothills of the Blue Ridge

Mountains the higher elevation made the days colder than what she'd experienced in Atlanta.

Garet watched June overturn a stone with a stick. Tess and Garet never held hands when they walked with June. They tried not to exhibit any kind of public affection in front of June, but Garet wondered if June already had a clue. She never said anything in front of Garet, but June was an astute, curious six-year-old. Garet figured it was only a matter of time.

"Garet, look!" June was too far ahead for her to see what she'd found.

"Oh, wow." It was part of a turtle shell bleached white from exposure to the elements.

June used the end of her stick to toss the broken shell into the river. Kids loved to see things splash in the water. It seemed June never grew tired of that either.

They walked on, farther than usual. Past the turnoff to the café, the trail became more secluded and rustic. They came across the rusted remnants of a forties era Ford almost completely buried in dirt and dead leaves, being slowly swallowed by the Earth. Likewise, a quarter-mile past that, an old cow barn that had barely any roof left. She tried to open the gray plank door to get a glimpse inside, but the structure had sagged so that she was unable to work it free.

It was always curious to Garet the things folks allowed to slowly disintegrate in the elements. Was that a Southern thing? Or just a rural thing? A thousand years from now, what would archeologists assume about what they unearthed?

Garet's mind wandered and she'd lost track of time. June seemed happy to meander and investigate, and she'd gotten caught up in June's enthusiastic exploration.

"Hey, June. Want to go get some hot chocolate now?"

June nodded. She took Garet's hand as they turned back toward the Riverside Café.

CHAPTER FORTY-THREE

It wasn't quite lunch time when Garet and June reached the part of the trail nearest the café. Garet's hands were chilled without gloves and she was looking forward to warming up with something hot to drink. June showed no signs of the cold, but she'd hardly stopped moving since they left the house. Darting here and there as they walked, June had probably walked three times as far as Garet along the same path.

They cut across the grass between the trail and the café. There was a gradual hill and steps that led from the parking area down to the café's outdoor deck overlooking the river. Garet glanced up just in time to see Charlotte at the top of the steps leading down to the deck. She waved when she saw Garet and started down, lowering the stroller slowly, one step at a time. But the flagstone steps were uneven and Garet worried they had ice on them. She hurried to intercept Charlotte, but she wasn't quick enough.

Charlotte's face contorted as she lost her footing and fell. It was like watching something horrible happen in slow motion. Garet lunged for the stroller just before it took off down the hill. Charlotte moaned and grabbed her ankle.

"Charlotte! Are you all right?" Garet stabilized the stroller on a flat bit of flagstone.

"It's my ankle, I think I broke it." Tears were on her cheeks. "I'm so stupid and sleep deprived. I saw you and June and I—" her voice broke. "I just wasn't thinking."

June was standing a few feet away watching with a shocked expression.

"Everything is okay, June." Garet touched her shoulder.

Charlotte was in pain. Garet retuned her attention to the twisted ankle. It didn't look quite right, but she wasn't sure how to tell if it was truly broken or just badly sprained.

"Can you stand?"

"Maybe." Charlotte braced against Garet, but the second she put weight on her ankle she crumpled, pulling Garet down with her.

"I'll call someone." Garet remembered she'd left her phone to charge at the cottage. She didn't think she'd need it because she'd planned to spend the day with Tess. "I don't have my phone. Do you have yours?"

Charlotte shook her head. "I left it in the car. I let the battery run down."

"Okay, hang on. I'll use the phone in the café." She placed her hands on June's shoulders and made eye contact for a second. "June, you stay here with Charlotte. I'll be right back."

Tucker started to cry. Charlotte reached for the handle of the stroller and rocked it a little to reassure him. Right before Garet reached the café door, Candi opened it.

"What's going on out there?" Candi held the door for Garet. She was only in a thin shirt and shivered in the doorway.

"Charlotte fell. Can we call the rescue squad or someone to come help her?"

"Yes, yes…Let me get the number."

Garet glanced out the café window as Candi dialed. Oh shit. She didn't see June.

She hurried back to Charlotte's side.

"Where's June?"

For a moment, Charlotte seemed confused.

"Oh, my God, she's down by the river!" Charlotte pointed. "I just took my eyes off her for a minute. June! Don't climb that!" Charlotte called to June as Garet sprinted down the hill toward the ice bank.

June was precariously perched on a rock outcrop beneath an old dead tree. The dry branches stretched out over the rolling water, and June was reaching up for something clinging to the lowest branch. As Garet got closer she could see there was a tiny black and white kitten just above June's head. June reached for it, overextending. Her foot slipped and she splashed into the water.

"June!" Garet's heart was pounding. Panic and adrenaline surged in her system as she lunged into the icy water. She gasped from the shock of the cold water swirling around her up to her waist.

June had managed to grasp the last bit of rock jutting out into the water. She was almost completely submerged. Garet reached her in a matter of seconds, but those seconds seemed like hours as she visualized June getting sucked out into the swollen waterway.

Garet grabbed June's hand first and then yanked her up and into her arms. June was scared and crying.

"I've got you. It's okay now." Garet held her close. "Everything is okay now."

June began to shiver. She needed to warm her up, and quickly. She noticed red flashing lights for the first time at the top of the hill. Two rescue squad members broke away from Charlotte and ran toward Garet with a blanket. She relinquished June and they swaddled her in the heavy wrap. Garet was breathing hard, her heart thumped loudly in her freezing ears. She braced on her knees willing herself to calm down. The entire incident had frightened her badly. Too many things happening at once, all of them potentially bad.

Tess pulled up in her Subaru just as Garet reached the edge of the parking lot. Her jeans were soaked which slowed her climb. Two men lifted Charlotte into the back of the ambulance on a gurney and then Tucker was settled onto her chest. June was perched at the edge of the open door of the medical vehicle, still wrapped in the blanket. Candi had given her something warm to drink.

"What happened?" Tess sounded alarmed.

"Everything is okay." Garet was still a little out of breath, plus, her teeth were chattering. "June is—"

"Why is June wet?" Tess turned on Garet, her eyes widened with concern.

"She fell in the river—"

"She fell in the river!" Tess's worry blazed into anger.

Tess rushed to June. She rubbed her arms briskly beneath the blanket and drew her into a hug. June was crying again.

"Mama..." Her words muffled as she pressed her face against Tess.

"Sweetie, are you all right?" Tess swept June's damp hair back to look at her face.

From the gurney inside the van, Charlotte groaned in pain.

"We need to take Charlotte to the hospital for x-rays." One of the rescue squad guys spoke to Tess. "Maybe you should ride with us, just to make sure June doesn't suffer from hypothermia. We can get her warmed up on the way."

Tess nodded. She obviously knew this man. Of course, she did. Everyone in Shadetree seemed to know Tess. No one was asking Garet if she was okay, no one seemed worried about her in the least as she stood shivering in the cold watching all the activity.

"I should never have left her with you." Tess's anger caught Garet by surprise.

"What?"

"You're careless and you almost let her drown." Tess's mouth tightened into a thin line. "How could you let that happen? I trusted you!"

"Tess, wait—"

But Tess didn't wait. She spun abruptly and climbed up into the van with Charlotte and June. The same man who'd spoken to Tess closed the doors. Garet was in shock. What had just happened?

"Here, we saved him for you." A woman in a sheriff's uniform handed Garet a small box.

Garet opened the flap to see the tiny black and white kitten inside. The kitten looked at her with impossibly large eyes and meowed.

"This isn't mine." But the woman was already striding toward her squad car.

The rescue squad van pulled away, with siren and lights blaring, leaving Garet holding the box, watching them leave.

Candi put a comforting arm around Garet's shoulders as she stood like a frozen statue and watched the flashing lights fade into the distance.

Candi patted her shoulder. "It's gonna be okay."

But Garet wasn't so sure.

❖

Tess had her arm around June, who was snuggled next to her on the sofa. A half-eaten bowl of chicken soup was on the coffee table. She kissed June's hair, probably for the hundredth time since leaving the hospital.

June was all right. Everything was all right.

She kept repeating those words to herself. Maybe her mind believed them, but her heart wasn't buying it. As far as her heart was concerned, everything was *not* okay. When she closed her eyes all she could visualize was June submerged in the icy river. Even thinking of how horribly things could have turned out made her ill. In fact, she'd thrown up the minute they got home. Her insides were a tumultuous sea of seething emotion. One minute afraid, the next minute furious, and the next minute feeling guilty.

June, the most precious thing in her world, fell into the fucking river and almost drowned. Garet had been the only target for her rage and she'd given her all of it.

If she stepped back from the scene and pictured Garet, she could see the hurt expression on her face, but this wasn't about Garet.

"Mama, Is Garet going to come over?" June's voice sounded tiny and far away.

"Not today, sweetheart." She squeezed June closer. The TV was annoyingly bright. She'd agreed to let June watch cartoons while she ate the soup. "You need to rest."

After another half hour, Tess coaxed June into taking a nap. June's forehead felt warm and she didn't want the winter swim to bring on a cold. She tucked the covers around June and settled Chester under her arm.

"Are you mad at me?" June's question made her want to bust out in tears.

"No, honey." Yes, she was furious, but not at June. And she was sorry if June thought that. "I was just scared and upset." She kissed June's forehead. "You rest for a little while."

Once she was back downstairs, she felt lost. There was nowhere to put everything she was feeling. The person she most wanted to call was the person she least wanted to need—Garet. She was so upset that she was unsure if she was overreacting or underreacting. Was her anger misplaced? She couldn't figure any of it out.

She sat at the kitchen table, covered her face with her hands, and cried. Sobs shook her shoulders. When they finally subsided, she felt a tiny bit better, lighter. She sniffed and searched for a tissue.

Tess reached for her phone and dialed.

"Mom?"

"Tess, is something wrong?"

"Mom, something happened to June..." And then the tears came again.

CHAPTER FORTY-FOUR

Garet watched her phone all day Sunday expecting a call from Tess, but none came. By late afternoon she could stand it no longer. She called to check on June. Tess didn't answer so she left a rambling voice mail. She regretted calling as soon as she left the message. Tess was clearly angry and just needed a little time to process what had happened.

Garet felt stranded in her own life, unable to move past it. She was worried about Charlotte and June and no one was telling her anything. She was alone with her thoughts, making it very hard to focus on anything else.

Monday morning ended up being no better. She expected to see Tess at school and was looking forward to getting a chance to explain what had happened. Surely, once Tess knew what had transpired she'd feel better. But Monday, Tess called in sick, and the same happened Tuesday. A local retired music teacher filled in for Tess on the last two days before Christmas break, the last two days before Garet was to leave for Atlanta.

By Tuesday afternoon, Garet's worry and confusion had shifted to anger. Tess had coldly and completely shut her out without hearing her side of the story. On some level she'd known that she would never be able to compete with June in Tess's heart. June came first. Intellectually, she knew that. But it made her no less angry to have been brushed aside so quickly. She cared about June too. Didn't that count for something?

The kitten batted one of her expensive graphite pencils to the edge of the counter and then onto the floor.

"Hey, cut that out." She was in no mood for anything cute or sweet.

All she wanted was Tess.

Garet picked up the kitten and set it on the sofa where he proceeded to fight with one of the throw pillows.

❖

Tess's phone rang. If it was Garet she should pick up. She'd been avoiding talking to her because she was so angry, not just at Garet, but at herself. Garet had left several voice mails. She could tell by the sound of Garet's voice that she was hurt, but Tess was hurting too and not sure how to deal with it.

June's winter swim in the river had given her a cold. Tess's concern and guilt made it impossible to leave June's side until she was feeling better. She'd called in sick to work partly to be with June but also because she couldn't bear to see Garet.

God, she was a fool. She'd completely let her guard down with Garet and she'd known better. She'd left June with Garet and look what had happened. She'd let her desire for a relationship ultimately endanger her child. She felt guilty, and lonely, and sad all at the same time. She was a mess.

She needed to talk to Garet, but she was waiting until she was calmer. She knew time was running out. Classes had ended today and Garet would be leaving, probably tomorrow.

Her phone rang again and she checked the screen. The call was from Charlotte so she picked up. She'd been so upset over June that she hadn't even called to check on Charlotte. She wasn't just a terrible mother, she was a terrible friend.

"Hi, Charlotte." Tess dropped to the sofa. "I'm sorry I haven't called to see how you are doing."

"I'm the one who should have called you…but with the crutches, and the baby…"

"No, don't worry about it. You have a lot going on."

"I do, but I sincerely apologize for what happened."

"What do you mean?" Charlotte suddenly had Tess's full attention.

"When I fell, Garet left June with me to go call the rescue squad." Charlotte's voice faltered. Was she crying? "I'm sorry, I'm so emotional these days." She took a shaky breath. "Anyway, I literally just looked away for a minute and…Garet acted so quickly…if Garet hadn't been there, I just don't know…"

Tess sat silently waiting for Charlotte to continue.

"If Garet hadn't been so fast, I don't know what might have happened." Charlotte sniffed. "Can you ever forgive me?"

"Charlotte, I—"

"Please forgive me. I feel terrible and I love you and June so much." Charlotte sobbed softly. "With the baby and trying to reach Tim on the way to the hospital, well, I didn't get a chance to tell you what really happened. I'm so, so sorry."

"Charlotte, I forgive you." Tears gathered along Tess's lashes. "It was an accident. It could easily have happened to me if I'd been in the same situation." The truth of her own statement hit her hard in the chest. She clenched the front of her sweater.

Garet had saved June. It hadn't been Garet's fault. She'd been so quick to blame her, probably out of fear. That was the truth of it wasn't it? She was afraid because she knew she'd fallen in love with Garet. She'd known for a while now and June's accident provided an easy escape from facing that truth and dealing with her own crippling fear of letting someone share their life. Letting someone in.

"Charlotte, I have to go." A sense of urgency gripped her. "Thank you for calling, but don't worry, okay?"

"Are you sure?" Charlotte sniffed loudly.

"Yes, I'm sure. I'll call you later."

Tess sat forward on the couch and checked the time on her phone. It was almost four thirty. Garet was certainly home from school. She dialed Garet's number but there was no answer.

"June!" She walked to the foot of the stairs. "June, get your coat!"

"Why?" June slowly descended from the second floor.

"We're going for a drive."

CHAPTER FORTY-FIVE

B y three thirty, Garet had decided there was no point in staying in Shadetree any longer than she had to. The cottage, everything reminded her of Tess, and if Tess wanted to shut her out then so be it. By four thirty she'd shoved her well-traveled duffel bag into the back and closed the hatch. There were only two things left to pack—the kitten she hadn't asked for and Lane's bike.

She stood for a moment strategizing how to tie the bike to the roof of the Volvo. She was glad that Hildy wasn't home. Garet was in a terrible mood and in no shape to participate in small talk. She'd leave the key and a note for Hildy in the mailbox and call her later from Atlanta.

As she lingered in the driveway, a wave of sadness threatened to capsize her. Was she really angry, or just hurt? An unwanted tear trailed down her cheek and she swiped at it with the cuff of her jacket.

She needed to see Tess one more time. Garet knew she wasn't going to get past this if she didn't see Tess one last time. Tess could yell at her if she liked, but Garet had things to say and she decided right then and there she wasn't leaving until she got a chance to say them.

She searched her pockets for the car keys. She'd drive over to Tess's and then come back for the bike and the kitten. With renewed resolve, she jumped in the car and turned the ignition. Nothing happened.

You've got to be kidding!

She tried the ignition one more time. Nothing, it was completely dead.

Not to be defeated, she got out of the car, fastened the bike helmet strap under her chin, and spun out in the direction of Tess's house. She'd feel like kind of a loser showing up on a bicycle, but there wasn't much that could make her feel lower than she already did, so fuck it. She pedaled hard down Front Street. There was a little daylight left. Cold air seeped in from her collar inspiring her to increase her speed.

Regardless of how this went down, taking action made her feel better, more in control.

She wasn't going to let Tess shut her out until she had a chance to tell Tess how she felt. Tess owed her that much.

❖

June was dragging her feet until Tess explained they were driving to Garet's house. The mention of Garet improved June's attitude almost immediately. Within five minutes, they were in the car and Tess was backing out of the driveway. She was just clearing the neighbor's wooden fence so that she could check for oncoming cars. It was almost dark, and seeing no headlights, she started to roll into the street.

"Mama, stop!" June yelled from the back seat.

Tess slammed on the breaks, but it was too late. She hadn't seen the bicycle coming and the rider was going too fast to stop. The front tire of the bike slammed into the side of the car with a loud thud, and the rider summersaulted across the hood and hit the ground on the other side.

"Stay in the car!" Tess spoke to June as she jumped out of the car.

Garet was lying on her back looking stunned.

"Garet! Oh, my God!" Tess knelt beside her. "Are you hurt? I'm so sorry, I'm so sorry."

Garet blinked slowly, unclipped the helmet, and tossed it aside.

"Garet, sweetheart, talk to me." Tess held Garet's face in her hands.

"I need to talk to you." Garet's voice cracked.

"I need to talk to you too." Tess kissed her forehead and her cheeks and then her lips. "Garet, I know what happened at the river wasn't your fault. Charlotte told me everything."

"She did?"

"I've been so sure that you would let me down, that you'd hurt me, that I think I created my own reality to make it all come true." Tess pressed her face to Garet's. She knew her cheeks were damp with tears. "I jumped to conclusions fueled by my own fears. But I'm not afraid any longer. I'm not afraid of you and I'm not afraid of us."

"You're not?" Garet was possibly in shock. She partially leaned up, braced on her elbows. Her expression grew serious. "Listen, Tess, I'm not gonna let you shut me out. I love you, and I love June. I've known I was in love with you ever since that day...that day of the mandolin lunch."

"You mean the Bluegrass Brunch?" Tess tried not to laugh because Garet was so sincere.

"Yes, then...that first time I saw you play." Garet reached for Tess. Her fingers were at the back of Tess's neck drawing her closer. "I'm madly in love with you, Tess." She sank into Garet, wrapped her arms around Garet's neck, and kissed her.

"I love you, too." She kissed Garet again for good measure. "I'm sorry it took me so long to say it out loud."

"I don't want to go back to Atlanta. I want to stay here, with you."

"I want you to stay. I can't imagine my life without you in it."

It was only then that she realized June was standing nearby, having witnessed the entire affectionate display. Garet followed Tess's gaze as they both slowly turned to face June.

June grinned. "Does this mean we can get a dog?"

EPILOGUE

Garet carried her last bag upstairs to the bedroom. She could hear the murmur of voices downstairs as June and Tess finished the last batch of holiday cookies.

There were two dressers in the bedroom, and Tess had emptied one of them for Garet. She smiled as she stood for a moment and counted four empty drawers. She was finished with her one-drawer rule. She quickly shuttled her things into each drawer, then tossed the empty duffel bag in the closet. She'd organize more later, but this was Christmas Eve and she didn't want to miss out on one minute of it with Tess and June.

Her aging Volvo had been put out to pasture for parts. She'd decided to wait for the second half of her book advance to go car shopping. They'd moved her stuff up from Atlanta in Tess's Subaru after Lane offered to continue subletting her apartment. There were still a couple of boxes of things in the garage, things she wasn't even sure she needed. She'd deal with those later.

Garet had shipped the final spreads to her publisher and was excited to take the holidays off. Not sure what her next book project would be, she'd agreed to stay on and cover the art classes until Charlotte's ankle mended.

It was funny how quickly life could change into something truly amazing.

She trotted downstairs. The smell of sugar cookies filled the air. A plump Christmas tree stood in one corner of the living room with a haphazard pile of packages underneath. Along the mantel hung three stockings.

Garet paused in the doorway to the kitchen to watch June attempt to shuffle the cookies from pan to plate with a spatula. She was using two hands on the utensil, with her tongue out for good measure.

This was what home felt like, Garet was sure of it.

And she hadn't even really known she was looking for it.

From out of nowhere, the kitten pounced onto the counter almost landing on the cookie pan. As it was, he sent a dust cloud of flour everywhere. Garet scooped him up with one hand before he could do any real damage.

"Those cookies smell so good." Garet tried to contain the rambunctious kitten.

"We have to wait until after dinner, Mama says." June was all business.

Tess kissed the top of June's head. Having finished her task, June rounded the counter and reached for the kitten. She snuggled it under her chin with a huge grin on her face.

"Have you named him yet?" Garet casually leaned against the counter's edge.

"I named him Rover. And he's going to sleep with me every night." June shuffled to the living room in sock feet, with the kitten in her arms.

"Was that dresser big enough for you?"

"Yes, more than enough drawers."

"I'm sorry I had to stop helping and finish the cookies." Tess wrapped her arm around Garet's waist.

"I'm not. Cookies trump unpacking every time." Garet kissed Tess softly at her temple. "This is going to be the best Christmas ever."

"I agree." Tess smiled warmly. "I'm so glad you were able to arrange everything so that you could be back before the holiday officially started."

They both turned when they heard the front door open.

June came racing back into the kitchen. "It's snowing! Come see!"

"Okay, okay." Tess accepted June's hand and June pulled her toward the door. She glanced back. "Are you coming?"

"I'll be right there."

Garet reached for her jacket but stopped mid movement. Something tacked to the refrigerator door caught her eye. In the center of the door hung one of June's drawings, this was a new one, a picture Garet hadn't seen before. She smiled when she realized what it was. With simple childlike brilliance, June had drawn herself in the center, holding hands with a kitten and a bear.

June had been right all along. She was the lost kitten from her own story and she hadn't even known it.

She shrugged into her jacket and met Tess on the front stoop. June was running in circles trying to catch the big, wet snowflakes on her tongue. Garet wrapped her arm around Tess's waist and Tess rested her head against Garet's shoulder.

The moon was bright against the purple blue of the nighttime winter sky. Warmth seeped past her from the open door and the yellow glow from the windows cast squares of light on the ground, which was quickly transitioning from brown to white.

This *was* going to be the best Christmas ever.

The first of many.

Love, it seemed, had delivered her home.

The End

About the Author

Missouri Vaun spent a large part of her childhood in southern Mississippi, before attending high school in North Carolina and college in Tennessee. Strong connections to her roots in the rural south have been a grounding force throughout her life. Vaun spent twelve years finding her voice working as a journalist in places as disparate as Chicago, Atlanta, and Jackson, Mississippi, all along filing away characters and their stories. Her novels are heartfelt, earthy, and speak of loyalty and our responsibility to others. She and her wife currently live in northern California.

Books Available from Bold Strokes Books

His Brother's Viscount by Stephanie Lake. Hector Somerville wants to rekindle his illicit love affair with Viscount Wentworth, but he must overcome one problem: Wentworth still loves Hector's brother. (978-1-63555-805-0)

Journey to Cash by Ashley Bartlett. Cash Braddock thought everything was great, but it looks like her history is about to become her right now. Which is a real bummer. (978-1-63555-464-9)

Liberty Bay by Karis Walsh. Wren Lindley's life is mired in tradition and untouched by trends until social media star Gina Strickland introduces an irresistible electricity into her off-the-grid world. (978-1-63555-816-6)

Scent by Kris Bryant. Nico Marshall has been burned by women in the past wanting her for her money. This time, she's determined to win Sophia Sweet over with her charm. (978-1-63555-780-0)

Shadows of Steel by Suzie Clarke. As their worlds collide and their choices come back to haunt them, Rachel and Claire must figure out how to stay together and most of all, stay alive. (978-1-63555-810-4)

The Clinch by Nicole Disney. Eden Bauer overcame a difficult past to become a world champion mixed martial artist, but now rising star and dreamy bad girl Brooklyn Shaw is a threat both to Eden's title and her heart. (978-1-63555-820-3)

The Last First Kiss by Julie Cannon. Kelly Newsome is so ready for a tropical island vacation, but she never expects to meet the woman who could give her her last first kiss. (978-1-63555-768-8)

The Mandolin Lunch by Missouri Vaun. Despite their immediate attraction, everything about Garet Allen says short-term, and Tess Hill refuses to consider anything less than forever. (978-1-63555-566-0)

Thor: Daughter of Asgard by Genevieve McCluer. When Hannah Olsen finds out she's the reincarnation of Thor, she's thrown into a world of magic and intrigue, unexpected attraction, and a mystery she's got to unravel. (978-1-63555-814-2)

Veterinary Technician by Nancy Wheelton. When a stable of horses is threatened Val and Ronnie must work together against the odds to save them, and maybe even themselves along the way. (978-1-63555-839-5)

16 Steps to Forever by Georgia Beers. Can Brooke Sullivan and Macy Carr find themselves by finding each other? (978-1-63555-762-6)

All I Want for Christmas by Georgia Beers, Maggie Cummings, Fiona Riley. The Christmas season sparks passion and love in these stories by award winning authors Georgia Beers, Maggie Cummings, and Fiona Riley. (978-1-63555-764-0)

From the Woods by Charlotte Greene. When Fiona goes backpacking in a protected wilderness, the last thing she expects is to be fighting for her life. (978-1-63555-793-0)

Heart of the Storm by Nicole Stiling. For Juliet Mitchell and Sienna Bennett a forbidden attraction definitely isn't worth upending the life they've worked so hard for. Is it? (978-1-63555-789-3)

If You Dare by Sandy Lowe. For Lauren West and Emma Prescott, following their passions is easy. Following their hearts, though? That's almost impossible. (978-1-63555-654-4)

Love Changes Everything by Jaime Maddox. For Samantha Brooks and Kirby Fielding, no matter how careful their plans, love will change everything. (978-1-63555-835-7)

Not This Time by MA Binfield. Flung back into each other's lives, can former bandmates Sophia and Madison have a second chance at romance? (978-1-63555-798-5)

The Dubious Gift of Dragon Blood by J. Marshall Freeman. One day Crispin is a lonely high school student—the next he is fighting a war in a land ruled by dragons, his otherworldly boyfriend at his side. (978-1-63555-725-1)

The Found Jar by Jaycie Morrison. Fear keeps Emily Harris trapped in her emotionally vacant life; can she find the courage to let Beck Reynolds guide her toward love? (978-1-63555-825-8)

Aurora by Emma L McGeown. After a traumatic accident, Elena Ricci is stricken with amnesia leaving her with no recollection of the last eight years, including her wife and son. (978-1-63555-824-1)

Avenging Avery by Sheri Lewis Wohl. Revenge against a vengeful vampire unites Isa Meyer and Jeni Denton, but it's love that heals them. (978-1-63555-622-3)

Bulletproof by Maggie Cummings. For Dylan Prescott and Briana Logan, the complicated NYC criminal justice system doesn't leave room for love, but where the heart is concerned, no one is bulletproof. (978-1-63555-771-8)

Her Lady to Love by Jane Walsh. A shy wallflower joins forces with the most popular woman in Regency London on a quest to catch a husband, only to discover a wild passion for each other that far eclipses their interest for the Marriage Mart. (978-1-63555-809-8)

No Regrets by Joy Argento. For Jodi and Beth, the possibility of losing their future will force them to decide what is really important. (978-1-63555-751-0)

The Holiday Treatment by Elle Spencer. Who doesn't want a gay Christmas movie? Holly Hudson asks herself that question and discovers that happy endings aren't only for the movies. (978-1-63555-660-5)

Too Good to be True by Leigh Hays. Can the promise of love survive the realities of life for Madison and Jen, or is it too good to be true? (978-1-63555-715-2)

Treacherous Seas by Radclyffe. When the choice comes down to the lives of her officers against the promise she made to her wife, Reese Conlon puts everything she cares about on the line. (978-1-63555-778-7)

Two to Tangle by Melissa Brayden. Ryan Jacks has been a player all her life, but the new chef at Tangle Valley Vineyard changes everything. If only she wasn't off the menu. (978-1-63555-747-3)

When Sparks Fly by Annie McDonald. Will the devastating incident that first brought Dr. Daniella Waveny and hockey coach Luca McCaffrey together on frozen ice now force them apart, or will their secrets and fears thaw enough for them to create sparks? (978-1-63555-782-4)

Best Practice by Carsen Taite. When attorney Grace Maldonado agrees to mentor her best friend's little sister, she's prepared to confront Perry's rebellious nature, but she isn't prepared to fall in love. Legal Affairs: one law firm, three best friends, three chances to fall in love. (978-1-63555-361-1)

Home by Kris Bryant. Natalie and Sarah discover that anything is possible when love takes the long way home. (978-1-63555-853-1)

Keeper by Sydney Quinne. With a new charge under her reluctant wing—feisty, highly intelligent math wizard Isabelle Templeton—Keeper Andy Bouchard has to prevent a murder or die trying. (978-1-63555-852-4)

One More Chance by Ali Vali. Harry Basantes planned a future with Desi Thompson until the day Desi disappeared without a word, only to walk back into her life sixteen years later. (978-1-63555-536-3)

Renegade's War by Gun Brooke. Freedom fighter Aurelia DeCallum regrets saving the woman called Blue. She fears it will jeopardize her mission, and secretly, Blue might end up breaking Aurelia's heart. (978-1-63555-484-7)

The Other Women by Erin Zak. What happens in Vegas should stay in Vegas, but what do you do when the love you find in Vegas changes your life forever? (978-1-63555-741-1)

The Sea Within by Missouri Vaun. Time is running out for Dr. Elle Graham to convince Captain Jackson Drake that the only thing that can save future Earth resides in the past, and rescue her broken heart in the process. (978-1-63555-568-4)

To Sleep With Reindeer by Justine Saracen. In Norway under Nazi occupation, Maarit, an Indigenous woman; and Kirsten, a Norwegian resister, join forces to stop the development of an atomic weapon. (978-1-63555-735-0)

Twice Shy by Aurora Rey. Having an ex with benefits isn't all it's cracked up to be. Will Amanda Russo learn that lesson in time to take a chance on love with Quinn Sullivan? (978-1-63555-737-4)

Z-Town by Eden Darry. Forced to work together to stay alive, Meg and Lane must find the centuries-old treasure before the zombies find them first. (978-1-63555-743-5)

Bet Against Me by Fiona Riley. In the high stakes luxury real estate market, everything has a price, and as rival Realtors Trina Lee and Kendall Yates find out, that means their hearts and souls, too. (978-1-63555-729-9)

Broken Reign by Sam Ledel. Together on an epic journey in search of a mysterious cure, a princess and a village outcast must overcome life-threatening challenges and their own prejudice if they want to survive. (978-1-63555-739-8)

Just One Taste by CJ Birch. For Lauren, it only took one taste to start trusting in love again. (978-1-63555-772-5)

Lady of Stone by Barbara Ann Wright. Sparks fly as a magical emergency forces a noble embarrassed by her ability to submit to a low-born teacher who resents everything about her. (978-1-63555-607-0)

Last Resort by Angie Williams. Katie and Rhys are about to find out what happens when you meet the girl of your dreams but you aren't looking for a happily ever after. (978-1-63555-774-9)

Longing for You by Jenny Frame. When Debrek housekeeper Katie Brekman is attacked amid a burgeoning vampire-witch war, Alexis Villiers must go against everything her clan believes in to save her. (978-1-63555-658-2)

Money Creek by Anne Laughlin. Clare Lehane is a troubled lawyer from Chicago who tries to make her way in a rural town full of secrets and deceptions. (978-1-63555-795-4)

Passion's Sweet Surrender by Ronica Black. Cam and Blake are unable to deny their passion for each other, but surrendering to love is a whole different matter. (978-1-63555-703-9)

The Holiday Detour by Jane Kolven. It will take everything going wrong to make Dana and Charlie see how right they are for each other. (978-1-63555-720-6)

Too Hot to Ride by Andrews & Austin. World famous cutting horse champion and industry legend Jane Barrow is knockdown sexy in the way she moves, talks, and rides, and Rae Starr is determined not to get involved with this womanizing gambler. (978-1-63555-776-3)